D1407284

REAPER

REAPER

Jon Grahame

MYRMIDON

Myrmidon Books Ltd
Rotterdam House
116 Quayside
Newcastle upon Tyne
NE1 3DY
www.myrmidonbooks.com

Published by Myrmidon 2011

ISBN 978-1-905802-52-4

Set in 11.75/15.5 Sabon
by Ellipsis Digital Limited, Glasgow

Printed and bound by
CPI Group (UK) Ltd, Croydon, CR0 4YY

3 5 7 9 10 8 6 4 2

For my agent, Mandy Little

China's reckless use of antibiotics in the health system and agricultural production is unleashing an explosion of drug resistant superbugs that endanger global health, according to leading scientists.

Chinese doctors routinely hand out multiple doses of antibiotics for simple maladies, like sore throats, and the country's farmers' excessive dependence on the drugs has tainted the food chain.

Studies in China show a 'frightening' increase in antibiotic-resistant bacteria such as staphylococcus aureus bacteria, also known as MRSA. There are warnings that new strains of antibiotic-resistant bugs will spread quickly through international air travel and international food sourcing.

"We have a lot of data from Chinese hospitals and it shows a very frightening picture of high-level antibiotic resistance," said Dr Andreas Heddini of the Swedish Institute for Infectious Disease Control. "Doctors are daily finding there is nothing they can do; even third and fourth-line antibiotics are not working.

"There is a real risk that globally we will return to a pre-antibiotic era of medicine, where we face a situation where a number of medical treatment options would no longer be there. What happens in China matters for the rest of the world."

Associated Press, February 10, 2013

An outbreak of SARS (Severe Acute Respiratory Syndrome) has been reported in Guangdong Province, China. It was discovered by Canada's Global Public Health Intelligence Network (GPHIN), an electronic warning system that monitors and analyses internet media traffic, and is part of the World Health Organisation's (WHO) Global Outbreak and Alert Response Network (GOARN). The disease comes on top of the problems caused by the violent earthquake that devastated the region two months ago. Members of worldwide aid agencies are still working in the area.

Guangdong Province previously suffered a SARS epidemic in 2002 although the Chinese Government did not inform WHO until four months later. It spread to 37 countries and there were 8,096 known infected cases and 774 fatalities. SARS is a viral disease that can initially be caught from palm civets, raccoon dogs, ferret badgers, domestic cats and bats. Initial symptoms are flu-like and may include lethargy, fever, coughs, sore throats and shortness of breath.

Les Knight, founder of the Voluntary Human Extinction Movement

(As quoted in *The World Without Us* by Alan Weisman, Virgin Books)

'No virus can ever get all six billion of us. A 99.99 per cent die-off would still leave 650,000 naturally immune survivors. Epidemics actually strengthen a species. In 50,000 years, we could easily be right back where we are now.'

Chapter 1

JIM REAPER STARTED TO PLAN MURDER as thousands began to die in a natural disaster that almost killed the world.

He had become a man of routine and habit. He still bought the *Independent*, as a sign of his social leanings and pretensions. He had bought the paper when Margaret was alive. The *Independent* for him, the *Mirror* for her. His and her papers, reflecting his and her intellects. Except that he had preferred to read the *Mirror* first, for the shorthand version of national and world events, and the sports pages.

On this day, he walked into the city, as he did every day, and bought the newspaper from the same shop in Reuben Street. He had a late breakfast at Wetherspoons.

He always started with a couple of coffees and then, seeing as he was in a bar, it seemed only polite to have a couple of pints. Maybe three or four. No more. He wasn't an alcoholic or dependent on the booze; he was dependent on the routine. On this grey day in the middle of February, he left to walk home, back through the city and into the suburbs. It was then he saw Frank Morris, large as life, coming out of a bar in New Street, a mobile phone to his ear, a girl on his arm, laughing and joking as if all was well with the world.

You only had to look at the morning headlines to see that all was *not* well with the world. The earthquake in China was proving more of a handful than expected. Thousands had been killed, infrastructure devastated and, on top of that, there had been an outbreak of a glorified flu virus. The world had started dying, although no one yet knew it, and all Reaper could think about was how to kill Frank Morris.

He followed him, almost without thinking, staying well back and hidden among the crowds. Morris and the girl went to the bus station and waited at the number 36 bay. Reaper kept his distance and watched from the anonymity of ever-changing crowds. A green double-decker arrived and disgorged passengers. The driver left and the bus waited empty, doors closed, until a new driver climbed on board. Now the doors opened again and those waiting could board and pay their fares. Morris and the girl went upstairs. Reaper got on the bus and asked for a ticket to the terminus, took a seat on the lower deck, and waited.

The girl had been attractive in a common way. The boots she wore and the fake fur jacket were probably high street expensive. The skirt was short and her legs long; her make-up blatant and her hair bleached straw blonde. She laughed too loud. He could hear her now from downstairs; she was laughing as if to show off to the world that she was with a real catch. She couldn't be more than 18. She didn't know any better.

He held the newspaper at eye level in case Morris looked in his direction when they came downstairs to disembark but, when they did, in the middle of the undistingushed Butterly Estate, the man was too intent on saying something suggestive to the girl, who laughed obligingly and flashed a challenging glance down the bus as if to relay the fact that they were now going off to do something scandalous and dirty that was far beyond the limits of her audience's boring lives. They got off as it started to rain. Two other people were also waiting to climb down, one an elderly woman who was taking her time. Reaper left his seat, helped her and got off himself.

The couple were running down the wet pavement, eager to be out of the rain, eager for each other. Reaper followed at a distance. They turned left and he ran to keep them in sight. They walked up the path of a semi-detached council house. He walked twenty paces down the street until he could confirm the number on the gate, turned away and began to walk back. The rain was getting heavier but he didn't feel the elements; he felt only the anger, deep, patient and uncompromising.

It was two hours before he realised he was approaching his own house. Without realising, he had responded to a homing instinct like a pigeon. The day was already darkening and he was soaked and needed to pee. He let himself in, stripped naked, used the lavatory and took a hot shower. He lost track of time and became aware, some hours later, that he was laying on his bed in a bathrobe.

His mind had short-circuited with the knowledge that Frank Morris was out and he knew where he lived. A sudden thought muddled his half-formed intention. Did the girl live with him? Or was she only an afternoon's diversion? He calmed himself. A lot of planning was needed. He would discover the necessary details, he would wait until the time was right, and then he would act. Justice would finally be done. So far, justice had been only noticeable by its absence. *Vengeance is mine, sayeth the Lord*. Reaper thought it was time the Lord had a little help.

Reaper stopped drinking and undertook a fitness programme of walking and jogging. Then he initiated a harsh regime of circuit training in his garage. After a month, he felt fitter than he had in a long time. He bought a nondescript second-hand van that wouldn't look out of place parked near his target's house and kept intermittent surveillance on Morris. He treated the rear windows of the van with transparency paint that let him see out but rendered the interior dark. He sat on a mattress in the back and logged the man's movements, not all and every day, but enough to build up an accurate framework of when he was at home. He had been right. The girl did not live at the house. Morris took several girls there, most of them on the verge of legality, very few of them more than once.

Morris had spent three years inside and looked to be in the peak of condition. He walked as if he had lifted weights and his muscles bulged his clothes. His hair was cropped, his features had an arrogance that some women might find attractive. He was six feet tall and 32 years old, two inches taller than Reaper and thirteen years younger. Reaper continued his own routine of exercise with a grim determination.

He no longer bought a newspaper and was unaware of the stories reporting the spread across the world of the pandemic, tagged 'Super-SARS'. He watched only films or dramas on television. He recorded many and re-ran them. His choice was eclectic: *The Railway Children* for lost innocence, *Unforgiven* for revenge. Most were violent. He had a joke with himself that they were training films. He watched brain-eating Zombies without flinching or laughing. He bought a punch bag that he hung from the ceiling of the garage and practised kicks and firmed up his fists upon it. The time was getting close. He felt he was approaching peak fitness and the moment of justice. Then Morris disappeared.

Reaper parked the van to make sure his target was keeping to his schedule, but Morris wasn't at the house. Had he stayed somewhere else overnight? He did not reappear the next day. Reaper spent longer in the van, using a bottle to piss in, but the man did not return that night or the day after.

Hunger and tiredness made him drive home and consider what might have happened, but after food and sleep he returned to his vigil. Morris was still absent, although the postman called. The thought that his mail was still being delivered gave him cause for optimism until he realised it could be junk mail or Morris could simply have left without telling his creditors. Why would he tell creditors? Who else would send him mail?

Driven to distraction by uncertainty, Reaper moved the van to a location well away from the house, then walked back and strode down the garden path as if he had a perfect right to be there. He pretended to knock at the door in case a neighbour was watching, and then peered through the front window into a room dominated by a large-screen TV. Newspapers and magazines were on a coffee table, a scarf and a jacket were thrown over the back of an armchair. The house did not look abandoned. He went round the back and saw a piece of toast next to the sink alongside a mug of half-drunk coffee. The clincher was a four-pack of Carlsberg Special on the bench. Morris would never have left those behind.

Even so, the following days were tense and Reaper's training suffered. When Morris returned after an absence of three weeks, he had a deep tan and a satisfied smile. Three weeks in the sun on no visible means of support. Reaper hadn't watched where Morris had gone during the days or nights; he had only wanted to know when he was at home. His hours of absence from the house had not fitted a normal work pattern: but then Morris had never had normal work; thieving, enforcing and drug dealing had been his trades, although the police had never been able to gather enough evidence to make a case.

Reaper returned to his regime of rigorous training and, towards the end of April, he was ready again, mentally and physically. Without turning mystic, he felt the karma of the moment ahead. It would happen the next Wednesday.

On Wednesday nights, Morris usually came home about 7:30 and stayed in alone. Usually this coincided with a football match on television. Everybody has routines. Reaper waited in the van and watched the house. A taxi stopped outside at 7:40 and Morris got out, walked down the path and went in through the front door. Reaper drove home, ate a steak, showered and prepared. He wore black to blend into the night. In a shoulder bag, he carried a meat cleaver, a hammer, a pair of plastic handcuffs and the nearest thing he could find in a toyshop to a vaguely convincing Colt .45, once he'd added a little paint here and there. At 10 o'clock, he drove the van back to the Butterly Estate and parked round the corner from the house.

There was an intermittent moon that played hide and seek with the clouds. It was a spring night; warm with the promise of a summer he planned to miss. He felt no excitement or fear or even anticipation as he left the van and walked down the street towards the semi-detached house; this was the final act. There was a light on in the front room. He went to the door and took the hammer from the bag. He knocked. Waited and knocked again. The light in the hall came on and he heard Morris speculating out loud to himself about who the hell was knocking at this time of night. The door opened, Reaper stepped forward and hit him with the hammer.

The speed of the attack made it successful. He connected with Morris' head and Morris went down, still conscious, but shocked and shouting. Reaper went inside and closed the door. He pushed the man onto his front and pulled one hand behind his back. As he tried to get the other, Morris realised what was happening and began to struggle. He was stronger than Reaper expected and the handcuffs wouldn't work. The plan to make him wait until dawn, tied to a chair, being told why and how he was going to be killed, was discarded. Reaper pulled the meat cleaver from the bag, swung it high and brought it down into the back of the man's head. It split his skull like a melon and blood spurted into his face.

Morris stopped struggling. His legs twitched and he gurgled, but he stopped struggling. Reaper sat with his back against the front door, looking down the worn carpet of the hallway towards the kitchen. The door to the living room was open and he could hear high-lights from a football match on the television. He took a deep breath and smelt the blood, could almost *taste* the blood. He got up and left the cleaver where it was and wondered if it was too early to call the police. Maybe he would have a cup of tea first? He felt tired, drained. All that preparation, all that concentrated energy and now it was over, in two blood-splattered minutes.

Would Emily understand? Would Margaret? He suspected Emily would approve. *This was for you, love.* But his wife had been aggravatingly religious, particularly towards the end. She wouldn't approve. Not that he cared.

He went into the kitchen and switched on the light. Now he was here, he couldn't be bothered making tea.

In the fridge were the cans of Special Brew. He wouldn't normally choose such a strong beer but there was no alternative. Besides, it was a special occasion, and he allowed the wisp of a gallows smile to cross his face. He took a can and popped the ring pull. A noise in the hall made him turn; Morris was trying to get to his feet. Reaper put the can down and opened kitchen drawers, found what he was looking for and picked a carving knife. He wrapped a tea towel round the handle to get a better grip, and stepped into the hall, measuring the distance. He judged his target was fairly close to death anyway, but he moved quickly and stuck the knife into Morris's stomach with an upward thrust. Reaper let go, stood back, and watched Morris fall, driving the knife further into his body as he hit the floor. This time he wouldn't get up.

The blood on Reaper's hand bothered him. It was on his face as well. He ran a tap at the sink and washed it off as best he could. Then, picking up the can of lager and stepping over the body, he went into the front room. The match highlights were still on. Newcastle were winning two nil. He sat and watched until it finished and a news bulletin followed. It was about Super-SARS, the flu virus that was sweeping the nation. It had been dominating newspaper billboards and TV headlines so much, even he had been unable to avoid the vague awareness of what was happening. The TV reporter was speculating on rumours that the Government was planning quarantine areas.

Reaper was tired. Killing had taken more out of him than he had realised. Maybe it was time to call the police.

Morris didn't have a land line and Reaper didn't have a mobile. He used Morris's mobile, left on the arm of the couch, where he had apparently been sprawled. Reaper dialled 999 and told them his name, and that he had killed a man. He told them the address and said he was armed and dangerous and would kill the first person who attempted to come through the front door.

He wanted them to bring guns. He wanted them to shoot him. *Death by police*. It had a certain satisfying symmetry.

The first car arrived within ten minutes. By that time, he had opened the front window and had hung the body half out of it so that the cleaver, still in place in the back of Morris's head, could be seen. That should give the police marksmen an incentive. The Armed Response Unit arrived 30 minutes later. By this time there were two police cars outside and a searchlight was aimed at the front of the house. Officers had tried to evacuate the homes on either side, although one family wouldn't go. He listened to them arguing: the son and daughter were in bed with flu and their mother wouldn't move them. He couldn't see much because of the light in his eyes but he waved the hammer and the replica Colt .45 to show his intent. No one fired. No one shot him. There was no release.

The light hurt his eyes and a disembodied voice that invited him to lay down his weapons and step outside annoyed him. He took another can of lager from the fridge – how many had he had? – and went upstairs to a back bedroom to rest in the dark. When dawn came, he would put on a show of provocation. He lay on a single bed that had no bedding, just a mattress. A second wave of exhaustion swept over him. He felt no emotion, no triumph, no regret. He had done what he had set out to do. What he had *had* to do. *Vengeance is mine* . . .

The police found him asleep. He awoke as they put plastic cuffs on his wrists to hold his hands behind his back. They were not rough with him and he suspected they knew who he was and the circumstances that had led him to do what he'd done. He corrected them when they charged him with murder. 'It was an *execution*. He should have suffered more.'

'You're probably right, but whatever you call it, you killed him.'

He was taken to Police Headquarters. He declined a doctor and was put in a cell. It was strange returning to his place of work for the first time in three years. He had planned to be on a mortuary slab by now. Even though his plan had gone awry, the satisfaction of the kill had eased the perpetual pain inside. It was four o'clock in the morning and he expected the place to be busier; have more officers, more clients, more drunks, more noise.

The next morning, he was questioned by a detective sergeant and made a full confession. He spent another night in the cells and then made an appearance before a magistrate. He was remanded in custody for two weeks. The wheels of justice were operating on a skeleton staff. No one was available to transfer him to a proper jail and he remained in police cells. Charlie Benson was the custody sergeant, an officer he had known for years. He brought him meals from the staff canteen. He was sympathetic. They all knew the background.

'I'd have been tempted to do the same,' Benson confided.

A second bobby in the corridor outside coughed. Benson called over his shoulder, 'Take your germs out of here. I don't want your flu.'

'It's not flu. I don't get flu. It's just a cold.'

'Everybody seems to be going down with this bloody flu,' Benson told Reaper, 'Even the villains, which is just as well. We're short-staffed ourselves.'

Reaper was not interested in the outside world. He hadn't been for a long time. Even before Morris was let out, he'd only read the papers out of habit and to pass the time. The release of the kill was fading and he was sinking into despair because he himself was still alive.

During the first week of remand, he noticed the situation within the station get worse. Even fewer lags, fewer staff. In the second week, there was a 24-hour period when no one came to his cell. Then Benson opened the door. His eyes were red rimmed and he was breathing through his mouth. He held a handkerchief to his face. He dropped a couple of pre-packed sandwiches onto the bed.

'They're out of date, but it's the best I can do. It's crazy out there.' He coughed. 'Bloody SARS! I'd like to get me hands on the swine who started it. Look, Jim. Everything's falling apart. The courts have stopped operating. All custody remands have been extended. I'm not going to lock that door again. It could be there'll be no one around to open it. There's even been a riot up at the infirmary – people demanding a vaccine. Bloody armed police to disperse them for chrissake! We're on our way to hell in a hand basket. God alone knows where it will end. I've opened all the cells. Sent three on their way. I'm off home to bed. God knows. You hear stories . . . you don't know what to believe. I'd stay here if I was you, Jim. Use the canteen. When things get back to normal, it'll stand you in good stead that you didn't do a runner.' He coughed again, long and harsh. '*If* things get back to normal.' He looked at his hand

and his handkerchief and said, 'I won't shake hands. All the best, Jim!'

Reaper nodded.

Benson left and Reaper opened the packet. He ate a cheese and tomato sandwich washed down with a glass of water. He sat on the bed, back against the wall, feet stretched out in front of him, and listened. Somewhere distant a door banged. Someone called out. Someone coughed in reply. Time didn't seem important. He lay down and slept. When he awoke he ate the other sandwich, ham and pickle. It was stale but it was food. He sat and waited. No one came. No more sounds except, like the song, *The Sound of Silence*. He got up and stepped outside his cell. The corridor was lined with cells. All the doors were open.

He walked to the end of the corridor and found the custody desk unmanned. The three other doors that led out of the area all had coded key-pads but they had been propped open. A noise on another level. A door? He went back to his cell and lay down.

Had he been mistaken? Perhaps he had really been shot and was he now dead, or dying in a hospital bed? Had the last week been a bad dream, an illusion? Was death a deserted police station? He had thought death was nothingness, blackness, sinking into an endless sleep. How did this equate? Maybe drugs. Maybe he had been shot and had been pumped full of drugs? Like that TV series, *Life On Mars*. He tried to burst back into reality, to tell the doctors to turn off the life-support system and let him go, but nothing happened. He fell asleep again, hoping that this time he would wake up in the real world.

His eyes opened and he stared at the ceiling. A nondescript ceiling. An institutional ceiling. A ceiling that could easily be in a hospital. He looked around and saw he was still in the cell. He was hungry and felt dirty. When was the last time he had showered? He got up and went to the custody desk. Still silence. Three open doors of silence. He shouted. 'Anybody there?' No one replied.

He went through a door that had been propped open with a waste bin, and walked along a carpeted corridor, past the interview room where he had made his confession, past small offices, through an open plan office that had been abandoned. The clock told him it was 11:50. He went round corners, along another corridor, and he was at the front desk, which was unmanned. Swing doors led to the outside. He stood near the glass and stared out onto the dual carriage ring road that ran past police headquarters. The sun was high. The body of a man in civilian clothes lay on the steps. There was no traffic.

He went back into the station, climbed some stairs, and saw a senior officer in an office. Reaper knocked, then went inside. The man was dead, slumped over his desk. Reaper carried on walking, exploring the station.

He found three more bodies. What had happened?

Hunger drove him to the canteen. He cooked bacon, eggs, beans and toast, and wondered how he could possibly have an appetite. It was as if whatever had happened was of no concern to him. He had stepped outside the bounds of society when he had killed Morris. He was alone and maybe there really was a God and His punishment was for Reaper to live in a land that had ceased to exist. Except for the bacon, eggs, beans and toast. Or maybe he was in intensive care in hospital and just tripping on morphine.

Reaper went back to his cell and lay on the hard mattress. He dosed, woke and lay in a state of vegetation for a long time, trying not to think. He had wanted a conclusion when he had set out to kill Morris. He had expected by now to have been consigned to the nothingness of death. Instead, he didn't know whether he was alive or not. He had a drink of water, used the lavatory and used the custody section bathroom to have a shower and wash his underwear and socks. He went behind the custody desk and found the locker that contained prisoners' property. An envelope with his name on it was the only property there. He opened it, took a single photograph from his wallet, replaced everything else and put it back in the locker. He went back to his cell, switched off the interior light from the outside, and went back to sleep.

When he next woke, he got up and had another

shower. He was delaying decisions through mundane routine. He dressed and retraced his steps of the day before, or was it two days before? The lights in the station were permanently on, but outside it was dark. He went to the canteen and cooked himself a bacon sandwich and drank tea. The bananas had gone rotten but the apples were edible. There was no rush. He drank more tea and wondered where he was; wondered if this was a different reality to the one in which he had killed Morris.

Had God banished him to an alternative universe? Probably not, because he didn't believe in God. He had lost that belief three years ago. The fact he didn't believe, of course, did not mean God didn't exist. Reaper could even see the humour in such a situation. Would he still deny His existence if he was ever called to account on Judgement Day? In the unlikely event of it happening, he would welcome such a confrontation. He would be able to ask where God had been when his family needed Him – and to hell with salvation: he knew all about hell and nowhere any God might send him could compare.

He walked down to the front doors and went outside. The body of the man was still on the steps. Streetlights were lit and he could see the roads outlined in orange dots as they climbed the hills opposite, beyond the limits of the city. House lights showed sporadically and in the clear night air he could see smoke rising from a fire down the valley. He could smell burning from a lot closer, probably a building in the town. He sat on the steps, a few yards away from the body, stared out at a night that was still and peaceful and listened to the sounds of insects and the rustle of leaves in the light breeze.

The possibility he hadn't wanted to face pushed forward from the back of his mind. The flu or SARS pandemic had crippled the country, possibly decimated the population. Perhaps people had retreated to safe havens or been herded into medical compounds for treatment. What was that report he had half heard? Quarantine areas? Perhaps the city had been so badly affected it had been declared off limits. Perhaps armed police and soldiers still protected the hospitals and were keeping the infected at bay until the disease had run its course. How long would it be before they returned to the streets to clear the houses of the dead?

Part of his mind said this was the only logical explanation, while another part refused to fully accept that England had fucked itself up quite so completely. What had happened? Hadn't the Government stockpiled enough Tamiflu or whatever it was that they needed? Had there been selective prescriptions? Perhaps that's why the police station was empty. Most of the officers could have been given the necessary drugs and were now in those safe havens, waiting for the time to return.

The irony was, of course, that he had survived without so much as a sniffle. If he had waited two weeks, the flu would probably have taken care of Morris without Reaper having to dispense his own justice. Too late now and anyway: he was glad he had killed him; glad it was his hand to have dealt the blow and not some anonymous virus.

The crash of breaking glass from somewhere in the town came as a shock. He twisted his head sharply like a crow and tried to work out the location. Breaking glass meant people. There was a male shout and a female scream – then another male shout and the female screams continued. His blood ran cold as he sat, remembering. He listened to the screams, interspersed by angry male shouts and guttural laughs. Eventually the screams died down to be replaced, first by sobbing and groaning, and then silence. On a still night when only the insects sang and no traffic disturbed the peace, sobs and groans carried a long way. Their echoes remained in his soul.

Still sleeping, God?

God was dead, had never lived in the forms imagined by Buddhist and Jew, Muslim and Christian and all those who had worshipped the sun and rocks and Mother Earth. God was an accident of cosmic energy who had grown from a dream and a hope by a mankind looking for a means of escape. A mankind unsatisfied with a temporary burst of life, had gone looking for eternity. They prayed that when they died, they would sit at the right hand of God and live forever in peace and harmony and love; states they had never been able to achieve in any real measure during their lifetimes. What a shock when they discovered the right hand of God was just a black hole of dreamless sleep.

Reaper went back to his cell, lay on the hard mattress and tried to rationalise the situation. He decided that he did not know enough to make an informed assessment. Come the daylight, he would find out more. He slept fitfully, the screams of the woman replaying in his mind.

Chapter 2

THE MORNING DAWNED SILENTLY OUTSIDE the police station that had become his womb. He showered, ate breakfast and stood by the reception desk at the front door for a long time before leaving the building's safety. The sun was shining and the office clock said it was 11am.

He stepped outside, walked to the corner and turned left towards the town. The street was lined with parked cars, but deserted. He felt vulnerable, as if someone might be watching from a rooftop or a window, and he crossed the road to be in the shadows. He went carefully, listening for sounds, looking for life – fearful of finding it.

Near the town centre branch of Sainsbury's, he heard

breaking glass. He approached from the far side of the street, hiding behind parked cars, but could see nothing except that one of the large windows had been smashed open and the shards cleared for easier access. This had been done earlier; it was not the recent sound of breakage he had heard. He crossed the road and peered inside. Stock had been spilled in the aisles and he could hear the clink of bottles. The sound of a trolley being pushed got louder.

'Why do I always get one with funny wheels?' slurred a man.

Reaper was watching for the trolley to appear and didn't see the woman come out of another aisle with boxes in her arms.

'Bugger off!' she shouted. 'This is ours!'

The woman was middle-aged and large and looked even larger in a fur coat. Her blonde hair sat strangely on her head and he realised it was a wig. Her face was flushed and she was angry. Possession was nine tenths of the law, her expression declared, and they possessed Sainsbury's.

'What is it?' shouted the slurring man, the trolley increasing in speed and suddenly coming into view. It was filled with cases of beer and bottles of spirits and wine. The man was Reaper's age and he wore white jogging pants and top and new trainers. He was tall with broad shoulders and a large belly. With him was a younger, smaller man in designer jeans and T-shirt.

He was skinny with ratty eyes and carried a Samurai sword. The large man stopped the trolley and lifted out a cricket bat that he wielded threateningly.

'What do you want?' he demanded.

The first on the streets were the pillagers and rapists. Honest folk would be cowering in their homes waiting for authority to reassert itself. Reaper said nothing, but backed away to the street and moved out of sight. He continued on his way, taking great care not to stumble upon another such group: people who, a few weeks before, might have been law-abiding enough because of the strictures of the society in which they lived, but now, because of shock, loss, lack of social cohesion and absence of police, had decided to take what they could, while they could. He suspected that if anyone stood in their way, they would have no hesitation in using whatever weapons they carried.

He heard other sounds of breaking glass in the distance as he walked. After some five minutes, the sound of running feet caused him to withdraw into the shadow of a shop doorway and he watched as a young couple scurried up a side street, followed a short while later by two older men. He reached Albert Square. Much of it was a paved area, with benches and flowerbeds and ornamental lamps. The railway station and its forecourt dominated the north side. The three-star Albert Hotel was to the east. The other two sides were imposing, with Victorian architecture in the grand style; office buildings on the west side, while South Parade had upmarket shops, café bars and restaurants at ground floor level, and flat conversions above for the young and upwardly mobile. There were still, surprisingly, three taxi cabs at the rank outside the station, but only one contained the body of a driver.

Reaper crouched by the taxis, waited and watched. Two of the bars on South Parade had smashed windows. He went into the Albert Hotel and heard a voice speaking in normal, conversational tones. He was surprised and felt a surge of relief – then disappointment when he realised it was coming from a television. He followed the sound into the Tudor Bar that had once served a fine pint of Timothy Taylor. The décor was mock Tudor with exposed beams, chunky tables and well-upholstered seating and a large TV screen was fitted to the wall. A barman, in pale blue jacket and black trousers, lay dead in a club chair, with a half empty bottle of vodka and a glass in front of him on a table. He looked peaceful. Perhaps the pills had helped; there was an empty blister pack beside the bottle.

The man on the television screen was vaguely familiar. Perhaps a minor figure in the Government? Reaper guessed what he was seeing was being repeated on a loop. There was a message of 'God bless and good luck', a fixed stare and the screen went blank before the loop started again. A message was shown and read by an anonymous presenter: *An announce-ment on behalf of Her Majesty's Government by the Right Honourable Geoffrey Smith*, it said.

The Right Honourable Geoffrey Smith looked out at what was left of the country with tired, defeated eyes behind heavy-framed glasses. He had a moustache that looked as if it had already died, and wispy hair combed across a bald patch. Vanity unto death. He read from a script.

'By now, you will all be aware of the terrible effects of the SARS pandemic. It is estimated that 50 per cent of the population has already died of this dreadful virus, and we fear that many more will succumb. Hospitals are full, and medical staff have fallen victim at the same rate as the civilian population. All known medicines have failed to stop the devastating effects of what scientists have described as "a virus aberration". No one could have foreseen this modern plague, and no one, it seems, can save us from it, not just here in Britain, but all around the world. We don't know when this pandemic will end. But we do know there are some who have a natural immunity. This small percentage is, at present, our only hope for the survival of the human race. All I can do is urge you all to make your peace with your god and remain in the safety of your homes as we truly face the apocalypse. God bless. And good luck.'

Reaper took a bottle of Mexican lager from a cold cabinet behind the bar, flipped off the top and drank.

The message repeated and annoyed him. When it started a third time, he threw the bottle at the screen, which smashed in an electric frizzle. Silence returned. He was getting used to silence. *Apocalypse? Survival of the human race?* He had seen some of the survivors and they hardly filled him with hope. He headed out, and had reached the front door of the hotel when a movement on South Parade caught his attention and he stepped back into cover.

Three people. An obese man with a shotgun carried carelessly over his shoulder, a young girl carrying plastic shopping bags and another male, well built, also with a shotgun, were walking in single file. The obese man held a long chain that was attached to a dog collar around the girl's neck. When she stumbled, he yanked upon the chain to make her keep up. Reaper's fists clenched and unclenched as he watched them go into the entrance of the flats opposite, and he suddenly realised what he had to do.

He left the hotel by the rear entrance and made his way back to the police station. It was a relief to return to somewhere familiar and he sank into the chair behind the reception desk. Had anybody been here in his absence? He hoped that wrongdoers would stay away, that they would want nothing to do with a police station. One thing he was sure of: that society, no matter what form into which it might evolve, would never take advantage of him again.

He went through the building to one of the bodies he had found on a lower floor. It was that of an armed police officer. Was he still contagious? Reaper didn't care. He unfastened the belt and holster from around the man's waist, took out the Glock handgun and walked a few yards further to an unmarked door. If necessary, he would shoot off the hinges. He didn't have to; to his amazement it was unlocked. He stepped inside the armoury. Another dead body lay on the floor inside the room. This one was riper. The flies were beginning to gather. He ignored the smell and the buzzing insects and wrested a bunch of keys from cold fingers.

Reaper thanked God – if He existed – that no one had beaten him to it.

He unlocked the cabinets and cupboards. He put on a Kevlar vest and smiled grimly at the familiar weight. He knew the Glock handgun had a 17 round capacity magazine of 9mm bullets. Why have only one when he could have two? Ten per cent of the population were left handed, and armouries usually had a similar percentage among their supplies. He found a left-handed holster and fitted that onto the belt as well. He fastened the belt around his waist. The handguns were held in Viper drop-leg holsters that strapped around the thigh at hand height. He loaded a second Glock with a full magazine and slid it home. He also took a Heckler and Koch G36 carbine with a 12 inch barrel and fitted scope that had a 30 round curved magazine. He put extra magazines for both weapons in the pockets of the vest and in his holster belt.

There were 10 carbines and twice that many handguns in the armoury, plus Kevlar vests and ammunition. He dragged the body of the officer in the corridor into an office supply store room, then went back for the armoury officer. He put him in the same place. Reaper intended to return to the weapons room and he preferred it cleared of ripe corpses. On impulse, he took the police cap that the armed officer had been wearing and put it on his head. He locked the door. Just in case.

Reaper went through the station to the rear of the building, to the yard where vehicles were parked. He found the Vauxhall Astra patrol car that matched the fob on the keys he had taken from the cabinet behind the main station desk. He placed his carbine in the passenger well and fastened the seat belt before he got in so that he could drive un-belted without the annoying warning noise. The car started first time and the fuel gauge registered half a tank of petrol. He reversed, manoeuvred and drove through the open gate into the side street. He had the windows down and could smell the smoke.

He joined the dual carriage ring road and began a slow circuit. Past the multi-storey car park, there was an accident. One car had rear-ended another and the vehicles sat, crumpled together, half on and half off the pavement outside a pub called The Horse and Jockey. He passed one or two cars that had been abandoned at the side of the road but none of them appeared to contain bodies. Side streets were orderly, lined with parked cars. Smoke rose from an industrial estate beyond the ring road. Between buildings, he could see more smoke from a smaller fire in the city itself.

A bigger shunt had occurred at the underpass and traffic had backed up behind. Half a dozen abandoned cars blocked the road. He drove across the central reservation onto the wrong side of the road and continued. By the time he had completed a circuit and was back outside the police station, he had seen three bodies at the side of the road, but no one alive. He turned into the town itself and cruised the silent streets that he had earlier travelled on foot. He stopped at the Sainsbury's near the bus station, but the trio he had seen earlier had gone. He guessed that, at the sight of a police car, those with dubious motives would stay out of the way.

He got out of the car, carrying the carbine in the crook of his arm. He stepped through the broken window into the store. The electricity was still on. He had been taking it for granted and suddenly wondered how long it would last. He walked the aisles and found broken products in the alcohol section and the result of what looked like a flour fight in baking. He went through a staff door into a warehouse and saw the bodies of a security guard, and a young man who was wearing the store's uniform. He picked up a basket and went shopping: long-life milk, crackers, biscuits, part-baked bread, tins of chunky soup, frozen steaks and chocolate.

He bagged his goods and took them to the car. The streets were still deserted. The rumble of a distant explosion shook shards of glass from the broken window and had him dropping beside the vehicle in a reflex motion. A gas leak? Smoke rose from the bus station in a mushroom cloud. He got back behind the wheel and drove up the street and watched the flames in the One Stop Café. Through the bus station entrance, he could see half a dozen double-deckers still at their ranks. The flames would spread to the rest of the one storey complex but was unlikely to jump to the buildings across the concourse.

Reaper continued his tour. Maybe most of the surviving population had been evacuated? The window of a fashion store had been smashed and clothing was strewn around outside. Every pharmacy he drove past had been broken into. Maybe they had been looking for Tamiflu. Or heroin. Or anything else that might help them escape the nightmare, either through temporary or permanent oblivion. For a fleeting second he considered the option. A couple of bottles of strong sedatives and a pint of whisky and it would all be over. Except that this was both his punishment and his destiny. This was why he had survived.

He avoided Albert Square but, elsewhere in the city, he stopped occasionally to wind down his window, sound the horn and listen for a response. Near the civic centre, outside a tower block of 1960s concrete and glass flats, he heard a voice. Feeble and female, crying for help. He got out and walked towards the cries that came from a window on the first floor.

'Hello?' he shouted.

'Help me! Please help me!' An elderly voice at the end of her endurance.

'What's the number of your flat?'

'Eighteen!'

'I'm coming!'

The door to the block was locked, entry gained by keying in a code. He levelled the carbine and fired three shots into each hinge. The wood splintered and the door sagged. He kicked it and it sagged some more. Another kick and it fell inwards. He climbed the stairs and found Flat 18. The door was locked.

'Are you there?' he called.

'Here!'

'Stay back. I'll have to kick the door in.'

One good kick levelled at the lock loosened it. A second crashed it open.

The room was overstocked with furniture. Framed photographs covered a mantelpiece and sideboard. A frail woman in her seventies or maybe eighties lay on the rug in front of the fireplace. Her gaze was pathetic.

'I've messed myself,' she said.

'That's all right, love.' He crouched by her side and stroked the hair from her brow. 'I'll sort it out.' Her lips were parched. 'When did you last have a drink?'

'Two . . . three days ago. I fell. I've broken something, I don't know what. But it hurts.'

He put the carbine down and put one arm, beneath her back and another beneath her legs. He could smell her.

'Shall I put you in your chair?' he said.

She nodded.

'If it hurts, I'll stop.' He lifted her gently and she winced and her face contorted in pain. She cried out, but it was easier to continue than put her back on the floor. He lowered her into an armchair that faced a blank TV set. She tried to ease herself into a more comfortable position but couldn't. He noticed the way her left foot lay askew. Leg or hip?

'I'll get you a drink.'

He ran the tap in the kitchen, filled a cup and brought it back. She drank gratefully.

'Thank you,' she said, and winced. 'Thank you. I thought I was a goner.' She nodded towards the photographs. 'My daughter and her family live in Manchester.' She kept nodding at the pictures. 'My grandchildren. God knows what's happened to them.'

'Manchester missed the worst of it,' he said. 'They evacuated people into Manchester. Chances are, they're all okay.'

'Thank God!' she breathed, and cried a little at the continuing pain.

'I'll call an ambulance,' he said. 'Get the medics here. You'll soon be in hospital and cleaned up. Get that hip sorted out.'

He picked up a photograph of a family group and handed it to her.

'That's my daughter Margaret,' she said. 'And John and Emma and Anna.'

Behind her chair, he took the Glock automatic from its holster and pulled back the slide to put a bullet in the chamber. He rattled the receiver from the phone. 'Hello?' he said. 'I need an ambulance.'

He pointed the gun at her head and pulled the trigger.

Reaper walked into the kitchen and looked at the poverty of the place. A grotty town centre flat, full of old furniture and memories; a kitchen with half a pint of milk and a piece of cheese in the fridge, and a container of some kind of homemade stew. Clean pans and empty cupboards, save for a few tins and a few crusts of stale bread. And she had survived, been unaffected by the virus, but had fallen and lived for the last three days in pain and uncertainty. He suspected she had made her peace with God a long time ago. He suddenly realised he didn't know her name.

A purse in a sideboard drawer told him she was Cecilia Bradshaw. She was 81.

Cecilia had dropped the photograph when he shot her and he picked it up. He put it into her lifeless hands and pressed it against her bosom before he left.

He went back to police HQ, baked bread in the canteen and fried steak on a griddle. He was still wearing the police cap and took it off when he sat down to eat. When he had finished, he didn't pick it up again. It didn't seem appropriate for mercy killings.

Cecilia wouldn't have made it. All he could have done was prolong her agony. He could rationalise all day but it didn't help. Best not to think about it. Maybe there was a god after all and this was part of his punishment.

In the early evening, he left the station on foot, still cradling the carbine that hung round his neck on a strap. Periodically, he would stop and shout, 'Hello.' His voice echoed back; the only response he got was from disturbed pigeons. There were few bodies on the streets or visible inside shop premises. Most people, it seemed, had gone home to die. Front rooms and bedrooms had become funeral parlours.

It started to rain. It was only a shower, but he had no coat and he looked for shelter. His attention was caught by The Great Outdoors, a specialist camping store. The door wasn't locked and he entered, making a search for the corpse of an owner or shop worker who might have underestimated the severity of his illness, but the place was empty. A tent might be an option for the future but right now he was more interested in a camping stove. He chose one that came with two burners and a grill and packed it into a rucksack, along with pans, utensils and gas cylinders. A glance outside revealed that the streets were still deserted, but he took bundles of clothing and boots from racks deeper into the store to ensure he could not be seen. He wasn't prudish, but he didn't want to be caught with his trousers down by anyone who might be a potential enemy.

He changed into navy-blue combat trousers with extra pockets, a pair of Doc Marten boots and navy blue T-shirt. The Kevlar vest went back on top and he strapped on the holsters. The boots were comfortable and strong enough to make kicking an optional weapon. The store had a lot of equipment and clothing he could use, if he lived long enough. He put a torch into the bag, along with a British Army all-purpose knife. A folding knife with a three-inch blade came in its own belt sheath, which he attached to his trouser belt. He also needed a watch too and unboxed one whose wrappings said *as used by US Special Forces*. Great. Now he could invade Afghanistan.

The rain was not heavy but it was persistent. He put on a long, navy-blue waxed coat with a storm cape over the shoulders. It was loose enough for him to hold the carbine inside its drape. He stuck a waxed hat on his head that would fold and go in a pocket when the rain stopped. Finally, he chose a pair of light-weight Tornado binoculars with a seven times magni-fication and a built-in compass. They were well over £100 but what the hell? They went into the bag too. He would return but, for now, he shouldered the ruck-sack and made his way back to Sainsbury's.

More shopping: this time for bottled water, tea bags, long-life milk, a stale loaf, pre-packed bacon and sausage, more frozen steaks. He stowed it all, shoul-dered the bag and took back streets to approach the Albert Hotel from the rear. There, a staff door was unlocked and interior lights were still on. He made his way into the kitchens and then stopped abruptly. A chef was hanging from a rope attached to a butcher's hook. A large chap in traditional white coat and check trousers. Flies circled his head. He had kicked a low stool away, presumably after consuming the greater part of the bottle of Remy Martin that was next to him on a stainless steel counter. An expensive bottle of courage.

Reaper wondered how many more had taken the same way out – after the despair of realising that the world they knew was at an end, that their loved ones were gone, that the future held nothing but uncer-tainty and pain. The chef was at the far end of the kitchen so he didn't need to disturb the body as he continued along a corridor and found a staircase to the ground floor entrance foyer. He went up again, crossed a mezzanine floor, and up one more flight to where the rooms started. There was a smell of death that he was getting used to, not strong but pervasive. The rooms at the front were suites and were locked, which was annoying. He left the rucksack and went down to reception. Thank goodness the hotel was old fashioned enough to have real keys and not electronic cards. He took a handful of the numbers he thought might be appropriate and went back upstairs. He found one that fitted and opened a door.

It was what he was looking for: a living room, bedroom and bathroom – and no previous occupant still in residence. He put the Do Not Disturb sign on the outside and locked the door. In the unlikely event of anyone else coming up here, they might think the sign had been there a long time and that something inside was dead and ripe.

He unpacked, set up the camping stove, lay out his food and placed a comfortable armchair by the window. It was just after seven. It hadn't occurred to him before, but he should have requisitioned a CD player too, while there was still power to use it. Maybe later. He made a mug of tea and took up his position in the armchair facing the row of bars and bistros to his left on South Parade. Bizarrely, many were still lit and half a dozen lights showed in the windows of the flats above. He checked them all through the binoculars then sat back into the gloom. He sipped his tea and waited.

They made their appearance at nine o'clock. Three men and a girl left the apartments and went into a bar called El Greco. There was no hesitation; it was a practised move. In front was the well-built young male. He wore jeans and a T-shirt and carried a shotgun against his left shoulder; over his right, he pulled the chain that dragged the girl. A short middle-aged man followed, looking decidedly incongruous wearing a suit while carrying a baseball bat. The third male was the obese younger man. He also held a shotgun.

Once they were inside, Reaper could see little, and so he put down his binoculars. He eased the window of his room open and heard music. Disco from a previous decade, not too loud. Perhaps they didn't want to attract too much attention. He checked the Glocks and cocked them both before leaving the room and locking it behind him. He did not take the carbine or his coat. He left the hotel the same way he had entered, through the kitchens. He did not look at the dead chef.

The rain had stopped and the air was fresh after the cloying interior of the hotel. It took only a few minutes to reach South Parade. He crossed a road where nonexistent traffic was still being controlled by

lights and smiled mirthlessly to himself when he realised
that he'd still looked both ways. The town felt dead,
abandoned by life and hope, and the muted sounds
from the bistro bar were an intrusion on the wake.

He took the guns from their holsters. For a while
he listened, back against the dark wall, next to the
light that spilled from the bar. A chair scraped . . .
someone laughed . . . another voice sang along to the
music . . . feet shuffled to the beat. He took a glance
inside but no one was looking his way. He assessed
the situation.

The middle-aged man in the suit was sitting in a
booth on his own, a grin upon his face as he watched
the obese youth move his considerable bulk in time
to the music. Fatman was swathed in gold chains, rings
and bracelets. The girl was dancing with him but in
a desultory fashion. She did not move away when he
ran his hands over her body, but neither did she appear
to be enjoying the experience. The middle-aged man's
eyes were fixed on the girl, who was dressed in a
parody of sexual sophistication. High heels and a short
black silk dress beneath which, Reaper could see, the
men had made her wear stockings. Living the fantasy
and who cared who suffered?

The girl was young but he was not good at judging
the ages of the young. They all looked pretty much
the same and he hadn't looked too closely in the last
few years. This girl was probably the first he had taken

an interest in since Emily. She was about five four – even in the heels, short brown hair, slim with nice features. An ordinary girl whose value as a commodity had increased simply by surviving.

Now he was this close, he realised that the younger man was not as young as he had first thought. Probably in his thirties. A hard muscled body and a hard face. The shotgun lay on the table in front of him and he was drinking from a pint glass. He was the one who was laughing as he made crude comments about the fat youth and the girl. The girl's face was impassive beneath extreme Panda-like make-up – their idea again? – that had streaked with tears. Her mind had gone somewhere else. But how long would it be allowed to stay there?

Reaper quietly opened the door and stepped inside. He kept his hands at his sides. The hard man stopped smiling and put a hand on the shotgun. Reaper stared at him and said, 'Don't.'

The hand remained on the stock but did not move. The middle-aged man looked frightened. The obese youth was flustered; he turned and backed towards the bar. His small eyes darted all over the place: looking for orders from his leader, looking for salvation, looking for escape. His shotgun lay on the bar.

The girl was confused and stopped dancing several beats after her partner. She looked at Reaper but had trouble assessing the changing circumstances. Maybe she thought he was a new addition to the group. Someone else she would have to service.

Reaper spoke to her.

'What's your name?'

Her gaze went from him to the hard man, looking for guidance.

'It's all right,' Reaper continued, in a soft voice. 'I'm not here to hurt you. What's your name?'

Now she looked back at him.

'Sandra,' she said.

'Do you want to be with these men, Sandra?'

More confusion. She looked round, uncertain.

'She's ours!' the hard man said. 'Fuck off and find your own!'

Reaper raised his right hand and shot the hard man in the chest. His body jumped in his seat and he slumped back against the red leather, his eyes wide in shock.

The obese youth turned and ran for a rear door. Reaper pointed the gun in his left hand past Sandra and shot him in the back. The middle-aged man was terrified. 'Please,' he said. 'Please!' He wet himself where he sat. Reaper shot him in the chest, too.

'They won't hurt you again, Sandra,' he said, quietly. 'No one will hurt you. I promise.'

Sandra had put her hands protectively to her chest, her eyes were as wide as the hard man's, though she was alive. Reaper stepped slowly to her and, gently and tentatively, put an arm around her shoulders.

'How old are you, Sandra?'

'Eighteen.'

'My daughter would have been eighteen. You're safe with me. I won't let anyone hurt you. Believe me. You're safe.'

The girl was too scared and too shocked to feel safe. The obese youth on the floor behind her was still moving and making strangled breathing sounds. Reaper turned and put a bullet in the back of his head. Now Fatman finally stopped moving.

'Come on,' he said. 'Let's leave this place.'

He led her across the square to the Albert Hotel and up to the first floor suite. He unlocked the door and ushered her inside. He switched on the light and said, 'What you need is a nice cup of tea.' He switched on the room's electric kettle to boil the water. She remained standing in the middle of the room, frightened, wondering what might be expected of her. The black silk dress had been expensive but looked wrong on her. Too small, showing too much. The men had not allowed her to wear a bra and he doubted she was wearing underwear. Just the stockings and a garter belt. He was angry enough to want to go back and shoot them again.

If he had left them alive, they would have become a danger. If he had killed only the leader, the other two would still have been guilty, and were weak enough to follow the next bully to come along or rape the next unprotected woman they found. A week before, they might have been ostensibly normal citizens. Since then, they had transgressed and their deaths had been necessary. Their deaths had been . . . *righteous*. Reaper was a man like any man. He had sexual urges, but he also had a moral code. Even more relevant, he had a dead daughter.

'Maybe you would like a bath?' he said.

The girl glanced at him and looked away. A bath might be welcome but it meant removing her clothes. He sat her on the sofa and made the tea. He loaded it with sugar that he found in sachets on the night stand.

'Here,' he said.

The girl took the mug.

'I'll see if the hot water works.'

To access the bathroom, he went through the bedroom. If the girl wanted to run, now was the time. He ran the hot tap and, wonder of wonders, it came out hot. He let it run for a bath and took a large white towelling robe back into the living room. She was still there, sipping the tea.

'You can put this on,' he said. 'And you can sleep in the bedroom. I'll sleep on the sofa.'

'Who are you?' she said.

'I'm the man who is going to look after you.'

'Why?'

He smiled. 'Because you need looking after.' He handed her the robe. 'Now, are you hungry?'

Again, she looked puzzled. This was not a conversation she had expected.

'How about a steak sandwich? Or bacon? Sausage?'

He smiled and for the first time, the mask behind which she had retreated, cracked.

'Steak would be good. They didn't do food.'

'Steak sandwich it is. And tomorrow, we'll go shopping.'

This time she smiled in response. A small smile, but a start.

Chapter 3

SANDRA WAS MORE TRUSTING WITH THE DAWN. Maybe it was because he had not attempted to molest her during the night. After her rescue and her bath, she had worn the towelling robe while he ate a steak sandwich in toast and drank more sweet tea. With the makeup washed away she had looked even younger. She relaxed a little, but had still been guarded, her eyes always wary for any untoward movement. He made none, nor did he ask what the men had done. He didn't need to; it was obvious.

Under gentle questioning, she said her name was Sandra Newton. She had lived on the outskirts of the city with her mother and had been a sales assistant in Top Shop. Her mother had died at home early in the pandemic, when undertakers were still working, and her body had been taken to a chapel of rest. The funeral had never been held, because the illness that had swept the land, had grown exponentially. Or, as Sandra put it, 'like Topsy'. Within a week, society broke down and shuffled to a close. In the latter days, those who ventured out stared at other people with fear and suspicion. She stayed at home until the food ran out and met the three men when she came into town. Not surprisingly, with all that had happened she was still in shock. Reaper guessed that those who had survived the sudden death of their loved ones, even if they had managed to avoid further trouble, would be in shock for a long time to come.

There had been a downpour during the night that he thought might have put out a few fires. The morning was dry but cloudy. While she was still asleep, he used a bathroom further along the corridor to shower and shave. He toasted bread on the stove's grill and fried bacon, and the aroma that woke her made the day seem almost normal. She opened the bedroom door and looked into the sitting room. For a long moment she stared at him, re-evaluated where she was and said, 'That smells good.' It was as if she had made a decision.

They ate in silence and, afterwards, he said, 'You need to go shopping for some new clothes,' and she smiled again at the concept of going shopping.

'What's your name?' she said.

'Reaper.' The singularity of the name somehow consigned his former existence to the past.

'Reaper,' she said, as if testing it.

'Sandra,' he said. 'Nice name.'

'My mum was a Clint Eastwood fan,' she said, but the reference passed him by. She looked up at him suddenly, her wide eyes catching and holding his. 'What are we going to do?'

'First, you'll get some clothes. Then we'll find others and start over.'

'Start over?'

He nodded.

'There's a place I know that would be good for a settlement.'

She stared at him and said again, 'Start over?'

'People will start over. Groups will get together, up and down the country. Some will have the best of intentions, others will want power, some will be like the men you met.'

She shuddered.

He smiled at her gently. 'We'll see who we find. Maybe no one will *want* to start over. Maybe they'll just want to drink Sainsbury's dry.'

'We always shopped at Tesco,' she said, and smiled at the small joke.

He smiled back. A small joke was a good beginning.

Reaper packed the rucksack and put it on his back.

He gave Sandra his long caped raincoat to cover her relative nakedness until she was able to choose new clothes. He noticed the way she looked at the weapons he carried.

'They're necessary,' he said. 'For us to have a chance, these are necessary. There always were bad people in the world and now they will be worse. Now there are no rules and men can be beasts. We both know that.' He tapped the carbine. 'Believe me, they're necessary.'

'I believe you,' she said.

They walked to the city's main shopping centre, Sandra uncomfortable on the high heels she had been made to wear. On the High Street, they entered Monsoon and she flipped through the racked dresses and skirts but shook her head.

'I need something like what you're wearing,' she said, and he nodded.

'Maybe later you can choose something nice.'

They stopped again at Marks and Spencer and she looked at him questioningly.

'Underwear?' he said, and she blushed.

They went in. Reaper grabbed packs of underpants and put them in the rucksack and then waited with eyes discreetly averted while she filled a plastic shopping bag and went into a fitting room to put on bra and pants. He was alert during the walk to the camping and outdoor store, but they saw no one.

Sandra picked out navy-blue combat trousers and

a T-shirt, like his, donned thick socks and Doc Martens and put her spare underwear in a rucksack along with a sweater and extra T-shirts. He added similar knives to the ones he carried, plus a torch and a pair of binoculars. She chose a caped coat like his, but shorter, and finished off her outfit with a navy-blue baseball cap. She looked at herself in a full-length mirror and then at Reaper.

'What do you think?' she said.

The clothes had given her confidence.

'I think we look like a team,' he said, and she laughed.

'Now where?'

'The police station.'

They entered the station through the yard and he took her to the armoury.

'Are you a policeman?' she said.

'Of a kind.'

Her eyes were wide as he fitted her with a Kevlar vest. She didn't complain about its weight or bulk but simply nodded when he asked if it felt okay.

'Have you ever fired a gun?' he asked.

'No-o,' she said, in a tone that implied 'don't be ridiculous'.

'I think you should learn.'

They exchanged a serious stare and she nodded.

'I'd like to.'

He fitted a belt and holster around her waist and took her into the police yard. He let her handle the

Glock unloaded to get used to its feel and weight.

'If you draw the weapon but don't have an immediate target, hold it in the ready stance. Upright, like this, in both hands.' He demonstrated and handed the gun to her and she followed his example. 'That way you won't shoot me and you can point when a target makes itself known.'

She nodded.

'Now the shooting stance. The target is on the other side of the yard. The white door? Stand like this.' She tried to follow his example. 'Feet apart, about the same width as your shoulders. You're right leg slightly behind the left, like a boxer.' He put his hand on her leg to move it into position. She did not flinch. 'Hold the grip firm and high and extend your right arm at shoulder height. That's it. Face forward. Now support your right hand with your left. The gun may kick and the double grip will hold it steady. That's it.' He walked around her and moved a leg fractionally, then her arm. 'If it doesn't feel right, it won't work. Does it feel right?'

'It feels strange.'

He smiled at her. 'Of course it does. Right, now let's try it loaded.' He took the gun from her and showed her how to load the magazine. 'It holds seventeen nine-millimetre cartridges. You put it in like this.' He took it out again. 'Now you do it.' She did it at the second attempt, then repeated the exercise. 'Always treat a gun as if it is loaded,' he said, 'and never point it at anything you are not prepared to shoot. Now, it's loaded but it isn't cocked. You need to rack the slide like this, to put a bullet in the chamber. Now it's ready for firing. Adopt the ready stance.'

Sandra did so.

'Now the shooting stance.'

She adopted the stance and Reaper stood behind her, aware of how small she was, and corrected her position once more.

'Look down the sight. Point, hold it firm.' The gun wavered a little. 'Now pull the trigger.'

She fired and the gun lifted a little, but not as much as he had expected, and a chunk flew off the white door. Sandra began to turn towards him with a smile on her face and the gun moving in his direction. He put out a hand to stop its traverse.

'Never forget what you are holding. Never point it at anyone by mistake. Always assume it is loaded.' She raised it to the ready and he pointed her back the correct way. 'Again.'

She fired again and again and hit the door five times.

He stood close behind her and could sense the excitement quivering within her.

'Again.'

She fired another five spaced shots, each time hitting the door. It was not a difficult target, but her success would give her confidence. She paused and looked at him over her shoulder.

'Now just blast away and empty the magazine,' he said.

Sandra did so, dropping more into the stance, feeling and being invigorated by the power, and hitting the door every time. Finally the trigger clicked on empty and she began to turn towards him but, as he stretched out an arm to stop the traverse of the gun, she corrected it herself and took out the empty magazine.

'How did it feel?'

'Brilliant.'

'Always remember it kills. Always remember the safety rules.' He smiled at the former sales assistant from Top Shop who was learning a new skill that might help her survive. 'Good shooting.'

They went through it again for an hour, until the safety aspects sank in, until she could draw the gun confidently and without fumbling, could load a magazine with cartridges, could load the pistol with a magazine. He explained how the gun could not be de-cocked. Each shot automatically put another bullet in the chamber. To de-cock it entailed removing the magazine and racking the slide to remove the last bullet. This was something she would do every day, prior to cleaning the weapon.

Finally, he let her fire again and watched her exhilaration. It was shortly after midday and he had just given a young girl lessons in how to kill. A month before, it would have been inconceivable. A month before, she may well have been totally disinterested to the point of ridiculing anyone who might have suggested it. Now she accepted it, embraced it. He thought that, after what she had already endured, she might already be willing and able to kill to avoid such pain and degradation occurring again.

'Hungry?' he said.

'Famished.'

They went into the police canteen, both of them now armed with Glocks, and he cooked sausages and oven chips. After they had eaten, they drank coffee.

Sandra began to cry and Reaper didn't know what to do. He reached a hand across the table and put it over one of hers.

'I'm sorry,' she said and sniffed. 'It's just that everything is mad.' She raised one hand to her eyes and removed the other from his hand to feel her pockets in vain. 'My nose is running now.'

He went to the counter and tore a strip from a roll of kitchen towel and handed it to her. She put it to her face and sniffed some more. He sat down opposite and waited.

'I'm sorry,' she said again.

'There's nothing to be sorry about. Anyone who survived will think it's mad. The world has ended. What else can it be?'

'It's just that . . .' she started crying again, the kitchen towel to her face and she reached her other hand across the table. He covered it with his own and felt happy that she had offered it. 'I cried when my mum died. I thought that was the end of the world. And I cried because I was on my own. I cried because I thought I might lose the house. I cried because I couldn't afford to pay for a funeral.' She laughed bitterly. 'And now everything's gone. None of it matters.'

'You're here. That matters.'

She wiped her nose, brushed a hand across her eyes to dry the tears and looked at him across the table.

'The men who found me. I knew one of them. The fat one. I'd seen him in The Red Light.' Reaper knew of the nightclub. 'He'd stand in a corner and watch the girls. He was a creep. He'd stand in a crowd at the bar so he could brush against you. You know?' Reaper nodded. He knew. 'The small bloke worked in an office. He was the worst. He . . .' but she stopped whatever revelation she may have been about to make and shook her head. 'Carl was the one with muscles. The leader. At least you knew where you were with him.' Her gaze had dropped while she was talking but she raised her eyes to make contact as she said, 'Drink, fuck, then drink until he fell asleep.' She was trying to be defiant, wanting comfort, understanding, forgiveness for something she had been unable to prevent. He gripped her hand tighter.

'Last night . . .' she said. 'When you shot them . . . You did it so quick. No questions.'

'There was no need for questions.'

'Did you have to kill them?'

'They could have come back. They could have killed me, taken you. Should I have let them go?'

They exchanged a long look.

'No,' she said.

He nodded. 'They deserved to die and they didn't deserve a second chance. If they hadn't come after us, they would have gone looking for someone else, another girl. They had to die for the protection of everyone else. This is a new order. The old rules are dead.' He took a breath. 'You know you don't have to stay with me just because I helped you out last night.'

'I *want* to stay with you!'

She seemed momentarily panicked at the thought of losing the first stability that had entered her life since everything had changed.

'I'm just saying, you're free to leave at any time in the future. We may meet a group that appeals to you. People with different ideas.' He smiled again. 'Maybe there'll be someone you find you like and who's closer to your age, who doesn't want to be part of my way forward. If that happens, it will be okay. I'm not going to be a dictator. More a . . .' He thought about it for a moment. '. . . a *facilitator*. I'll help anyone who wants to survive and start again at the place I know.'

'Like a sort of policeman,' she said. Reaper kept his

smile, but shook his head. 'An armed guard?' He laughed at the thought.

'No,' she said, as if she had made up her mind. 'A one-man army.'

He laughed loudly this time and immediately thought it a strange sound to be echoing through a police head-quarters empty but for the two of them and a handful of dead bodies.

'You're forgetting,' he said. 'There are two of us, now.'

Sandra had overcome her tears, taken back her hand and sat back in her chair.

'Where's this place you want to go?'

'Further north. The other side of York. It used to be a country house and the owners converted it into flats. Then they built holiday cottages in the grounds to make a sort of self-contained holiday village. They even made one of the cottages into a pub. It's in a lot of grounds, all enclosed by a high wall, and has a small farm. I went there once on holiday. To be honest, I found it a bit claustrophobic. I'm not good with people. But it could be an ideal place to start a new community.'

'When do we leave?'

'Tomorrow.'

'What about other people?' She smiled cheekily. 'What about this man who is more my age? Where will we find him?'

'We'll find people on the way.'

'So what do we do next?'

'Choose our mode of transport.'

'Sorry?'

He grinned. 'Rolls Royce, Transit van, motor home?'

'Could we really go in a Rolls Royce?'

'We could, but it would be impractical. A Transit might be best.'

She pulled a face. 'I've never been in a Rolls Royce.'

'How about a motor home?'

'Is that like a caravan?'

'Sort of. We'll go and look at some.'

They took the police car he had used the day before and drove into the suburbs. A firm specialising in motor homes and caravans was located on the rural edge of the sprawling conurbation. As they approached a cross-roads at a small shopping centre, they saw two people in the distance scurry away and hide. Perhaps they had already suffered at the hands of strangers and didn't want to risk another encounter. They drove down tree-lined streets at a pace slow enough to be noticed and Reaper kept a look in the rear view mirror in case someone came out in response to their presence, but no one did.

The occasional stray dog or small pack crossed their path and he wondered about the pets that had been locked inside their homes when their owners fell ill.

Their plight evoked a pang of sorrow that he hadn't felt for the human race.

Winslow's was at the top of a hill four miles from the city centre, a large sprawling site filled with caravans and what were termed RVs or Recreational Vehicles. He parked and they looked around to get their bearings. Reaper cradled the carbine, just in case. When they moved, they started off in different directions. Sandra headed towards where the biggest and most luxurious vehicles were parked, while he went towards the smaller, compact and more manoeuvrable vans. He sighed and turned to follow her. After all, he had offered and then denied her a Rolls Royce in the same breath. The least he could do was allow her some choice.

He talked her out of anything that was too big to be practical and she was persuaded to settle for a five-berth van with luxury fittings. Reaper liked the three-litre diesel engine, five gears and plenty of storage space, while Sandra appreciated the splendour of the interior. It had a double bed above the driving cabin in a bubble that reminded him of Japanese capsule hotel rooms he had once seen on TV. There was a double bedroom at the rear and a bench seat in the living area provided the fifth bed. The van was equipped with oven, fridge and a slim-line bathroom that, while seeming to be no bigger than an aircraft lavatory, included a shower. The dashboard had the look of a Boeing 747 and the armchair front seats also swivelled to face inward.

'You want this?' he said.

'Yes.'

'I'll make the man an offer.'

He found the keys in an office. The fuel pumps on site still worked and he filled the tanks. He checked that the two propane gas bottles that were fitted were full and added two more as spares, then filled the fresh water tank. He also scouted around for a length of tubing in case he had to syphon more diesel from another vehicle during the journey.

'What about the car?' she said, meaning the police Astra, when he climbed behind the wheel and started the engine.

'We are living in a disposable society,' he said.

Sandra got into the passenger seat and he drove out of the compound. The six-wheeled vehicle drove more easily than he had imagined and the engine felt full of power. The seats were high and comfortable and gave an impressive view. He just hoped the van was not so noticeable as to become a target.

On the way back, he took a detour into the mostly empty car park of an Asda supermarket. He approached cautiously, drawing the van side-on up to the front entrance of the store. Two cars were parked or had been abandoned in an erratic fashion directly outside: a Range Rover, with its front doors left open, and a

Jaguar; the sort of cars that might have been chosen by looters. No windows had been smashed in the store.

'What do we need?' Sandra asked.

'Bottled water. Food for the road.' He eyed the building suspiciously. 'Let's be cautious, okay?'

'Okay.'

She sensed his unease as they stepped out of the van. The carbine hung on its strap around his neck as a deterrent. If there was trouble inside, a handgun would be easier to use, but the sight of the heavier weapon might make potential attackers think twice. They reached the front of the store and the doors hissed open automatically. Sandra unfastened the safety strap that held the Glock in its holster.

Without speaking, she got a trolley from a rack and they moved down deserted aisles. In places, they showed signs of pillaging, particularly when they passed the alcohol section. He raised a hand. They stopped, and from somewhere in the store they heard scurrying footsteps. He held the carbine at the ready and they continued. When they reached the water, he pointed to Sandra, then to her gun and made a fist like he was holding a pistol. She nodded and took out her weapon, racked the slide and held it in the ready position in both hands, raised in front of her face. He put the carbine across the top of the trolley and filled it with packs of two-litre bottles of water.

They moved on to tins and bake-your-own bread,

tea, coffee, sugar, whitener. At the sweet section, he added chocolate raisins and chocolate bars for energy and Sandra threw in more chocolate, Midget Gems and Smarties for fun. At the frozen food, he stopped abruptly and Sandra, seeing his reaction, stepped closer and looked into a refrigerator that contained packets of peas, Brussels sprouts and a dead body. An elderly man with a fatal wound to his head lay on his back. He was very pale, his eyes stared and his lips were frosted.

Reaper looked at Sandra. The hands that held the gun trembled momentarily. She returned his look and nodded with determination.

'Time to go,' he said.

He hung the carbine round his neck again, slid it under his arm into the small of his back, took a Glock from its holster and cocked it. He pushed the trolley with his left hand and the weight of his body. It was heavy and a little unwieldy and they slowed as they approached the entrance to the store, a tall aisle of toys on their left and displays of clothes on their right.

He felt the threat in the air. Maybe they should have gone to a smaller shop. Too late now.

'We're leaving!' he shouted. 'No need for anyone to get hurt.'

No one answered. Perhaps there was nobody there. Perhaps he was being paranoid. But sometimes, paranoia kept you safe.

'Okay?' he said softly to Sandra.

Sandra glanced at him and nodded again. He pointed his weapon to the left, she dropped into the shooting stance and pointed hers to the right and together they moved forward out from the protection of the aisle. He stared down a row of abandoned tills and checkout stations. A bottle smashed somewhere from that direction and he sensed Sandra might turn. 'Stay,' he said, and she corrected the movement, fired a single shot, gasped and fell against him, landing on the floor on her bottom.

At the same time items came over the top of the aisle of toys, long kitchen knives, a television, heavy kitchen pots. He avoided them and fired four shots through the shelves, confident the flimsy construction wouldn't stop them. Sandra fired more shots but he didn't count them. He crouched and turned to her. He heard curses and footsteps and crouched beside her.

'Are you all right?'

His eyes tried to cover everywhere and she gasped, 'They threw an axe at me.' He glanced down and saw the axe on the floor next to her. Footsteps were loud in the aisles. Three, four people? Coming back? 'I'm okay. It hit the vest, but it hurt my tits.'

He hauled her to her feet and said, 'We'll use the trolley as cover.' He turned it round and pulled it one handed behind them and they retreated side by side towards the front doors, handguns covering the unseen dangers of the store – the glimpse of a face taking a peek and he fired. It ducked away. The doors hissed open behind them. He stepped out briefly to check, but no one was outside.

He dragged the trolley across the deserted car park and round the front of the van.

'Load the stuff in the side door,' he said. 'I'll cover.'

He holstered the automatic and swung the carbine round, training it on the front doors as they hissed open again. A group of men and women appeared carrying a variety of weapons. Bottles were hurled towards them; they smashed on the ground and sprayed liquid. A teenager in a designer suit was lighting a rag that was stuck into the neck of a bottle of vodka. But Reaper's attention was caught by a man who now appeared at their rear, carrying a crossbow, held at shoulder height. Reaper shot him and the man fell backwards, the bolt flying high over the van. The others scattered back into the store, all except the teenager with the now lit Molotov cocktail. Reaper shot him as he swung his arm back for the throw. The bottle went back into the store and the youth fell, a bullet in his chest. The Molotov cocktail exploded and flames enveloped the clothing section. There were screams. A woman ran out, her clothes on fire, and Reaper shot her. No one else ran out. The store's sprinkler system activated and began to douse the flames.

Sandra was at his side, her gun once more held upright in the ready stance.

'Time to go,' he said. 'I think you scared them.'

He entered the van through the passenger door and clambered across into the driving seat. He lowered the window and pointed his gun, while Sandra covered the manoeuvre. Then she joined him, crouching behind his chair to cover the store entrance while he reversed. No one came out to watch them go, or attempted to stop them, and Reaper wondered what had possessed the group to pick a fight with two armed people. Jealousy because of the motor home? Possessiveness? Did they consider the Asda to be *their* store? Had turf wars started already?

They drove in silence back towards the police station.

'You did well,' he said. 'You did bloody well.'

'They threw a fucking axe at me.'

'Language, Sandra,' he said, and they both burst out laughing, releasing the adrenalin, although he saw the fragility in her eyes.

She had been through a lot. He knew all about the after effects of rape, the shock and disbelief, feelings of alienation, withdrawal, depression. Even self-blame. In a perfect world, she would have time to come to terms with her emotional trauma and receive proper treatment. Not that that always worked. In a perfect world, it would never have happened in the first place. In this world, she didn't have time to recover. She had to survive. Maybe a diversion would be good.

Reaper made another stop: right outside a record store in the High Street in the middle of the pedestrian way.

'DVDs? CDs?' he announced.

The van was equipped for both.

They got out, handguns drawn. The shop door was open, hanging off its hinges. He pointed and, with hand signals, positioned her to stand by the counter and keep him covered as he went quickly through to the back of the store and checked out the staff room. They were in sole possession of the shop. He returned to the counter where he found a box that he handed to her.

'Choose something.'

'What do you like?'

He shrugged. 'The Beatles . . . Clapton . . . Laurel and Hardy?' Sandra looked blank. 'You choose.'

She went down the aisles, dropping films and music discs into the box. He kept watch out of the window but saw no one, and his mind drifted back to the Asda store. It could all have ended so differently. If that axe had been higher, Sandra could have been badly wounded or dead. Had it been a risk too far? Christ, everything was a risk several miles too far. He jumped when she rejoined him and touched his shoulder.

They got back in the van and drove to the police

station where he parked in the compound around the back. Reaper found a key in the guardhouse and locked the gates behind them. Sandra was in the yard waiting for him. She looked quite the warrior, although he knew that was only image. Maybe she would believe in the image long enough for it to develop into reality. He hoped her new persona would help her get over all she had suffered. She had left girlhood behind.

Reaper began to relax now that the gates were closed, and he could see some of the tension draining from Sandra too.

'Okay?'

'Okay,' she said, and came into his arms.

He was surprised, but pleased. He held her for a moment then kissed the top of her head. The embrace was not sensual. It was of friendship, comradeship. She could have been his daughter, and yet she had come through so much in the last few days and hours.

'You did well,' he said. 'Now, what we need is a nice cup of tea.'

Chapter 4

THEY HAD SHED THE KEVLAR VESTS AND WERE sitting in the canteen when they heard the commotion. The echo of a door slamming, a voice, then the same voice raised in panic followed by screams and yells. They drew their handguns and ran.

Reaper led the way along the corridor and down the stairs, taking them two at a time. They followed the noise coming from the front reception office. This was a carpeted room with a bench seat to one side and a door that led to an interview room. The reception desk was high to dissuade anyone attempting to jump over it. A door with a keypad lock led into the office space at the rear of the reception desk and another keypad door was to the side to allow officers access and egress to the station proper. Both doors had been propped wide open.

He stopped in the doorway that led into the public part of the front office. A woman was on the floor, a man on top of her. She was screaming and fighting as he tried to pin her arms above her head. A second man, standing by the double doors that led outside, caught sight of Reaper, and threw a knife at him. He stepped sideways to avoid it and heard Sandra shoot. The man's head exploded and sprayed blood on the glass doors. His body was flung backwards and slumped down against them. The man on the floor stared up at Reaper, eyes wide with surprise, raised his hands and began to get to his feet. Reaper shot him in the chest, flinging his body back across that of his companion.

Reaper glanced sideways and saw Sandra behind the desk, right arm straight, left arm slightly bent to help hold the gun steady. Her eyes were wide and the gun was not steady. It wavered. He stepped back and went to her. Gripped her shoulder. She was breathing heavily. Then Reaper spotted the boy, maybe four years old, crouched in an alcove beneath the desk, eyes unblinking, mouth open.

'Sandra,' he said. 'The boy.' He got her attention. 'Put the gun away. Look after the boy.'

She did as she was told and crouched in front of the youngster, his distress outweighing her own, and reached her arms out to him. Reaper went back into the front office to the woman who was now sitting up, gasping, still fearful. Her scoop neckline top was torn to reveal large breasts.

'You're okay now,' he said. He didn't want to stare; he went to the door and looked out. 'Were there any others?'

'No. I don't think so. I think they were the ones who took Mrs Jones. She lives at number five. I hid with Ollie. Is Ollie . . .?'

'He's safe.'

He held out a hand and she took it to pull herself to her feet. She was late thirties, blonde hair in a nondescript style. She was short and stocky and wore jeans that were tight around her hips. A pleasant, slightly chubby face with a turned-up nose. Her cleavage was her best feature, which was probably why she had worn the top – fine when times were normal, but dangerous now. She was recovering quickly.

'I'm Jean. Jean Megson.' She held out a hand and he shook it. 'I saw a police car go past earlier so took a risk and drove here. After seeing them take Mrs Jones, I didn't know what else to do. They must have been waiting because they followed, only I didn't know until we got here. Then we just ran.'

After the relative quiet he'd shared with Sandra, Jean Megson, it seemed, could talk for England.

Reaper said, 'I'm Reaper.'

On the other side of the counter, Sandra had picked up the boy who clung to her with both hands around her neck.

Jean seemed to notice her torn blouse and tried in vain to make it cover her exposed bra.

'Oh! I'm sorry,' she said. 'I have another in my bag.'

He glanced outside and saw two cars parked on the grass.

'In the car?' he said.

She nodded, then she noticed the bodies as if for the first time. She shuddered and turned away. He ushered her through the doorway, and turned to Sandra, 'I'll only be a minute. I have to get their bag.'

He went back into reception, pulled the bodies away sufficiently so that he could open one of the doors, and checked outside. It was clear. He ran to the first car, a three-year-old Ford, and saw two bags on the back seat. He opened the door, grabbed them and ran back into the station. Sandra was standing behind the counter, gun raised, in the ready stance. The boy was now in Jean's arms. Reaper dropped the bags in the corridor.

'Take them to the canteen. I'll secure the building.' Sandra raised an eyebrow as if about to argue. He leaned closer so only she could hear. 'Best they have protection. It will make them feel better.'

She nodded, put away her gun and picked up the bags.

'This way,' she said, and Reaper nodded at Jean, indicating she should go with Sandra.

He returned to the front office, but could find no way of locking the glass doors. Instead, he lay the bodies across them as a deterrent and to make it difficult for anyone to push them open. He removed the jams from the two interior doors so that they locked. If anyone tried to batter through them, they would hear. He went to the basement corridor that led from the cells to the courts that were located next door. That door also had a keypad lock, but was propped open. He removed the prop and let the door close. A side door for maintenance was already locked, so his last call was at the rear. He secured the back door that gave access to the vehicles.

'Yo!' he shouted as he approached the canteen, in case Sandra was nervous. 'It's me.'

Sandra had brewed more tea, which Jean was sipping gratefully. She had changed her torn top for another with a similarly scooped neckline. The boy was eating a chocolate biscuit and drinking a can of pop. Sandra was once more in control of herself. *Good.* She was still playing the tough soldier role. Keep playing it, he thought. Eventually it would work. Sandra went to the counter, poured a mug of tea, added whitener and handed it to him. Togetherness: she knew how he took his tea. They stood side by side in their matching outfits and looked at their first two survival candidates for starting over.

'I thought you were police,' Jean said, 'but Sandra says you're Special Forces.'

Reaper smiled and sensed a moment of discomfort for his partner.

'That's right,' he said. 'We're special forces.'

As Jean relaxed, they learned a little more about her. Her home had been in one of the tree-lined suburbs through which they had driven on their way to choose a motor home. A semi-detached house, a good job in Human Resources, a divorce eight years ago and – no, thank you very much – she had not been looking for another relationship since. Although, Reaper pondered, her choice of blouse might have suggested differently. There had been no children, something for which she was now thankful. She was not the maternal type, she assured them. Her father was dead and her mother lived in Cumbria but hadn't answered her phone for days, that is, when they were still working. She accepted the likelihood that her mother was dead.

She had taken Ollie Collins, the four-year-old, into her care when his mother became ill.

'His father was away on business,' she explained in a low voice, while Ollie sat on the floor and played with a car he had taken from the bag Jean had packed for him. 'He's away a lot. Germany, Switzerland – anywhere in Europe. Anyway, he didn't come back and Geraldine got the flu and . . . that was it, basically.

By then, we all knew what would happen, and it did. She died ever so quickly.

'I took Ollie to my house. We went to the shops when they were still open, when people were still behaving normally – or trying to. Mr Jenkins at Village Stores just let us take what we wanted. He could see the writing on the wall. We all could. 'Stock up,' he said. His wife was ill and he had started coughing and I think he knew. He just let us take what we wanted. Never asked for a penny, although I left money on the counter. Next time I went, the shop was open but he wasn't there. The only people I saw was an old chap and a teenage girl. Not together, separate, stacking stuff in trolleys. The girl had strong lagers, alcopops and cigarettes. She put a bottle of whisky in the old chap's trolley and said, go on, treat yourself. It might never happen.'

Jean laughed . . . but the laughter turned swiftly to tears.

'"It might never happen." But it did. Didn't it?'

Sandra put an arm around her. The 18-year-old comforting the older woman. Part of the role. The art of the role.

'When I stopped seeing people in the street, I felt frightened. One car came down the street, cruising . . . *very slow* . . . men inside, looking at the houses – and I hid. It came back later and stopped. Three men – two of them were the men downstairs – started breaking in the houses opposite. I didn't know what they were looking for but they found Mrs Jones at number 15. A nice young woman. Her husband's an architect for the council.' Jean smiled an apology. '*Was* an architect for the council. They took her away in the car. She didn't want to go but what could she do? What could I do? We just hid. We prayed.'

As Jean was close to tears again at the thought of what might have become of her neighbour, Sandra changed the subject: telling Jean about the safe haven they had in mind, where a group could start a new community, and that they had a motor home outside for the journey. The thought that a fresh beginning might be possible diverted Jean and cheered her up. The way Sandra told it, everything was already in place for a new Eden. Reaper didn't disillusion anyone. Not yet.

He suggested that Jean might like to prepare a meal while he and Sandra checked the motor home. Jean was eager to be of assistance and to take charge of the still-functioning kitchen. Reaper took Sandra to the armoury and handed her a carbine.

'I think you should learn how to use one of these, as well,' he said, and he could tell she was pleased at his confidence in her. And yet it was not just confidence that motivated him. It was necessity. She had already proven to be a girl with gumption and, besides, he had no one else. He showed her the basics: how to load the magazine, how to hold the weapon. She was a quick learner. 'It may feel a bit heavy at first but you'll soon get used to the weight.'

'What are we going to do with all this?' she said, gesturing at the small arsenal that surrounded them.

'Take it with us. Also, I want to collect all the Asps.'

She looked quizzical.

'The batons. They can be deadly at close quarters. It will mean breaking into the lockers.'

'What do we do first?'

'The lockers.'

He led the way to the locker rooms. The locks were not particularly strong and he used the blade of his British Army knife to force the first, feeling just a little like a grave robber. Sandra followed his example. Personal possessions were on the top shelf. A photograph of a young couple was stuck in a crack in the metal: a good-looking young couple who leaned in close for the camera, their heads and hands touching.

'Take the equipment belts,' he said, gruffly.

The Asps were attached to the belts in leather holders, along with handcuffs, a CS Spray can, a torch, an unused pouch and a key holder for the cuffs. He stopped looking at the top shelves and photographs and instead took the belts and they dropped them in a pile on a table. They had 32 when he called time.

'Jean will be getting worried,' he said. 'You go back upstairs and I'll find something to carry these in.'

He found boxes of files in an office, dumped the files on the floor, filled two boxes with the belts and carried them to the back door. Also in the locker room was a metal battering ram, known as an Enforcer. He took that as well. Carrying the whole load took him two journeys. By the time he was done, it was early evening and the sun was low but still bright, the sky tinged with red. An artist's sky. What did red sky at night mean? Sailor's delight? Smooth waters for tomorrow's adventure?

Reaper suddenly felt hungry. There was still much to do but he needed to eat, needed to be back with Sandra and Jean and the boy Ollie. These were now his people.

The smell greeted him at the canteen door.

'I made a stew, baked some bread,' said Jean.

'It smells great!'

The food was from tins but she had made it taste delicious – that, or he was hungrier than he had realised.

Later, they moved to a chief inspector's office that had a TV with a built-in DVD player. Sandra brought a handful of films from the van and Ollie chose *Ice Age 3*. Jean and the boy settled down on easy chairs to watch the movie while Reaper and Sandra went back to the armoury. They found more boxes and two holdalls, from which they tipped footballs and cricket gear and loaded up their arsenal and ammunition.

They packed it all into a rear storage area of the motor home, along with the boxes of belts and Asps. He took two Asps and torch holders from the belts and they fitted them on the holster belts they wore.

Reaper showed Sandra the beauty of the Asp. How to flick it open so that it extended to 22 inches of steel. 'Aim for the arms, hands, knees. You'll break bones. If you land a hit on the head, you'll cause serious damage.' He put the tip on the concrete floor, pushed down and retracted it.

They sorted out the supplies of food and water they had obtained that afternoon, putting it in cupboards and the refrigerator of the van.

'Tonight, we'll sleep in here,' he said. 'Jean and Ollie can have the bedroom.'

'How long will it take to get there, tomorrow?' Sandra asked, and he grinned.

'We've not even started and you're already asking if we're there yet.'

She poked him in the ribs. 'How long?'

'A few hours. Straight up the M1 then onto the York road.'

'Is that allowing for traffic jams?'

He smiled, but he had already considered them. Not slow moving traffic but possible barriers across the road. That was why he had decided not to take the route through country lanes and villages to the motorway. The roads were too small for emergency manoeuvres in this van. They would stick to major roads. He was already regretting choosing the motor home because it was such a target. A workaday Transit would have been better, but then there wouldn't have been anywhere to put Jean and Ollie. He had to accept that every step into the future was a risk. What was one more?

The interior of the van was snug and provided a false sense of security with all the blinds in place. The bogeyman was locked out, so they must be safe. Jean and Ollie were pleased to have the bedroom and, despite the woman professing she had no mothering instinct, she was doing a pretty good job with the little boy.

They closed the door and Reaper nodded towards the bunk above the driving cabin.

'That's yours,' he said. 'I'll take the bench.'

'It looks very narrow.'

'It pulls out.' He pulled it out. 'I'll be fine on that. But first, I'll do a tour.

'I'll come with you.'

He was about to argue that someone should stay to protect the van but he thought it was fairly secure. The gate and walls were high and had razor wire along the top and, so far, no one had come visiting. That would change when someone out there realised there might be guns in here. Hopefully, by then, they would be gone.

They put on the protective vests and picked up the carbines.

'Jean!' he called, softly, leaning close to the door.

'Yes?'

'We're going to check the perimeter. We won't be long. We may fire a couple of test shots, so don't be worried when you hear them. We'll be back soon.'

'Okay.'

They left the motor home and checked the gates, looking through them into the street, still lit by the overhead lamps. Nothing moved. The other access points were all secure. They made the tour in silence and Reaper led her up a final staircase and onto the flat roof of the building. At its edge, they stared out over the city, still bright with neon, shop windows and street-lights. It was strange; overall it was so very, very quiet, and yet this served only to make individual sounds so much more clear and distinct: drunken voices and a strand of music hung among distant buildings. Smoke from another fire rose lazily in the distant gloom. Lights still shone with false hope on the hillsides beyond.

'Time to try the carbine,' he said. 'It's accurate up to 200 metres. We'll try something nearer.' They walked across the roof to the back of the building and looked over the side, down into a landscaped area of grass, flowerbeds and a few trees that was meant to make the frontage of the 1960s concrete magistrates court look more attractive. It had failed a long time ago. 'That tree,' he said. It was about 50 metres away.

Sandra raised the gun to her shoulder.

'In close combat you could fire from the hip or from the shoulder without the sights. Aim and point. But normally, you'll use the laser sight. Hold the weapon into your shoulder.' She did so. 'Now try to make sure that the red dot fits the cross hair of the sight. Is it properly sighted?'

'Yes,' she said. 'They fit.'

'Good.' He thought they would. The carbine sights would have been aligned and ready to use. If any of the guns needed re-aligning, it was an easy enough job adjusting the mounting screws with an Allen key. 'Now. Hold it tight into the shoulder.' He adjusted her stance. 'Lower your weapon until the sight moves over the tree. If you were resting the gun on a ledge or a wall, you could hold the target in your sights, no problem. But you're taking a shot from a standing position. The gun will waver. Lower the sights onto the target. As it moves onto the tree, squeeze the trigger.'

She moved the red dot of the laser beam over the tree a couple of times for practice, then fired at the third pass. The bullet clipped the bark. 'Good shot,' he said. 'Try a couple more.'

Sandra missed with her next shot, but hit the target squarely with the third.

He put his hand on her shoulder and she raised the weapon and slipped on the safety.

'How did it feel?'

'Comfortable,' she said. 'But then, I'm only aiming at a tree.'

It was a valid point. A handgun you pointed and fired, often in a taut situation like that they'd already experienced in the supermarket or the front office of the Police HQ. A carbine or rifle you had time to aim; time to look down the barrel at your target, at the human being you were about to kill. It took a different kind of nerve, of courage, of commitment.

'That's enough for tonight,' he said.

They walked along the perimeter of the roof, back towards the door that would lead down into the building. They stopped again to stare over the city and at the hills beyond the ring road. It all looked so normal. You could almost pretend it hadn't happened. Then, without warning, the lights went out. Suddenly, block by block, the city became dark, and died. Glass smashed somewhere in the distance. The strand of music stopped abruptly. Cursed obscenities and moans of despair arose from what had become an underworld.

Sandra gasped and he put a hand on her shoulder.

'It had to happen eventually,' he said. 'Now we enter a new phase.'

Back in the van, they disarmed and removed the Kevlar vests, but not their clothes. The darkness outside had made the night ominous.

'I'm not going in the bunk,' Sandra said.

He looked at her questioningly.

'I'll share yours. I need a hug.'

She lay tight against the wall and he lay alongside her. The night was warm but he still draped a blanket across them to provide the illusion of normality.

'Put your arm round me,' she said. He lay on his side and did as he was told. They lay silently for a long time although both remained awake. Eventually she said, 'I killed a man.'

He squeezed her and kissed the back of her head. 'You had to. He was trying to kill me.'

'It was easy. I didn't know it would be so easy.'

'It's not easy,' he said, and held her and she cried.

'No,' she whispered. 'It's not.'

Periodically during the night, he slipped from beneath the blanket, took a Glock from a holster, and checked the yard and the building. The city was silent. Maybe it was in shock because of its loss of power. The lights had gone out and the music had ended. The apocalypse was now real.

Chapter 5

IN THE MORNING, THEY USED THE WOMEN OFFICERS'
showers and bathroom; they had to preserve what they
had in the van and Reaper already regretted not
stacking more gas cylinders. Jean used the motor home's
oven to grill toast and make tea for breakfast and,
before they left, she returned to the canteen and came
back with a box of tinned foodstuffs. Reaper checked
the street outside and opened the gates. He drove down
the street and stopped at The Great Outdoors. Sandra
stood outside with the carbine across her chest as he
entered. He collected two boxes of gas cartridges for
camping stoves and three six-kilogramme cylinders for
the van, two double sleeping bags and a single.

Both Reaper and Sandra were nervous, but no one

was about. Jean stored the new additions to their supplies as he drove onto the ring road, heading for the M1. The roads were empty, apart from parked cars and the occasional crash – some, he suspected, had been caused by joyriders after the cataclysm. He kept to a steady speed through the urban areas, ever watchful, and he and Sandra saw occasional faces peering from bedroom windows; the remnants of a confused and frightened population waiting for someone to restore order. An old man in his garden waved as they passed but they kept on going.

The road ran into countryside for a while and he increased speed. Back into a built-up area and more signs that others were still alive. They came suddenly upon a bonfire at a crossroads outside a pub, around which maybe a dozen people were standing: men, women and children. The group stared in surprise and someone threw a brick. Reaper did not stop.

Back into the country and a car approached from the other direction. A Range Rover. Reaper guessed no one would be driving old wrecks any more. It slowed at their approach and, at the last minute, drove into their path, perhaps hoping to force him off the road. Anticipating such a move, Reaper drove onto the other side of the road, clipping the rear of the Range Rover. For the first time, he was glad that they had so much weight onboard.

The Rover turned and followed. Reaper did not

attempt to outrun the pursuing vehicle. He took out a pistol and lowered his window. Sandra lowered her window. He glanced at her and her face was determined. She held the carbine upright in her lap and he nodded. He kept the van on the wrong side of the road, forcing the driver of the Range Rover to approach on the inside. As it nosed almost level, Sandra leaned out and fired the carbine. Four, five, six shots. He watched in the wing mirror: the men inside the car panicking; the car's windscreen shattering; the car veering, hitting the pavement and going through a fence into a field that was below road level, hitting it hard, nose down, and then flipping, end over end. Reaper kept on driving.

He glanced at Sandra again. She was sitting straight in the seat, the gun once more upright in her lap, taking deep breaths. She looked at him and gave a tight smile and nodded. He nodded back, returned the handgun to its holster and pressed the button for the window to go back up. A moment later, she did the same and lay the carbine in a more comfortable position with its butt on the floor. In the back, Jean had diverted Ollie by inviting him to choose another DVD.

'Ice Age 3 again?' she said, before slipping it into the DVD player in the bedroom.

Thirty miles to the M1 took an hour. They joined the motorway and headed north. The highway was empty and invited speed, but he did not exceed 50.

They passed a car that had crashed into a concrete bridge support and another that had taken off from the tarmac and landed a distance away in a field. A car approached on the other carriageway travelling fast. A Bentley. A man and woman were inside. They exchanged stares of curiosity but made no other acknowledgement of each other.

After an hour, two Transits approached at a reasonable speed. They slowed, Reaper slowed and he lowered his window. Sandra climbed out of her seat and crouched in the back of the van behind his seat, the carbine out of sight. The two Transits and the motor home stopped on different sides of the concrete and steel barrier that ran down the centre of the motorway.

'How's the road south?' shouted a large man who seemed to be all pale skin and muscles. A woman and child sat with him in the cab.

'Clear for the next fifty miles,' Reaper said. 'How about north?'

'We joined twenty miles back. It's clear that far. Where you heading?'

'North Yorkshire. Fresh air and hills,' Reaper said, attempting geniality. 'You?'

'We heard a rumour about some kind of government in Cambridge.'

Reaper nodded and they sat and stared at each other. They were each committed to their own destinations but, for Reaper at least, and he guessed for the man opposite, this was about as normal a conversation as he had had since it started. The van behind had pulled almost alongside the first van and he could see it contained two white women and an Afro-Caribbean man.

'You got some place to go?' the pale man asked, making conversation.

'There's a place I have in mind,' Reaper said. 'Other side of York. Could be good.'

The man nodded.

'Good luck!' he called.

'You too.'

They each moved off slowly, as if sorry to be breaking the small touch of social contact. Sandra waved and one of the women waved back. Should he have done more, invited them along? He guessed that was what Sandra might be thinking, but the middle of a motorway was the wrong place to make a pitch for survival in a walled holiday village, especially on a moment's acquaintance.

'Normal people,' he said. 'They exist.'

'Thank God,' she said.

'I hope they make it.'

'Me too.'

Another forty miles and he slowed and Sandra lifted the carbine to the cradle position. Ahead, two vehicles were parked at the side of the road in the slow lane. A middle-aged man who had been sitting

in a folding camping chair between the cars stood
up. He carried a shotgun, broken for safety. Now he
closed it but held it casually in his right hand, the
barrel in the crook of his left. Reaper slowed the
van so that they approached at a pace that would
not alarm.

'Keep the carbine down,' he said, and Sandra slipped
the safety on and lowered it back onto the floor.

When they were level, Reaper stopped the van in
the outside lane. They could now see a group of people
sitting around a camping stove on the hard shoulder,
protected by the vehicles, a Volvo Estate and a battered
Shogun. Another, younger, man with a beard, two tired-
looking women and two children. They all got to their
feet. Sandra lowered the window.

The man with the gun nodded warily, trying to see
inside the van, trying to see if it held danger.

'Where are you going?' Sandra asked.

'Yorkshire,' he said. 'The moors.'

'*Heartbeat* country,' she said. 'I loved that
programme.'

The man smiled at that comment coming from such
a young woman.

'What about you?'

'We're going to Yorkshire, too. Other side of York.'

'Had any trouble?' he said, glancing at the crumpled front nearside where Reaper had bounced the
Range Rover.

'We've had trouble,' she said. 'There's a lot of trouble around. You?'

Reaper had been scanning the open countryside beyond the hard shoulder. No cover for an ambush. But then who would stage an ambush when you might expect to get one car every two hours. Paranoia, paranoia.

'We've been lucky,' the man said. 'We saw plenty in Nottingham. That's where we've come from. So we got out. I suppose every city is the same.'

One of the women stepped forward and said, 'We can offer you a cup of soup. If you've got your own mug.'

Reaper heard the side door of the van open and Jean stepped out. He felt a momentary flush of panic that eased when he looked again at the rather forlorn group between the cars.

'Never mind soup,' she said. 'I've got an oven in here. Why don't we all have lunch?'

The woman hesitated and Ollie climbed out of the van and stood next to Jean, holding her hand. He looked at the children, a girl about ten and a boy about six.

'Do you want to watch *Ice Age 3*?' he said, and the tension evaporated. Reaper realised they were the first words he had heard the boy speak.

Reaper leaned across to speak to the man through the window.

'We're armed,' he said. ' But don't be alarmed.' Sandra

climbed down from the van and took the carbine with her, hung by its strap around her neck. Reaper guessed she looked intimidating. 'You're welcome to look in the van,' he said. 'There's no one else. Just Sandra, me, Jean and Ollie.' The man nodded, looking at the hardware, protective vest and Doc Martens worn by Sandra. 'Look. I'd better pull the van in closer in case someone else comes past. Okay?'

'Okay.'

He reversed and then pulled the van into the middle lane and stopped it parallel to the gap between the two cars. Jean slid open the double doors and invited the women and children inside. Reaper went round the front of the van, his carbine slung across his back. Sandra had not gone with the women.

'I'm Reaper, this is Sandra,' he said as they shook hands.

The man he had first spoken to said, 'I'm Gavin. Gavin Price.' He was late fifties, slightly stooped, with a lugubrious face and bald head.

The second man said, 'I'm Nick Waite. The Reverend Nick Waite.' He was late twenties, slim and a lot of hair. His beard was trimmed to his jaw-line. He looked like an extra from a Hollywood epic. After revealing his calling, he paused, waiting as if to see if Reaper would make a comment. Blame him or his God for what had happened. But Reaper didn't believe in God. He didn't believe much in vicars, either.

'. . . You've come prepared,' said Price, nodding at the weapons.

'It's necessary,' Reaper said.

The man nodded. 'Hell in a hand basket,' he said.

Reaper remembered the comment being made before. 'Are any of you related?' he asked.

Waite said, 'No. I met Judith and Rachel at the community centre. I lived nearby and they'd gone looking for help. We found each other and stayed low. The boy is Sam. His parents were neighbours.'

'Then I turned up,' Price said. 'The little girl is Stella. I found her wandering down the street in shock. I took her to the community centre and found Nick and the others.'

Reaper said, 'You've all lost people?'

'I lost my fiancée,' Nick Waite said. 'Judith is a widow.' Judith was in her late fifties or early sixties, tall with striking grey hair and a natural elegance. 'Rachel lost her husband.' Rachel was mid-twenties, blonde, medium height and had a fragile prettiness. 'They'd been married four years. No children.'

Price said, 'I lost my wife. We'd been married nearly 25 years. Silver wedding in August. But you either give in or go on, don't you? I'd found Stella, so I had to go on. She lost her family. Her parents, two brothers and a sister. She nursed them all until they died. They were all in bed. I went back with her to make sure, pack a few things. The house was immaculate, the bedrooms neat and tidy . . . mum and dad together . . . the baby girl in between them . . .' He pursed his lips against swelling emotions. 'The brothers in twin beds . . . they were five and seven. She'd put their teddy bears in with them.' He shook his head. 'No wonder she was in bloody shock.'

They said nothing. Stood in a sad group, the imagery vivid. The world uncaring except for the people Stella had found.

Waite said, 'By the time we left, gangs were forming. Decent people are having a difficult time.'

Reaper nodded. 'Same all over,' he said.

'What about you?' Price said.

'Sandra is my daughter,' Reaper said, and the words surprised him.

'You're lucky,' Price said.

'Yes, we are,' Sandra said, stepping closer to him. Reaper put his arm around her shoulders.

Reaper said, 'We were based at a police station when Jean and Ollie found us.'

'Based?' said Waite. 'You're police?'

'They're not police.' Jean was suddenly among them. 'They're Special Forces.'

The young vicar, Nick Waite, widened his eyes in disbelief as he looked at Sandra. 'Don't they have an age limit?'

Reaper felt Sandra tense beneath his arm.

'Listen,' Jean said. ''Don't be taken in by that butter-wouldn't-melt look. She saved my life. Killed the man calm as you like, one shot. In the head. Bang. Gone. Anyway, lunch is almost ready.' And she turned and went back to her stove.

Waite stared with a new respect.

'Is that true?' he said.

'It's true,' she said.

Reaper said, 'Why don't we eat?'

Jean had conjured another instant stew and they still had bread she had baked the night before. The children sat on the bed and watched *Ice Age 3* while they ate. The adults had their food outside. Reaper and Sandra remained standing and kept watch in both directions, spooning stew and juggling the bread. The two men accepted that they were professionals who knew what they were doing, and Jean, in full stream, was probably expanding on their special abilities.

'I don't know why I said you were my daughter,' Reaper said.

'I'm glad you did,' she said. 'It's a way of starting over, isn't it?'

'Yes. It's a way of starting over.'

'What about this lot?'

He raised an eyebrow, but knew what she meant.

'What do you think?'

'Decent people.'

'I think so, too.'

'Are you going to ask them?'

Jean shouted across: 'I've been telling them about the place we're going. They can come, can't they?'

'Sorted,' he said to Sandra with a smile. And, in a louder voice, 'Of course they can come, if they want to.'

They wanted to, that was obvious. They had been reassured by Jean's description of a new Eden and the belief that the special force wielded by Reaper and Sandra would help them survive. The food was finished, camping chairs were stowed and the entire group was preparing to leave when Sandra said to Reaper, 'Incoming.'

He looked at her and said, 'Incoming?' Where the hell had she got that from? He followed her gaze and saw two vans approaching from the south. They slipped the carbines around from their backs and held them ready. He was aware that Sandra now had an audience. The role she was playing was getting deeper. She would be fine. Particularly as he recognised the approaching vans.

'We passed them miles back,' he whispered, and he and Sandra stepped to the front of the motor home while the others hung back in a worried group. The vans slowed and stopped twenty yards away. The big man who was all pale skin and muscles got out and walked forward. He was unarmed apart from the tattoo of a bulldog on his left forearm.

'Bloody hell!' he said, when he got closer. 'You're packing.'

Others were getting out of the vans behind him: the Afro-Caribbean man, three women – one of them with striking red hair – a child, and a black Labrador dog.

'Change your mind about Cambridge?' Reaper said.

'Long way, Cambridge. We thought about Yorkshire.' He licked his lips. 'Thought we might go together.'

Reaper looked at Sandra, a question in his eyes, and she nodded. 'Sounds good to me,' he said.

Chapter 6

THEY CONTINUED DRIVING NORTH, THE MOTOR home in front, followed by the Volvo, the Shogun and the two Transits. Jean, who was standing in the van behind the driver's cab, said, 'Looks like we've got us a convoy.'

Reaper glanced over his shoulder and saw that she was smiling. 'You remember that old film?' he said.

'Kris Kristofferson. How could I forget? I had a thing for him once. Sadly, it wasn't reciprocated.'

She moved back to Ollie who remained sprawled on the bed, watching the following cars out of the back window. They had formed a loose alliance but that did not yet extend to allowing the other children to all travel in the van. Reaper didn't blame them.

They had been aware of heavy clouds over to the

northwest for some time, but when they crested a hill they saw the flames that tinged the clouds red.

'What's that?' Sandra said.

'That's Leeds burning,' said Reaper.

They carried on, passing the occasional car heading south on the other carriageway. They didn't slow, but raised a hand in passing. The turn onto the M621 that led to the city of Leeds came and went, and they stayed on the M1, which veered east around the suburbs. They left the smoke behind them. A Porsche went past them at well over 100 miles an hour but did not slow or threaten and was soon out of sight. They were in open country, which made Reaper feel better. The road linked up with the A1(M) and, a few miles further on, Reaper slowed to leave the motorway on the A64 to York.

As he negotiated the roundabouts, he checked in the mirrors to make sure the convoy was still intact, then increased speed to 50 along the straight road across the plain of York. They were maybe an hour or an hour and a half from their destination and he now began to feel nervous in case it was not as he remembered, or in case someone else had taken possession of it. What the hell? Nothing could be guaranteed and they were lucky enough that a dozen disparate souls had joined together with the intention of making the best of whatever lay ahead. There would be safety in numbers – at least at first.

Hopefully, they would be able to expand and maybe become modestly successful. That would bring other problems. Success and stability would make them a target for the wild groups that would continue to roam and raid and establish fiefdoms. Reaper had no illusions about the future. Others might think differently, but he believed a medieval war was about to descend upon them. Their party offered a variety of skills, not all of them useful: the bearded Nick Waite was a vicar; lugubrious Gavin Price a motor mechanic; Judith, the tall elegant lady with grey hair, was a retired vet; Rachel, the blonde in her mid-twenties, had owned a dress shop. The chunky bloke from the Transits was Pete Mack, a long distance lorry driver. His party included Ashley, a joiner in his early thirties. The Labrador, Lucky, was his. The women were Jane, mid forties and a district nurse, Ruth, early thirties, who had worked in a bank and red-headed Kate, late thirties, who had been a bar manager. The child, Emma, was seven and unrelated to any of them, another orphan of the storm.

A district nurse was good news, although Reaper would have preferred a doctor, a vet was also a bonus along with a motor mechanic. Pete would no doubt have practical knowledge and Ashley's skills as a carpenter would be invaluable. Better a carpenter than a philosopher or a graduate in media studies. Jean, meanwhile, seemed to have commandeered cooking duties. Altogether, it was not a bad mix – except for a vicar. What the hell use was a cleric when half the remaining world seemed intent on rape and murder and the other half was just trying to get by?

Pete was divorced and had teamed up with Ruth more than a week before. They had not known each other previously but now seemed to have a comfortable relationship. They had holed up in a house they had broken into and spotted the child, Emma, while out looking for food. Emma had lived with her mother and stayed in the house with her mother's body for five days before venturing out for help. Fortunately, she had found Pete and Ruth. They had met Ashley while choosing a Transit on a car dealer's lot. He was doing the same thing, looking for transport. Ashley had met Jane and Kate at his local pub, The White Swan.

'The pub was more like a social club,' Ashley said. 'A really good pub. Good beer, good company. A real cross section of people would get in there after work. When the shit happened, I went there looking for friends.'

When the shit happened, he lost a wife and son, a grief he seemed to keep in a separate and very private compartment. Jane had also been a regular at the pub and had gone there for the same reason – looking for friends she could rely on after losing her husband. Kate was the manager and had lived alone above the premises. She was divorced and her grown-up daughter had lived in Australia – until the virus took her.

They bypassed York and carried on towards Scarborough and the East Coast. They drove past the sign that pointed towards the stately home of Castle Howard, past the Second World War museum with its POW huts and a Spitfire displayed on its wing tip. Near the market town of Malton they could see the framework of the pleasure rides at the holiday village of Flamingo Park on the skyline. A few miles further on, Reaper slowed, turned off the main road and drove into the lush and rolling countryside of North Yorkshire. The lanes were narrow and he went slowly. Sandra lifted the carbine into her lap, probably as anxious as he was that they were in confining byways. At least the height of the vehicle gave them good observation. They drove past the occasional cottage and tracks that led to farms and the land seemed peaceful.

Eventually, they were driving alongside a tall brick wall.

'This is it,' he said.

The memories returned of when he had last been here, when times were normal, when Emily had been alive. Long sunshine days and smiles and love. You never remembered the tears or tantrums that a twelve-year-old could engage in, just the smiles and laughter. He realised it had been six years ago and he wondered if the place had changed that much. It couldn't have done. They had kept sending him brochures well after they had stopped being a family. Long after Emily had gone.

A big double gate was ahead. It was closed. Reaper stopped the motor home and jumped down. A sign at the side of the gate said: *The Haven*. The gate was secured by a padlocked length of chain. The convoy had stopped and Nick Waite and Gavin Price got out of their cars.

'Is this it?' asked the clergyman.

'This is it.'

Reaper shook the chain.

Pete approached and saw the problem.

'Hang on,' he said. 'I've got some cutters.'

The three of them waited without speaking, all wondering what lay behind the gate and the high wall. Pete returned with heavy-duty bolt cutters and severed the chain.

'I'll put it back when we're through,' he said.

They pushed open the gates and Reaper led the convoy into the grounds. The road was not much wider than the motor home and, periodically, there were lay-bys so that traffic coming in the opposite directions could pass. They drove to the top of a hill and he stopped just on the other side. On the lower slopes of a gentle descent was the purpose-built village of twenty cottages.

The road ran between the cottages to a crossroads at the bottom that was marked by a six foot stone cross on a plinth, erected as an echo to the past; a pretend artefact to give the pretend village an aura of reality and historical substance. The last building at the bottom of the hill had a pub sign outside: The Farmer's Boy. It was not a real pub, as this was not a real village, but a social centre for the holidaymakers who stayed here. On the opposite side of the cross-roads was the original manor house. From the crest of the hill, they could see farm buildings and stables at its rear. To the right of the manor house was a large barn. Reaper remembered the village as claustrophobic. Now it promised to be a safe Haven. He pushed the other memories from his mind.

'It looks great!' said Sandra, a touch of wonder in her voice.

'Look.'

A JCB was working in a field on the other side of the barn. It stopped. The man in it stood up and pointed at their arrival. A man standing by the side of the machine, turned and stared. People were already here, but who were they? And would they object to an influx of immigrants? Reaper drove down the hill and parked in the square between the cottages and the manor house. The other vehicles lined up alongside. Everyone got out, glad to have completed the journey.

Reaper motioned Sandra to follow him. He said to Nick Waite and the others, 'We'll go and see the residents.'

'Shall I come with you?' suggested Waite. 'A peaceful emissary?'

'No,' said Reaper. Why should he be polite to vicars?

He and Sandra went past the front of the house to the right where they had seen the JCB. They turned the corner and saw two men walking towards them through a herb garden. The men stopped when they saw the guns he and Sandra carried. Reaper let his carbine swing beneath his arm and raised both hands to reassure them. One of the residents was a young man in jeans and riding boots and a blue button-down shirt open at the neck. Probably mid-twenties. Good looking. Reaper smiled inwardly at how he immediately assessed potential members of the group that was growing around him. He wondered whether this one might appeal to Sandra. With him was a chap who could have been anything between mid-fifties to mid-seventies, a face and body worn by working the earth. Old cord trousers, old work boots, old shirt and a waistcoat, and an old hat upon his head.

'I'm sorry if we startled you,' Reaper said.

The two men stared back warily. 'This is private property,' the young man said.

'Unfortunately, not anymore,' Reaper said, gently. 'I'm not sure what that expression means anymore. The people we have with us are ordinary folk. They are just looking for somewhere to live. The cities and towns are no longer safe. These are decent people.

Men, women and children.' He took a deep breath. 'These guns?' he said. 'We needed them. Otherwise we would have been killed.' He offered his hand to the young man. 'My name's Reaper.'

After a moment's hesitation, the man took it. 'Jamie Hinchliffe,' he said. 'This is Bob.'

Sandra introduced herself and Reaper noticed the interest in Jamie Hinchliffe's eyes as they shook hands.

Jamie said, 'I'm estate manager. *Was* estate manager. Bob farms Inglewood. It's next to the estate. We've been burying our dead.'

'The JCB?' Reaper said.

'Yes. We had families in two of the cottages. They had hoped to escape the virus. Unfortunately they didn't. All the staff here and at the farm died, too. I'm the only one left. I thought it both decent and sensible to bury the others. Bob and I were doing it together.'

'Did you finish?'

'Almost. Another level of earth to put back.'

'We have a vicar with us. Maybe he could say a few words?'

Bob said, 'It would be grand if he could. I've got friends down there. Arnie and Mary were big church-goers. They'd appreciate it.'

Reaper nodded.

'Will you object to us staying?'

'I'd be rather foolish if I did, wouldn't I,' said Jamie, with a smile. 'No, I think it would be a splendid idea.'

'I'll get the vicar while you finish.'

He walked back to the front of the building, Sandra slow to follow. He supposed she would have preferred to stay and get to know Jamie Hinchliffe better. There was going to be another headache, when the group started pairing off, as he knew they would. The others were waiting patiently, although Pete Mack appeared from The Farmer's Boy. He held up his hands to show they were empty.

'Just checking,' he said. 'It's well stocked.'

Reaper said, 'We're welcome here. The sole survivor is called Jamie Hinchliffe, he's the estate manager. With him is a local farmer. What we saw, when we came over the hill? They were burying the dead.' He looked at Nick Waite. 'I told them we had a vicar. They would be grateful if you would say a few words.'

'Of course,' said Nick, moving towards the Volvo. 'Excuse me a moment.'

'As we're taking over this place,' Reaper said, 'maybe we could go along. Say goodbye to the past. Maybe those who know a prayer could say one.' He glanced at Sandra and they turned and went back towards the side of the house. Everyone else followed, a straddle of mourners, Nick bringing up the rear, now wearing a dog collar and carrying a prayer book.

It was an unusual funeral service. The grave was twelve feet wide. The group stood respectfully along one side, Jamie and Bob the farmer, his hat held in his hands, at one end, with the Reverend Nick Waite. Reaper and Sandra stood at the other end. Jean Megson and Judith, the vet, had coerced Ashley into cutting them a branch from a nearby hawthorn tree that was heavy with blossom. This they now lay upon the turned earth.

Nick began a short service: *'I am the resurrection and the life, saith the Lord; he that believeth in me, though he were dead, yet shall he live: and whosoever liveth and believeth in me shall never die . . .'*

After the ritual words, he said, 'We come as strangers, but we come in peace and we mourn your passing, as we mourn the passing of our own loved ones and the world we knew. We shall try to live in peace and make sense of the challenge that God has set us. And we shall tend your grave because it represents the grave that so many will never receive.'

They all dipped their heads in silent contemplation. Nick looked at Jamie and Bob, asking without words whether they wanted to add anything, but they shook their heads. He looked around and said, 'It would be nice to sing a hymn? Does anyone have a favourite? One we might all know?'

There was an awkward pause and Kate said, 'I know *Amazing Grace.*'

'I can't think of anything more appropriate,' said Nick. 'If you start, I'm sure we'll join in when we can.'

Kate coughed, shuffled a little self-consciously, and

began to sing, her voice low but growing in strength as she found the pitch and the confidence. As she reached the third line, others were already joining in.

She sang the next verse alone, a delicate and beautiful soprano, head back, red hair glowing in the light, feeling the words. Almost everyone came in for the chorus and the hymn caressed the countryside on that balmy summer afternoon. Kate sang no more and they remained with heads bowed, each contemplating their own loss and grief, until Bob the farmer said, 'That was grand, lass.' He held his hand out to shake Kate's. 'That was right grand. Arnie and Mary would be fair chuffed.'

Reaper picked up a handful of soil that had missed the infilling and threw it onto the grave. He hadn't prayed but he had been moved. Sandra leant against him, one of her arms around his waist, and sniffed back tears. He held her with an arm around her shoulder.

He looked around as the group moved slowly away from the grave, some still lost in thought, others pointing at the houses, speculating perhaps where they might live, and he realised that what had gone before had only been a prelude. What was to come would be the hard part.

The manor house had power that ran from a generator. Reaper was of a mind to get them to switch it off to conserve the oil it was using but was already preparing to step back from a role of command. Let someone else make those decisions. When the time came for them to sit in conference, which they would do, informally at first, he would state his case. He had brought them here, now it was up to them to make it work. He would remain as a facilitator and protector. He would forage for supplies, perhaps bring in new settlers, scout for enemies and, when necessary, fight them. He would be in charge of their armoury and train others in the use of firearms.

He had his own plans for helping this settlement survive. One was more weapons, another was more medical help. And where were you likely to find a doctor? In a hospital. He intended to scout Scarborough as soon as possible on both counts. As for recruits to form a defensive corps, Jamie Hinchliffe was an obvious choice, as were Pete Mack and Ashley.

The house contained guest apartments, staff quarters and estate offices. A consensus decided that the men and women should be accommodated separately. All except Pete and Ruth, the former bank worker with whom he had been travelling. It appeared they had already cemented a relationship with which they were both content. They chose to move into one of the cottages. Emma, the seven-year-old they had been looking after, wanted to go with them. The others agreed to pair off, the men sharing twin rooms, the women, not being so fussy, taking doubles or family rooms, so that the children could stay with them. Jean Megson and four-year-old Ollie had a room together.

Reaper asked Sandra if she would rather stay in the house.

'You'd be closer to Jamie, that way.'

She thumped him. 'I'll go with you,' she said.

He explained his plan to take the motor home back over the hill to gain a defensive view of the road into the estate.

Jean commandeered the kitchens at the manor house and, aided by Ashley and Rachel, the blonde with the fragile good looks, prepared a roast chicken dinner. Jamie opened the wine cellar and served the best vintage they had. As they waited in the dining room for the food to be served, Reaper told the group where he and Sandra would be staying and the reasons why. This brought a momentary silence, as if they had forgotten the dangers that existed outside the walls of the estate.

'We'll do a night patrol,' he said. 'Just in case.'

They seemed suitably reassured and Pete said, 'Need any help?'

'We will do. But not tonight. Maybe we can talk about it tomorrow?' He addressed his words directly to Pete.

'Any time.'

They dined well. One or two of the ladies drank

too much, but that was perhaps understandable, and Reaper was pleased that the men drank only moderately, as if aware of the changed circumstances of their lives. Afterwards, they had the first informal debate about the future. Reaper took the opportunity to explain his thoughts about his own role.

'Decisions will have to be made,' he said. 'Democratic decisions, rules about how we live, what work we do. We'll abide by them,' he said, including Sandra in his commitment. 'But my primary aim is to make sure this place remains secure.' He glanced around at them: some nodding in agreement or relief, one or two still coming to terms with being part of a local democracy. 'There'll be a farm to run, neighbours like Bob to find and cooperate with, machinery to mend, workshops, a school to set up.' He smiled at Nick Waite. 'Wedding services to conduct.' This provoked guffaws and embarrassed laughs. 'I'll work,' he said. 'So will Sandra. But first and foremost we'll keep you safe.'

He didn't say *try*; he said *would*. It was his purpose, the reason he had been spared. He would fulfil that role if it meant his death. Only he no longer planned to die. He would stay alive as long as these people needed him.

Reaper parked the camper van over the hill from the village in the shadows of a copse of trees. The night was clear, the darkness was the half-night of late spring and they could see all the way down the narrow road to the gates.

They disarmed and removed the Kevlar vests. Sandra stretched in appreciation.

'You take the bedroom,' he said. 'Get comfortable for once.'

'Thanks. I will.' She gave him a hug that he reciprocated. 'Thanks, Reaper.'

He didn't ask what she was thanking him for and she stepped into the bedroom.

'Jamie seems okay. What do you think?' he said.

She paused in the doorway and stared back to see if he was making fun of her but he wasn't.

'He seems nice.'

'I got the impression from the way he was talking to you that he's interested.' He shrugged. 'Could be a good thing.'

'You mean there may not be many choices to go around?'

'There is that.'

'Whatever happened to true love?'

He almost said, 'it died of a virus', but didn't. From the look on her face, he didn't have to.

'You're forgetting your kit,' he said, and handed her the weapons and vest she had just taken off. 'Keep it close at all times.'

'I know,' she said. 'In case.'

Reaper made himself comfortable on the pull-out

bench. He lay a long time with his head propped on pillows, but couldn't sleep. He didn't want to think. If he thought too deeply he might discover what he was creating was unreal and had no purpose. Were the reasons his mind had devised only there to give him false hope when he deserved none? After a while, he got up, put the vest back on, strapped on his weapons, picked up the carbine and went out into the night. He walked through the grass towards the gate and felt himself strengthen, his inner purpose returning. The doubts evaporated, along with the black thoughts.

Chapter 7

THEY DROVE BACK TO THE VILLAGE IN the morning, showered and had breakfast in the dining room. They were greeted by smiles and by children who laughed as they played. The group was adapting quickly. They felt comfortable in this safe haven. They were settling.

Reaper and Sandra were armed in their blue combat uniforms and looked ominously dangerous as they stood at the top of the steps of the manor house in the sunshine. Another warm and pleasant day. The Reverend Nick, Pete and Jamie joined them expectantly.

Reaper said, 'Sandra and I are going into Scarborough. We'll assess the town, and we'll look for two things specifically: weapons and a doctor.'

'Where are you going to find those?' Nick asked.

'We'll look at the hospital for a doctor. There may still be one alive whose Hippocratic oath induced him to stay with his patients.'

'What about the weapons?' Pete asked.

'The police station. If others haven't already been there. Scarborough will have a Police HQ that will have an armoury. It may be small but there should be guns there.'

'Is that necessary?' Nick said. 'To get more weapons?'

'Reverend, it is very necessary. Like it or not, we need the guns for protection, and it would be better if we took them to save them getting into the hands of those with less noble motives.' He looked at each of the three of them. 'Have any of you fired a weapon?'

'I was in the army cadets at school,' Jamie said. 'And you should know there are four shotguns in a gun cabinet in the wine cellar.'

'The cabinet's locked?'

'It is.'

Reaper looked at Pete Mack. 'How about you, Pete?'

'I've fired a shotgun. Clay pigeons. But that's about it.'

Reaper took the keys for the motor home and gave them to Nick.

'Look after these. There are weapons in the rear storage compartment in the van. I would prefer them

not to be used in my absence, until those handling
them have had some training. But, if we don't come
back, you may need to learn how to use them on your
own.' Nick looked at the keys as if he had been handed
a poisoned chalice. Reaper looked at the other two.
'Democratic decisions apply. Okay?'

Pete nodded. 'Okay,' he said.

'Okay,' said Jamie. 'But try and make sure you both
come back. Oh, and I should tell you, I've kept a radio
watch. You know, tuned in to short wave for radio
hams and checked on the main frequencies. So far
nothing, but you never know. And I only do it from
time to time.'

Reaper nodded. 'Maybe we could organise a shift
system,' he said. 'At least, listen in for a few hours a
day. What do you think, Reverend?'

'I think that's a worthwhile idea,' Nick said, 'I'll
organise something.'

'One other thing,' said Reaper. 'We need transport.'

Jamie said, 'There's a Ford MPV in the garage. Two-
litre engine, plenty of room and the tank is full.'

'That will do fine.'

'I'll show you,' Jamie said.

'You go with him, Sandra. I'll catch up.' Reaper
looked around at the signs of normality. Four-year-old
Ollie was kicking a football with six-year-old Sam and
seven-year-old Emma. 'This could be a good place,' he
said. 'We fucked up the world, excuse the language,

120

Reverend, but we have another chance here. Let's not fuck up again.'

'Amen to that,' said the clergyman, and Pete grinned,

Reaper took his time before he followed Jamie and Sandra. He collected the steel Enforcer battering ram that he had left in the motor home. As he strode towards the garages, he was surprised at the sound of a car engine. A Ford Galaxy with Sandra behind the wheel turned the corner in front of him and stopped. Jamie had a quick word with her and got out of the passenger side.

'Take care,' Jamie said to Reaper. 'Take care of her.'

Reaper got in, throwing a pair of binoculars onto the back seat. He buckled up and Sandra drove them out of the village, one or two people waving as they went, up the hill and down towards the gate. Reaper said nothing, but he sensed meaningful words might have been exchanged between the two young people. And why not? There might not be the chance for a slow romance. The moment had to be seized. He got out and opened the gates, she drove through and he closed them again, draping the cut chain, as Pete had done, to make it appear that they were padlocked together.

When he got back in, Sandra gave him a map.

'Scarborough,' she said. 'Guide me.'

'I didn't know you could drive.'

'You didn't ask.'

He winced as she swerved towards the grass verge then swerved back into the road again. 'Do you actually have a license?' he said.

'No. Does it actually matter?'

'Only if you kill us on the way to the seaside.'

He directed her into Scarborough along the A64. Pleasant rolling countryside followed by nondescript outskirts that could have belonged to any town. They went along a road of retail premises and hopeful private hotels and guest houses as they dipped towards the coast.

'Stop there,' he said, pointing at a shop with a display of suitcases in the window.

Sandra stopped and kept the engine running. He tried the shop door, found it locked, so kicked it in. He took two medium sized suitcases on wheels and loaded them into the back of the car then returned for two more, before climbing back in.

They continued down the road and eventually went past the railway station that would have once been busy with visitors but was now deserted. They turned left onto Northway, a dual carriageway that was a town centre hub. The police station was a five-storey red brick building.

They parked and got out, Sandra taking the keys with her. Reaper humped the Enforcer, and they went into the police station. Being a public building, few people had actually died on the premises and there was a minimal smell of putrefaction, but it hung there, nonetheless, like the lingering perfume of an overripe femme fatale. The doors had keypads. One had been forced and Reaper though they might be too late in this particular mission. Sandra held her carbine at the ready and they proceeded with caution. Other doors had been bashed in, obviously with a great deal of effort, and offices had been wrecked, but the deeper they went, the less damage they discovered. The security, it seemed, had put off whoever had been before them.

Reaper led the way to the basement where he opened locked doors with the Enforcer. On the fifth attempt, they found the armoury: ten carbines and fifteen Glocks, ammunition, cleaning kits and ten tazers. Reaper realised that he had been over-optimistic.

'Four suitcases?' Sandra said.

'I know.'

She gave him the keys and he carried the enforcer back out of the police station, put it in the back of the car and lifted out two suitcases. Movement across the street caught his attention. A drunk of indeterminate age, with long white hair and straggly beard and wearing jeans and a cloak, leaned against a wall and sipped from a bottle and watched. If someone moved the wall, Reaper guessed the bloke would fall over. He locked the car and took the cases into the station.

'We've got company outside,' he said, loading everything quickly.

When they were full, they pulled one each, the carbines hanging behind them, each holding a Glock. Sandra left her case to scout outside, glanced left and right, and nodded to him that the way was clear. Across the road, the man in the cloak had been joined by another man with long hair and a middle-aged woman, both as intoxicated. The woman leant back against a wall and slid gracefully to the floor, a wine glass in one hand and what looked like a large joint in the other. She never spilt a drop.

Reaper loaded the cases and they got into the vehicle. As he had the keys, he took the driving seat, which he had to adjust for his size, and Sandra didn't object. He was about to drive away when the younger man staggered across the dual carriageway towards them. Since the only weapon he appeared to be carrying was a bottle of Jack Daniels, Reaper lowered the window. He came close enough for Reaper to smell the liquor on his breath and the fumes of the ganja he was smoking.

'Hey, man. I don't, like, talk to police. Y'know? But you should know. Something bad is happening at the Imperial. *Real* bad.'

Reaper said, 'What's happening exactly?'

'There's a gang. They take what they want. They

took these girls. From that posh school? Took them yesterday.' He frowned. '*Maybe* yesterday. It's bad, man. I heard the screams.'

'How many?'

'Girls?'

'In the gang.'

The man shrugged. 'Maybe five. Maybe six.'

'Thank you for your information. You are a responsible citizen.'

'Shit. I'm not responsible for anything. Just don't tell them I told you. Y'know.'

'I won't.'

Reaper drove away, turned the vehicle and went back past the police station and the three responsible citizens. Two hundred yards further on, he stopped and inspected the map. He worked out a route, started the car and turned left towards the sea. He drove slowly, silently, easing the car down narrow lanes behind a shopping mall, past civic buildings, round the rear of hotels, occasionally stopping to check the map. Sandra said nothing. She knew his intention. He finally stopped at the rear of a hotel.

'The Imperial is on the other side of this one,' he told her. 'If we go in here, we should be able to take a look across the square and suss the situation. Okay?'

'Okay.'

They entered through a kitchen door. The light was dim and he had to use a torch, but it got better as they climbed a flight of stairs that brought them into a smart and bright reception area with wooden floors and red furniture. There was a dead body in a chair facing a dead TV, but the smell was not too bad. Putrefaction had yet to set in, although the flies were gathering. He led the way up carpeted stairs to the first floor and back into gloom: quiet corridors of deep shadow; that pervasive smell of death. The first door he tried was unlocked and, as he opened it, light blazed in through the window. They could tell by the absence of stink that it was unoccupied. The torch went back in his belt and they crouched low to cross the room. A double bed, a wall mounted TV, tea and coffee, and an open door that led to a bathroom.

Reaper looked across the square at the bedroom windows opposite and down at the main entrance: stone steps beneath the arched sign that said *The Imperial Hotel*. He used binoculars to look through the large windows on the ground floor. Interior light was dim but good enough, and he could see partway into the foyer, although he detected no movement. He scanned the windows above and saw a figure move past, a fleeting glimpse that could have been a girl. He kept the binoculars focused on the window but the figure did not return.

'The bedroom directly above the sign,' he said. 'I thought I saw someone.'

Sandra was staring at the hotel through the scope on the carbine.

Then there was movement from near a Bentley that was parked outside. A man, who must have been sitting on the floor with his back against the limousine, got to his feet. Late teens, maybe twenty, unkempt, new clothes. He carried a double-barrelled sawn-off shotgun. He walked a few yards, turned and stretched, then sat down on the steps of the Imperial and lit a cigarette.

Reaper stood up, staying out of sight, and reached forward, unfastened the catch and slid the window up. It was well-maintained and made minimal noise. Now they had a clear shot if they wanted one. But first, he had to find out where the others were and what they were doing. With the window open, they could hear the soft sounds of the sea and the cry of the gulls. They shouldn't be crouched here, plotting murder. They should be walking on the Promenade, enjoying an ice cream, eating fish and chips. Then another cry, different to that of the gulls. A cry of despair. Followed by laughter. This was why he had been spared. He didn't need any more reason to act.

'Can you shoot him from here?' he asked. It was about a sixty metre shot.

'I can try,' Sandra said.

'Just remember what he's done.'

She licked her lips and nodded.

'I'll get in round the back. When you hear shooting, take him down.'

'Right,' she said, and he remembered how young she was and that this time she wouldn't even have an audience of one to perform for. And this time it wasn't a tree.

He dropped the car keys on the floor next to her.

'If I don't come out, get back to the Haven. No heroics.'

She looked up at him and said, 'You'll come back.'

'Yes I will.' He touched the top of her head. 'Give me twenty minutes. Relax until then.'

He left his carbine on the bed. Two handguns, 34 bullets and a knife. That would be enough.

He moved quickly, left the building the way they had entered, ran down the block and crossed the road at the bottom of the square, using the cover of parked cars. The sun was warm, the day made for holiday-makers. Would they ever come back? The kitchen door at the back of The Imperial was unlocked. Were all kitchen doors unlocked? He went through a dim area that smelt of grease and spoilt food, and up a flight of service stairs that were even darker. He went past the ground floor and on up to the first floor, eased a door open and stepped into a corridor that was almost pitch black. At the far end was a faint glimmer of light. He used the torch to guide him along the length of the corridor and, as he neared its end, saw that the light came from a small window in a closed fire door. He switched off the torch and put it back on his belt.

Reaper looked through the window at the first floor landing. Wide stairs led down into the reception and foyer area. It aspired to grandness, but the red plush of the baroque seats was faded and the carpet worn. The chandeliers looked embarrassed. The Imperial, like the Empire, had seen better days. A balcony ran around both sides leading to first floor rooms and suites. He glanced up and saw the balcony was replicated twice more on third and fourth floors. The excellent lighting came from a glass-domed roof. The movement he had seen had been in a room directly above the front entrance.

He cocked both guns, opened the door and slipped out into the open space, suddenly feeling vulnerable. Music was playing downstairs. Mungo Jerry playing *In The Summertime*.

Someone, also downstairs, shouted. 'His name's Jerry Dorsey!'

'No it isn't.'

'It fucking is! Jerry Dorsey was the lead singer. The bloke with the gap in his teeth.'

'You know what they say about girls with gaps in their teeth, don't you?'

'No, it is. It's Jerry Dorsey!'

Reaper moved around the balcony, keeping well back

and out of sight. Bottles clinked, there was a slap on bare flesh and a girl cried out and he heard footsteps ascending the stairs. He stepped round a corner and into a short corridor. A girl wearing only a shirt appeared at the top of the stairs carrying two bottles of beer. Her head was down and she moved quickly, as if frightened of being late.

'You're wrong, pillock brain!' said a different voice from below. 'His name is Ray Dorset.'

'Bollocks! You're making it up.'

The low-key squabble continued and Reaper stepped out from cover in front of the girl. She stopped and gasped, her eyes wide. She dropped the bottles, but the carpet cushioned their fall and they did not break. He took her into his arms before she had the chance to turn and run and whispered, 'It's okay. I've come to save you. You're going to be safe.' But the girl just shook in his arms. He found it impossible to tell how old she was: maybe sixteen or seventeen. She was blonde and plump and her flesh trembled with fear.

'You need to tell me who is in the room,' he said urgently. 'How many?' He shook her shoulders gently but firmly but she still couldn't speak. 'What's your name? You're going to be alright now, but tell me your name. What's your name?'

'Helen,' she said, the word coming out as a sob.

'Helen.' He caught her gaze and kept it, looking

deeply and sincerely into her eyes. 'Helen, you have to help me. Who is in the room?'

'Caroline.'

'Caroline is in the room. Is she your friend?'

The girl nodded.

'Who else is in the room?'

'Stacey.'

'Is Stacey your friend, too?'

She nodded again.

'Good, that's good, Helen. How many men are in the room?'

'Jerome. They call him Jerome.'

'Just the one man?' She nodded. 'Okay. Now what I want you to do is take the beers into the room and leave the door open. When you go inside, walk to one side and stay there. I'll come in behind you. Okay?' She stared at him for a moment, uncomprehending. 'You go inside and walk to one side. Okay?'

She nodded again and he holstered the guns, picked up the bottles and gave them to her, took out the knife and flicked the blade open.

Helen opened the door but it didn't open properly and she eased herself in sideways. He peeked in and saw it was a sitting room and that, apart from the debris of a drinking session, it was empty. He should have realised it was a suite. He pushed the door open a little wider and entered. Helen took the bottles into the bedroom and Reaper began to close the door and then recoiled in horror.

Hanging from a hook on the back of the door was the body of a young girl. Her shirt had been torn but apart from that she was fully dressed and seemed unmolested. Her school tie was around her neck and had been fastened to a hook on the door. Her tongue protruded and her face was discoloured. He went numb, hardly hearing the exchange of words in the bedroom. Hate pulsed through his veins. A searing memory returned. His mind screamed silently.

'Stupid bitch!' he heard from the other room, and he was striding towards the bedroom door without thought for caution. He entered a large room with a king-sized bed, the sheet crumpled and the bedding thrown into a corner. Helen was to the left of the room, still holding the bottles. Crouched on the floor by the bedding was a dark-haired girl who seemed to be naked. On the bed, lounging against pillows, was a large naked man in his forties, blue tattoos livid against the white flesh of both arms, his head shaved to the skin. All he wore were boots and socks.

'Who the fuck are you?' he said, but Reaper was already on the bed and plunging the knife into his stomach, withdrawing and plunging again, aiming upwards beneath the ribs. The man struggled but the strength drained from him under the viciousness of the attack and the repeated blows. As he lay back with his life oozing from him and a startled look upon his face, Reaper knelt over him and stuck the knife into his throat and the blood gushed afresh. The knife stuck there and would not come loose.

Reaper rolled away and sat on the edge of the bed. His breath was ragged, his body was shaking – not with revulsion but anger that the man had died so quickly. He had wanted him to suffer more. He noticed the girls looking at him, horror in their faces. He raised a hand. His voice rasped.

'I'm not going to harm you,' he said. 'You'll be safe. Don't worry, you'll be safe.'

He got up and looked at his hands and went into the bathroom. He washed them. He didn't want them to be sticky for the next part of the operation. He also washed the butts of his pistols which had become smeared with blood. When they were dry, he held one in each hand and returned to the bedroom.

'I'm going downstairs now. How many are there, Helen?'

'Five.'

He looked at the other girl.

'Caroline?' he said, and the girl acknowledge the name. 'Are there any more of your friends down there?'

'Miss Hall,' she said.

'Miss Hall?'

'Our teacher.'

'What's her first name?'

'Jennifer. Jenny.'

'Okay. You wait here and I'll be back soon.'

They continued to stare at him in utter shock and there was no point trying to assure them that they were safe. He turned to leave the bedroom and saw himself in a full-length mirror. No wonder the girls were horrified; the sight shocked him. His face was a mask of blood; his arms and chest still dripped red. He was the devil incarnate. And he wanted more blood.

He checked his watch. It had been 25 minutes since he left Sandra. She would be getting nervous. He left the suite and walked unhurried around the balcony to the grand staircase. Mungo Jerry had finished and a Beach Boys song was playing. He began to descend the stairs and just past halfway down he shouted, 'Jenny Hall! Get down and stay down!'

A young man was lounging full-length on a red plush banquette that directly faced the stairs, empty bottles at his feet. Reaper shot him in the chest. Reception was to the right, the entrance to a bar was to the left. He entered the bar and was confronted by another man who was so alarmed that he dropped the bowl from which he had been spooning food. Reaper levelled and fired another chest shot and the man went down. The third man had picked up a full-length shotgun from the bar and was swinging it in his direction but it was too unwieldy. He should have had a sawn-off. Reaper raised his left arm and blew him backwards. Two others. One outside. Where was the last one?

He was by a cigarette machine in the corner. He fired a revolver at Reaper but the shots were wild. One hit the CD player on the bar and *Surfin' USA* came to an abrupt end. As Reaper levelled his right arm and aimed, the man seemed to sense the outcome: he dropped the revolver and raised his arms. Reaper shot him in the head.

His ears were ringing from the shots but there was still the fifth man to make sure of. Reaper went to the front door, staying out of direct line of sight, and saw the young man with the sawn-off lying on his face on the steps with a bullet-hole in his back.

'Sandra!' he shouted through the open door. 'It's over!' He stepped into sight with both arms raised at the top of the steps and stared across the square, finding her outline in the first floor window. He put the guns back in their holsters. 'You're needed, Sandra!'

He paused in the fresh air, trying to get his anger to dissipate. Eventually he went back inside.

'Miss Hall?' he called. 'Miss Jenny Hall?' A woman came from the bar. She too wore only a shirt, which she now held together in front of her. 'Jenny? Don't worry. You're safe now. Helen and Caroline are upstairs. I think they need you.'

'Who *are* you?' she said, gazing at the bodies and the lingering gun smoke.

'I'm Reaper,' he said.

She shook her head and murmured, 'The Reaper.'

He did not correct her.

'Where did you come from?'

'We have a place that's safe. Men, women, children. We'll take you there. If you like?'

'We?'

Sandra entered through the front door, carrying the two carbines. She was pale but in control and Reaper guessed that having an audience again had helped her composure.

'This is Sandra,' he said. 'Jenny . . . the girls?'

'Yes.'

Jenny Hall went upstairs to find Helen and Caroline. Sandra looked at the bodies. She visibly relaxed and handed him his carbine.

'You okay?' he said.

'I'm fine.' She was looking at the gore on his face and arms. 'What happened to you?'

'There's another one upstairs. He bled a lot.' He took a deep breath. 'Good shot.'

'It took two.'

'But you got him. When you learn what they did, you won't regret it.'

He went outside and sat on the step next to the dead body. Sandra sat next to him.

'Should we go help them?' she said.

'One of the girls, Stacey, she's dead. She's been dead some time. She's up there. I'll go and get her in a while. No need for you to see.'

He could sense she knew there was more to it than that, but she didn't ask

Instead, she said, 'How many of them?'

'Two girls and the teacher.'

There was a silence between them and he wondered if Sandra was remembering her own ordeal. He reached out and took her hand.

'It's okay,' she said. 'I try to blank it, but it's difficult. It'll be difficult for a long time. I came out with my life. I suppose a lot haven't.' She smiled at him. 'Playing soldier helps.' She looked at the body of the man she shot. 'That doesn't bother me. I remember. And I know he deserved it.'

'These girls are going to need looking after.'

'We'll look after them.'

'I'd better go upstairs,' he said.

'I'll come with you.'

This time he didn't try to dissuade her.

Jenny Hall, Caroline and Helen were on the landing. They had dressed in an assortment of clothes, some ripped, some complete. They still looked confused and nervous.

Sandra said, 'You need some proper clothes. We'll sort it.'

The two students stared at Sandra in wonder. The girl was not much older than them but seemed so much more assured and mature. She carried her weapons with an unforced ease. Reaper wondered if the turmoil the world had just gone through had accelerated development. More likely it had forced people to accept or give up. Sandra was not about to give up.

Reaper said, 'We have transport.'

The girls still looked more uncomfortable than he would have expected. Was he missing something?

Sandra said, 'Why don't we go across the road. The hotel we were in, it's okay. You could have a bath, a shower, clean up.'

That was it. How dumb could a man be?

They went across the road, Reaper and Sandra keeping watch, but the square was clear. Sandra led them upstairs and into the bedroom they had used. He stopped at the door.

'I'll bring the car round,' he said.

'There's something else you could do,' she said. 'Wait there.'

She closed the door and left him in the shadows. What now? He went to wait on the landing where the light was better. After a few minutes, she came to him and handed him the car keys and a sheet of headed hotel notepaper.

'Their sizes,' she said. 'It might be good if you got

them something to wear. Fresh clothes, fresh start.'

·'Got it,' he said, happy to take orders. 'I won't be long.'

He went out of the back entrance of the hotel and drove the car down a lane, took a left, and left again, ignoring no entry signs, and went past the fronts of the hotels. At the top he turned right towards the centre of town and the shops. He went past a large department store with a plate glass window that seemed to have been smashed out of pure vindictiveness. He paused at a junction: pedestrianised shopping centre to his left; more shops and pubs straight ahead; and a steep road down to the Promenade on his right. He turned left and drove up the pedestrian way. Someone dodged down a side street at his approach. It was inevitable people would be cautious while gangs led by animals like Jerome wandered the town.

Near a shopping mall, he found a camping store and filled bags with boots, socks, T-shirts, trousers, sweaters, baseball hats, rainproof coats like the one Sandra had chosen, all in blue, and a handful of sports watches that promised to work up to thirty metres under water. He chose new kit for himself, because of the blood. He found a staff bathroom, stripped and washed, then dressed in clean clothes. He packed everything up and stared at the shopping mall. Great place for an ambush, but how many gangs like Jerome's would Scarborough have? Besides, these were girls and they might not appreciate looking like conscripts in his private army.

He hefted his carbine and went in, heading straight to the Debenhams store at the back. Now he chose jeans, plain blouses, soft sweaters, tracksuits, white socks and trainers. He added packs of underwear. Sandra had added bra sizes and he spent an embarrassed few minutes trying to choose something that might be practical and inoffensive. How could he get embarrassed when he was on his own? Sports bras seemed a safe option.

One bag he kept apart from the others. This was for Sandra. Sweater, slacks, even a dress, although he thought he had probably got the size wrong. To make sure, he took the dress in two sizes. He remembered her shoe size from when she chose the Doc Martens. He picked her a pair of trainers, a pair of pumps, and a pair of summery high heels to match the dress.

He loaded everything into the back of the car and drove back up the pedestrian way. On impulse, he stopped outside a jewellery shop. The door had been forced but it was surprisingly tidy inside. He chose a Christian Dior Christal ladies watch with a price tag over £4,000. Sandra deserved a present.

Reaper was surprised that the shopping had taken so long. He parked outside the hotel and carried in the bags. Sandra was waiting in the foyer. Her eyes widened when she saw the amount of goods. She helped him carry them upstairs, knocked at the door and put her head round it. He waited while she took the bags inside.

'How are they?' he asked when she returned.

'Stunned, shocked. But they'll be okay. They'll have to be, won't they?'

It was a brutal reality, but she was right.

'I got you a present,' he said.

'What?'

His statement had taken her by surprise. He gave her one of the sports watches and saw her disappointment.

'That's for operational purposes,' he said. 'This isn't.'

The disappointment turned into delight when she opened the box he gave her and saw the Christal watch.

'It's beautiful,' she said. 'But when will I wear it?'

'Whenever you like,' he said. 'Old rules don't apply any more. Remember?' She gave him a kiss on the cheek. 'Oh yes, and there's a bag of stuff in the car for you.'

Sandra stared up into his face and said, 'Reaper, you are amazing.'

He looked away, changing the mood, then looked back.

'I'm going across the road to collect any weapons they had. And there's something else. The girl, Stacey. Did they tell you?'

'They said she couldn't face it. That she hung herself.

The man they called Jerome left her hanging there. He thought it was funny. She was fourteen.'

He nodded, getting his emotions under control, then said, 'There's a church up the hill. I'm going to take her there.'

'You don't believe in God,' said Sandra.

'No, but she probably did.' He paused. 'When the girls are ready, they might want to come. I'll wait outside.'

He went back to the car, took one of the suitcases from the back and pulled it into the Imperial. He opened it in the foyer and put in it two sawn-off shotguns, a Webley revolver, ammunition and two large knives in sheaths. He steeled himself to go upstairs, not because of the sight of Jerome, but because of Stacey. The man had a sawn-off shotgun, a Walther PPK and ammunition, and a 10 inch Bowie knife with a leg sheath. He strapped the sheath and knife onto his own right leg. The guns and ammunition he took downstairs and put in the case, which he stowed in the back of the car along with the full-sized shotgun.

Now, for the final part of what he had come to see as an act of cleansing . . . He went into another bedroom and found a clean sheet. He lay it on the floor of the room where the young girl hung. He stood for a moment before her and, in his mind, apologised for having to touch her. He promised he would be gentle and that she would now be able to rest in peace.

It was as close to a prayer as he could manage. Tears sprang to his eyes as he took her light weight over his shoulder, using the Bowie knife to cut the school tie from which she hung.

Reaper lay her on the sheet and arranged her clothes decently. He knelt by her side and, leaning forward, kissed her on the forehead, then carefully wrapped the sheet around her. He took the tie-backs from the room curtains, but they were not long enough. In the next suite, he found two white bathrobes and took the belts. As gently as he could, he tied the belts around the girl's chest and thighs to keep the sheet in place.

He swung the carbine onto his back, knelt down and picked up the body. She weighed hardly anything at all. A small victim in the aftermath of the end of the world. He glanced upwards. Are you there, God? Can You make sense of this? He carried her downstairs and lay her on the wall outside the hotel and waited in the sunshine beneath an egg-blue sky and the sound of the gulls.

Sandra brought the girls across the street. The two young girls were wearing jeans, sweaters and trainers. Jenny Hall was wearing combat clothes. They carried the Debenhams bags of spare clothing.

'There's a church not far away,' he said. 'I'll carry her. Sandra, why don't you drive the girls there? Then we don't have to come back.'

He picked up the body and strode off up the road.

Behind him, he heard the doors of the car open and close as they stored their gear and climbed aboard. Footsteps caught him up and he glanced to his side to see Jenny Hall.

'If you don't mind, I'll walk with you.'

He nodded.

The car started and followed in low gear.

The day was right for a walk. Good weather promising a bright future. If only they could survive the present. The girl was light but grew heavier in his arms. He welcomed the weight, wanted the journey to be painful, to remind him what had happened, to make the journey his Calvary. A re-commitment to cleanse the land. He had killed five men without compunction. One he would willingly have tortured before death. Two of the others he had put down without giving them a chance to defend themselves. Executions. He would do the same again wherever he met their kind and the reason why lay in his aching arms.

Jenny talked as they walked.

'I taught at St Hilda's,' she said. 'It's a public school about five miles away. When the illness started, some of the girls went home. Most of them stayed. Most of them died. I was the only teacher left. Helen was head girl. She's seventeen. Caroline is sixteen. We waited for help to come to us but it didn't. Two days ago we decided to look for help and came here. We met Jerome and his crew.' She took a breath, maybe to get the explanation done. 'They told us what they were going to do. They put Stacey in the room at the hotel and took Caroline, Helen and me downstairs. For a party, they said. Jerome said he was saving Stacey for later. For something special. When they went to get her they found she had hanged herself. Maybe she heard the screams. She was only fourteen. She thought that was a better way out. Maybe it was.'

She sounded on the edge of tears.

Reaper said, 'You're alive. That's better than being dead.'

'Is it?'

If he were to give her an honest answer, he would have to say he didn't know. He knew only that he had been spared for a purpose and that this was a limbo he was living through, a penance he was paying.

'I failed her,' Jenny said.

'No you didn't. You walked into events outside your control.'

'But I led her, and Helen and Caroline, on that damn silly walk into danger. We could have stayed at school.'

'Not forever. The bad elements are always the first to rise to the surface. It's happened in other towns, other places. But they will be put down eventually.'

They walked in silence for a while and then she said, 'You said I walked into events outside my control.'

'You did.'

'I don't want to do that again. Next time, I want a chance to protect myself. Like Sandra.' He supposed Sandra, booted and equipped, looked invincible to someone walking away from multiple rape. 'Will you teach me?'

'I'll teach you.'

It took twenty minutes to reach the church of St Paul's, a Victorian building of grey stone in a walled churchyard of 100-year-old graves. They walked up the path and the birds seemed to stop singing. Maybe his disbelief had shocked them into silence. One gull wheeled overhead and gave a last mournful cry. Sandra had parked the car. She, Caroline and Helen now walked behind them.

Jenny Hall opened the door and he stepped into the cool interior. He had half expected to find refugees inside, but it was empty and undamaged. Why vandalise a church when there were high street shops to plunder? He paused and felt the religion of the building. Not in God's presence but in the worship of generations who had knelt here and offered prayers in the hope of a better life, now and forever. He walked slowly down the aisle and stepped up onto the carpeted area before the altar. The imagery, candles and crucifix told him it was High Church. The paraphernalia seemed appropriate to the gesture he was making.

Reaper lay Stacey's body gently on the ground before the altar and the crucified figure of Christ. The four young women had knelt in pews. He glanced back at them. Helen and Caroline were crying. Jenny was distraught. Sandra looked at him as if to suggest, 'say something'. A few words?

He knelt on one knee, his left hand cradling the carbine, his right resting on the body, and he looked up again at Christ on the cross. If Christ thought He had suffered, He should look down here. But that was not what the girls wanted.

'This is Stacey,' he said. 'She's a young girl. Too young to have committed any sin. Too young to have properly lived. She didn't deserve this end, but at least now she has no more pain. No more fear.' He paused. What was he talking about? He had no authority to spout these words. 'Stacey's friends are here. They remember her. They'll always remember her. They're sorry they couldn't look after her. But now, they'd like you to look after her. Let her rest in peace.'

As he got up, the girls softly said, 'Amen'.

He took a last look at Stacey's shrouded body, nodded farewell, turned and walked out of the church, his boots echoing in the empty space that had swallowed his prayer, and blinked the moisture from his eyes.

Chapter 8

JENNY HALL AND THE GIRLS DID NOT TALK on the way back to the estate and Reaper and Sandra kept the silence with them. When they arrived, Jean Megson, her bosoms heaving, ushered the two girls indoors. Judith, tall and grey haired and looking more like a teacher than Jenny Hall, went with them. Nick Waite watched with sorrow in his eyes. Without being told, he had guessed at least part of the tragedy.

Reaper told him about Stacey as he unloaded the guns and ammunition from the car and, with the help of Sandra and Jenny, transferred them to the cellar of the manor house that would be their armoury. Jenny declined Nick's offer of prayers or silent contemplation, but he put his dog collar on anyway.

'A man is probably not the person the girls want to see at the moment,' he acknowledged, 'but perhaps a priest?'

He gave Reaper the keys of the mobile home and left them to join the two girls and the two women. Reaper unlocked the rear storage of the RV, and they moved the weapons that had been stashed there into the armoury, too.

Everyone else was out, inspecting the farm or houses and working out what needed to be done for the future. Reaper noticed Sandra kept glancing around, for Jamie he assumed, but there was no sign of him. To his surprise, he found he was also keeping a look out and realised the person he wanted to see most was Kate.

When they had finished, Reaper moved the mobile home back over the hill into the lookout position. Sandra and Jenny went with him.

'You two make a good team,' Jenny said.

'Yes, we do,' said Reaper, and watched Sandra try to hide her pleasure at the compliment.

'I meant what I said. I'd like to learn how to use a gun. I'd like to join you.'

'We need recruits,' said Reaper, 'and I'll teach you how to shoot. But we also need a teacher. A *real* teacher, for the kids we have here.'

'I won't teach again. Maybe Helen will teach, but not me.'

He nodded and looked at Sandra.

'Can we use her?' he asked her.

Sandra was standing at ease, carbine cradled. She looked the part and was enjoying being one of the perceived elite. But she looked at Jenny with a serious expression, one victim to another, and said, 'I think Jenny will be a fine recruit.'

'We'll start tomorrow,' Reaper said. 'If we start shooting today, everyone will think we're being invaded.

Reaper prepared the mobile home as a defensive position and Sandra brewed tea. Jenny talked about her background. A middle class home: father a doctor, mother a 'lady who lunched'. She had grown up in Redditch, went to Birmingham University and gained a disappointing 2:2 in History and English.

'I was never an academic but my parents expected me to go to college and discover a career. What I discovered was a tutor who majored in impressionable young girls who were away from home for the first time. I scraped a degree but left with my emotions somewhat in tatters. My dad agreed I could continue to study and this time I did something I was good at: sport. I took a course in Sports Psychology and Coaching Sciences at Bournemouth. That was what got me the job at St Hilda's, teaching history and sport. I was never a good teacher, although I liked sport. It always seemed as if I was doing the job until something else came along.'

'And then something came along,' said Sandra, softly.

'Yes.' Jenny was wistful. 'Dad phoned. Both he and mum had the flu. I think he knew what was happening. He told me to stay put. There's no point coming home, he said. No point. By then it was really bad and all the teachers were trying to help the girls. Not that it did any good. There were just the four of us at the end. At first we intended to go to Rutford School. That's the boys' school. We had links, both being public schools. But we decided to try Scarborough first. If only.'

Sandra said, 'There's no room for "if only" anymore. What happened, happened. It's not unique. It happened to me, too. You have to get over it and get on with it.'

Her face was tight and Reaper wanted to go and comfort her, but she was being hard, building the toughness into her performance as Lara Croft. Even so, he could tell she was on the edge.

'Oh,' said Jenny. 'I had no idea.'

And the knowledge that both were victims made Jenny give way at last and cry. Sandra went to her and put her arms around her. Reaper stepped outside the motor home and walked to the front gates to stretch his legs, breath fresh air and avoid emotion.

The growing community gathered in the dining room to eat the evening meal together. Reaper and Sandra left their guns on the high shelf of a Welsh dresser,

151

out of the reach of the children, and dispensed with the Kevlar vests. He gave Nick the key to the armoury in the cellar.

Sandra took him to one side. She had disappeared earlier into the house with the bag of clothes he had selected for her.

'You have great taste,' she said.

'I have?'

She kissed his cheek. 'Thanks, Reaper.'

Jenny and Sandra sat together and Reaper hovered until Jamie took the seat on the other side of Sandra. Reaper sat next to him. By chance, Kate was sitting opposite. Her red hair was lustrous, as if she had just washed it, and she smiled shyly across the table at him. Since when had a lady who had run a bar been shy? Caroline and Helen sat on the other side of Jenny.

There were also three newcomers who had been found by Jamie and Bob when they had toured the nearby farms and villages. A young farmer's son in his late teens, a middle aged butcher, and a fifty-year-old woman who had retired to the area with her husband only two months before. Now she was a widow and still slightly bereft of her senses, but extremely grateful to be with people again, after living alone with her husband dead in the master bedroom for the last two weeks. Jamie and Bob had buried him in the back garden.

Talk was about the future. Jamie and Bob would

continue to look for survivors in the countryside and ways to expand what they had. The estate was a walled thousand-acre enclosure but this was surrounded by neighbouring farmlands that included grazing and arable land. They had both dairy and beef cattle, sheep, hens and five estate horses that had been used for riding by paying guests. Bob knew of pig farms not too far away and a few miles up the road towards York were fields of pick-your-own vegetables and fruit. The estate had its own spring and river for a water supply.

Reaper said, 'Petrol and diesel won't be a problem for the foreseeable future. It gives us time to work out long term solutions.'

The farm had diesel tanks, as did many other farms. They could syphon fuel from the many abandoned cars. There was more fuel beneath petrol forecourts. With no power, the computerised electric pumps wouldn't work, but Gavin had a rotary pump: unlock the delivery cap in the forecourt, drop a hose inside and you could pump out however much you needed. For repairs, there was a small but well-equipped garage at a village only three miles away, which Gavin would use when necessary.

Everyone was asked to list their skills and everyone, when necessary, would have to work the land and tend the animals under the supervision of Bob and David, the young farmer.

Old Bob had one additional suggestion.

'We need cats and dogs,' he said. 'We'll need them to control the mice and rats.' He chuckled when some of the women shuddered. 'When I was growing up, we never bothered about mice running across the bed. It were normal. They're just God's creatures. But now we've moved back, like, in history so to speak, we're likely to see more of them. Put a cat in every house and that'll keep 'em down. They don't even like the smell of cats. And dogs, too. Terriers make good ratters.'

It was agreed that, the next day, Bob and Jamie would explore other areas in the countryside they had not yet visited. Gavin and Pete would go looking for more hand pumps, so that all their vehicles would be able to refill at petrol stations rather than rely on syphoning. Others would start getting to grips with animal husbandry and learning how to grow crops. Deirdre, the grateful lady who had just joined them, said she had been a market gardener, and Ashley had had an allotment where he had grown his own vegetables.

Nick, who still wore his priestly collar, looked pleased at the progress being made until Reaper said, 'We still need protection. Jenny and Pete have volunteered for weapons training. Jamie?'

'Of course, if you think it necessary.'

'I do. Anyone else?'

'I'd like to learn.' Kate's offer surprised him.

'Good,' he said. He glanced round the table, but Ashley dropped his eyes. 'Tomorrow at nine. Out front. So the rest of you, don't worry if you hear shooting. After that, Sandra and I will go out again and look for a doctor. If anybody wants us to collect any supplies, make a list and let me or Sandra have it in the morning.'

The meal ended and people broke into groups. Reaper joined Ashley.

'Tell me to mind my own business, but I'd say you've been in the services,' Reaper said.

'That's true, man. No point denying it.'

'You'd be an asset.'

'I've given up guns, Reaper. I'm sorry, but guns are not for me.'

'What happened, Ash?'

Ashley took a long look at Reaper and nodded his head imperceptibly, as if coming to a decision.

'You've got a right to know. I suppose I saw too much. Afghanistan, Iraq. Not just mates being blown up, civilians too. Women, kids, old folk. War doesn't discriminate, Reaper. Especially at 10,000 feet. It wore me down. I served my tours and, when I could, I got out. There was nothing dramatic in my leaving. I just left. And afterwards, I wondered why. Why had it been necessary? Was it a just war? Or just politics? Whatever, I didn't want to fight again and I'd prefer not to now. I saw too much, Reaper. That's all.'

Reaper nodded his acceptance of the explanation.

'Can't argue with that, Ash. But some time in the future, you might reconsider. I won't be pushing it. But maybe you might change your mind. Your decision.'

There was no wine tonight, no beer. Reaper drew Sandra to one side and said, 'Have you thought about where you'll be staying tonight? I don't think the motor home is suitable long term.'

'You're right. I thought I'd stay in one of the flats here with Jenny and the girls. There's a family apartment they've taken.' She looked into his face and he realised she wondered if he would be disappointed. 'I thought I'd try it. If it doesn't work, we could always take one of the houses?'

'I was going to suggest you stay here. We should have at least one armed person on the premises,' he said. 'Keep your weapons safe. I'll be okay in the motor home for a while. Maybe later I'll move in here and we'll alternate a guard. We'll see.'

She accepted the role he had created for her gratefully and he let her drift to the waiting Jamie.

Reaper eased himself away from the crowd, collected his weapons and looked back from the door. Nick caught his eye and nodded goodnight with a smile. The only other person who was watching him was Kate. Her smile was slight but it was a smile and she, too, nodded. He returned the farewell and left, walking through the village and over the hill to the motor home.

*

Another fine day, more blue skies and a warm sun that would be hot later. He had slept with the windows open to hear any noise and had got up twice in the night to walk the grounds and make sure the chain was in place across the gates. He showered, had a cup of tea, ate a tin of mandarin oranges and made two Thermos flasks of coffee.

The walk over the hill was pleasant. On the stroll down the other side, he could see people already active. His group waited for him outside the manor house. Sandra, Jamie, Pete, Jenny and Kate. The Reverend Nick came down the stairs and held out the key to the armoury.

'You'll need this,' he said.

'First,' said Reaper, 'we need trestle tables or benches, something waist high.'

'Patio tables,' said Jamie. 'They're round the side. In the season, we put them outside the pub.'

They were good quality rectangular wooden tables with folding legs. They carried three round the house to face the barn twenty yards away. Then he led them to the armoury and kitted them out in Kevlar vests and holster belts with Asp batons and cuffs and a Glock, and handed each a carbine. Jamie seemed comfortable with it; Pete handled his with interest. Jenny and Kate held them as if they were alien weapons, which, to them, they were. He put clips of ammunition in a cardboard box and led them back to the barn.

'Anyone working beyond there?' he asked, and Jamie confirmed no one would be in the way of stray shots.

Reaper broke up the cardboard box so that it made a target about 18 inches wide and two feet long. He used coloured pins he'd taken from the notice board in the lobby of the house to attach it to the side of the barn wall. He indicated that the four recruits should stand behind the tables and place their weapons on the wooden surface. Sandra, without being asked, joined them.

'Now . . . we'll start with the Glock handgun.'

He went through the procedures. Explained the magazines, the calibre, the power and showed them how to load and how to stand. Sandra followed his instructions as he gave them so that the four trainees had two of them to watch. For Sandra it was also a refresher course. After all, she had only been 'special forces' for a few days.

Pete got the stance straight away, but Jamie had to be corrected. The two girls also needed guidance, and Sandra helped Jenny, while Reaper moved Kate into position. Her hair shone in the sun and he was careful to touch her only lightly.

He put them through their paces one at a time. Getting them to shoot, correcting them, and having them shoot again, until each had used up the magazine.

'We're not going to waste ammunition,' said Reaper, 'but that was pretty good.' They smiled. 'That's because these weapons are the best and shoot where you point them.' Their smiles faded. 'But you were pretty good, too.'

And they had been, all hitting the target on several occasions, but then, the target was static, made of cardboard, and not shooting back.

They switched to the carbines and went through the procedures again, by the end of which each had used a full clip.

'That's it,' he said at the end. 'You are now fully-fledged members of our special forces. I know it's rudimentary, but you've got the basics. When you have time, practice stance and practice loading, both the magazines and the guns. But be careful, because guns kill – that's their purpose after all. I know it's been said before, but it is true and we don't want you killing yourself or each other: only ever point a gun at something or someone you intend to shoot.'

They relaxed and talked amongst themselves, pleased with the way it had gone.

Jamie said, 'Shall we put these back in the armoury?'

'No,' Reaper said. 'From now on, they're yours. It's up to you to clean them, practice with them, look after them and, if necessary, use them in the protection of yourself or this group. Pete? You're going out with Gavin later?' Pete nodded. 'Then I'd advise keeping on the vest and go prepared. There are nasty people about.'

Jamie said, 'I don't want to scare people in the villages. Maybe I'll leave the vest in the car.'

'Your call,' Reaper said. 'Jenny? Kate? Why don't you come with us? We'll take the MPV, find another vehicle on the way and split into two teams. Now, back to the armoury and get fresh magazines.'

Reaper drove the car with Sandra riding shotgun in the front seat. She had the list of provisions people had asked for, including bottled water, chocolate, cooking oil, toilet paper, tinned foodstuffs, matches, rubber gloves and Wellington boots. On the way out of the estate, he stopped at the motor home and picked up a holdall, which he put in the back. As they approached Scarborough, Reaper parked outside a car dealership and let them inspect the vehicles on the forecourt. Sandra chose a year-old red Vauxhall Astra van.

'This is good,' she said.

Reaper went into the showrooms and, after rooting about in an office, found a drawer full of keys. He brought the right one back and handed it to Sandra.

'You'd better check it for fuel,' he said.

She got into the car, adjusted the seat and started the engine. It fired first time.

'It's less than a quarter full,' she said.

'Bring it onto the road and we'll syphon some fuel.'

He went to the MPV and got a hammer and a rubber tube then walked down the street to a Renault saloon whose petrol cap was on the side of the car accessible from the road. The door was locked so he smashed the window with the hammer, reached in and opened it, and found the petrol cap release. 'Turn it round!' he told Sandra.

She did so and he guided her until her petrol cap was alongside, although a couple of feet away. She switched off the engine. He removed the cap on the Astra, pushed the tube into the Renault and sucked at the other end. He got a mouthful of petrol, spat it out, and held his end of the tube in the mouth of the petrol tank of the van. It ran for quite a time. The Renault must have been almost full.

'Three quarters,' said Sandra, and thirty seconds later the stream dribbled to an end.

He put the tube and the hammer back in the MPV. 'How are we going to—' he began, but Sandra said, 'Jenny can come with me. Kate, with you. Is that okay?'

'That's fine,' he said.

'I've got the list. I'll find a supermarket first, then go looking for Wellington boots.'

'We'll have a drive around town then head to the hospital.' He checked his watch. 'It's half eleven. We'll meet at the harbour at two. Then I thought we'd try Rutford School. Do you know the way, Jenny?'

'I know the way.'

They nodded to each other and Reaper said, 'Take care.'

'You, too,' said Sandra.

He and Kate got into the MPV and he was more aware of her sitting next to him than he had ever been of Sandra. Maybe it was because he didn't know her. They were both unknown quantities to each other.

'Okay?' he said, glancing into her face and noticing her hazel eyes.

'Okay.' she said.

Reaper followed the red van until it turned into a Sainsbury's. He stopped the car, remembering the last time, then followed it into the car park but stayed well back from the shop entrance. Sandra stopped the van at the front, glanced back at him and raised an arm in acknowledgement, then spoke to Jenny. The two girls approached the store cautiously, the carbines at the ready. Windows had been smashed and they stepped through broken glass and disappeared inside.

He waited a few minutes longer.

Kate said, 'Is anything wrong?'

'We had trouble in a supermarket. People can get proprietorial about them.'

Another minute and Sandra reappeared at the window and gave them the thumbs up. He raised a hand and drove away. The major danger would be from a gang like the one led by Jerome. Then again, even many ordinary people were prone to have become a little crazy after everything that had happened. The ones he and Sandra had fought in Asda might once have been essentially law-abiding citizens.

They toured the town slowly, the car windows down. He stopped on Northway, near where he had seen the three inebriates the previous day, and honked the horn. A couple of minutes later, his long-haired friend poked his head round the corner, saw who it was and staggered into view. He was carrying a bottle of lager.

'Hey, man,' he said.

'How you doing?'

'Me? I'm fine. Responsible citizen like me? I'm fine.' He raised the bottle so he could point a finger at Reaper. 'Good job, man! You did a good job.'

'You helped.'

The man shook his head. 'Nah. You did a good job, man. Needed doing and you did it.'

'What's your name?'

'Shaggy. What's yours?'

'I'm Reaper.'

Reaper held out his hand and, after staring at it for a moment, Shaggy took it in his own and they shook.

'Great name, man. You choose that? Reaper. Great name.' He squinted into the car. 'You've got a new lady. Is the other one okay?'

'The other one's fine. This is Kate.'

Shaggy waved. 'Hi, Kate.'

'Hi, Shaggy.'

'Any friend of Reaper's is a friend of mine.' He stepped,

or rather staggered, back a pace and refocused. 'Do you want to come for a drink? We're in The Alma. It's round the corner. You'd be welcome, man.'

'Thanks, but not today. We've got things to do.'

Shaggy nodded sagely. 'More patrolling and stuff.'

'That's it.'

'That's good.'

'How many of you meet in The Alma, Shaggy?'

'There's four of us.' He looked at the fingers of one hand and said, 'Five of us. Call in any time. Any friend of mine is a friend of Reaper's.'

'Any more trouble?'

'Trouble?'

'Like Jerome and his gang?'

'Don't know, man. People are frightened. Sometimes angry. Sometimes fight. I stay out of it. I stay in The Alma.'

'Shaggy, you and your friends take care.'

'We will. We will, man.'

Reaper offered his hand again, but this time his arm was upright, and Shaggy took it and gripped it, as if they were ready to arm wrestle.

'We'll be around,' said Reaper.

'That's good, man. That's good.'

Reaper drove away and Kate waved. Shaggy staggered as he waved back, his coordination a little unsteady as he was trying to drink from the bottle at the same time.

'A character,' said Kate.

'Believe it or not, he's one of the good guys. Now, where to next?'

'If I'm going to carry a gun, I'd like kit like you and the girls.'

'Okay.'

He drove to the camping shop.

Reaper didn't think it would be dangerous but there was no point taking chances. Besides, it was an opportunity for Kate to get used to being careful. She followed his example as they left the car, holding the carbine at the ready and checking the streets before cautiously entering the store. He showed her where the pants, T-shirts and boots were and kept a watch by the window. She picked her size and went into a cubicle with a loose curtain across it to change.

He noticed a display of knives that had nothing to do with camping and went round behind the counter to take them out and inspect them. Throwing knives, small, neat, sharp and, he had no doubt, in the right hands extremely deadly. But just how much weaponry did he want? He snorted to himself. *As much as bloody possible.* He picked a set of three stainless steel knives and a wrist sheath. He also slipped a sheath that held a single blade around his neck on a chain so that it hung down his back beneath his T-shirt and vest.

He began to put the sheath on his arm, glanced up and realised that, from his new position behind the counter, he could see Kate in the mirror of the changing room through the gap where the curtain didn't reach the wall.

She was wearing only her underwear: white briefs and bra, and his throat went dry at the sight of the curve of her spine, the fullness of the side view of her breasts, and the roundness of her rump. He panicked in case she saw him. She would think he had taken up this position on purpose. What could he say? *I was looking at knives. I wanted to be Ninja. Honest.*

He stumbled trying to move too fast from behind the counter, and kicked a box. He straightened up, once he was back in his safety zone, and looked towards the cubicle. Kate was peering round the curtain at him, alerted by the kicked box, and her glance seemed to read the situation.

Reaper held up the wrist sheath and said inanely, 'Knives.'

'Knives,' she said, and smiled, before retreating behind the curtain to continue changing.

Shit! thought Reaper, fumbling with the straps of the sheath. He had it in place by the time she came out, in what was becoming the regulation uniform of his special forces. On her, they looked good. She got a plastic bag and put her own clothes and trainers in it and put a navy-blue baseball cap on her head. The colour of the clothes and the cap suited her, making her hair colour look even richer.

'What do you think?' she said.

'I think you look great,' he said, instantly embarrassed for speaking the truth in such a heartfelt manner, and then wondering what he had started, when young women were dressing in military fatigues and pretending to be soldiers. Maybe he would regret it when one of them was killed. Maybe not, because it was necessary. 'We'd better go to the hospital,' he said.

The visit was not one he was looking forward to. Before they left the store, he took a handful of surgical face-masks from a display on the counter. In the weeks before the end, every shop had stocked them.

Chapter 9

SCARBOROUGH GENERAL HOSPITAL WAS A meandering complex of buildings. The main facade was redbrick. Ambulances sat beneath a yellow canopy outside Accident and Emergency. Reaper followed the sign to the main entrance. The car parks were full and there were bodies everywhere: sitting in wheelchairs, on benches, in vehicles, on the ground where they had fallen; hoping for help that had not arrived. Flies hovered in small clouds around the dead. He gave Kate a surgical mask and fitted one over his own mouth and nose and they went inside.

Inside was worse. Much worse.

As a policeman, Reaper had twice seen bodies that had lain undiscovered for a week or more. A householder notices a bad smell and realises they haven't seen their neighbour for a while. It was up to the police to discover the worst. He remembered the smell and the flies. A pathologist had given him a run-down on the process of decay.

For the first few days there are no outward signs of decomposition, but the flies are already laying their eggs. Then the body becomes bloated with gases, the mouth, lips and tongue swell, the skin becomes fragile. Maggots, flies and insects are all busy. Putrefaction has started. Maybe ten days after death, maybe a bit more, the body collapses, the abdominal gases escape, insect activity increases. After twenty days, the body is flat and begins to dry out and beetles take over. Mummification can begin.

They walked into noise and smell. The noise of clouds of flies, the smell of putrefaction. This was a horror show and he realised that he should have waited another two or three weeks before undertaking his search for a doctor.

'Are you okay?' he asked.

Only Kate's eyes could show any expression. They were wide in shock, but she nodded.

Bodies sat in chairs, on couches and the grey carpet of the waiting area. One man was sprawled across the display of dead flowers outside the small hospital shop where sad, partly deflated balloons were still tethered saying, *Congratulations* and *Get Well Soon*. And around them all the flies were busy, landing, laying eggs that would become maggots that would become flies, part of the process of nature and death.

They followed the signs along a corridor towards departments and wards, and the smell got worse, even through the mask. The death process here was more advanced and maggots writhed in ravaged faces. Why hadn't he waited? Given nature more time to do its work? They stayed alert, carbines at the ready, because a hospital, even in this state, could be a magnet for anyone wanting drugs for non-medicinal purposes.

'Hello?' shouted Reaper, and the word echoed back at him.

They walked past lines of trolleys that contained more of the dead; among them, lying on the floor as if taking a nap, were a nurse and a male hospital orderly, who had stayed at their posts until the very end. He occasionally turned full circle as they walked, to ensure no one was behind them, and Kate began to alternate the move so they were covered at all times. He hoped she was looking for the living and not at the dead.

'Hello?' he shouted again, and again there was no reply.

They entered a ward. The beds were full. The flies swarmed at the intrusion and then returned to their business. Mattresses had been placed on the floor to accept even more patients. Another nurse lay dead among her charges. Side rooms were full, with extra beds made up on the floor, all occupied. A doctor in a white coat and a stethoscope around her neck, sat in a high chair at the nursing station in the middle of the long ward, her body slumped across the counter. Through an open office door nearby, Reaper saw the body of another nurse.

'Hello?' he called again.

They retreated the way they had come and climbed stairs to the next level. Why, when they knew no one living could still be here? More bodies, hundreds of bodies. Kate shouted this time. Maybe someone would respond to a woman's voice? No one did. He wondered, at the height of the pandemic, what had happened to patients suffering from other diseases. Had they all succumbed to the virus or had some survived to die slowly in bed in the middle of a mausoleum?

When they saw the sign to a children's ward Reaper had had enough.

'We should go,' he said.

Kate nodded. Her eyes were numb. Tears welled simply at the sight of the nursery characters painted on the walls leading to the ward. They left quickly, trying to blot out the sights and the smell. They didn't even trouble to look for bandages or even the most basic or accessible of medical supplies.

Outside, they pulled off the masks and breathed the relatively clean air. The bodies out here hadn't been as dead as long and the putrefaction was not as advanced. Kate began to shake and leaned on the car for support, the carbine swinging round her back on its strap. Reaper stepped to her and took her in his arms for comfort, nothing more. A human contact after all the corpses. She put her head on his shoulder and her arms around him. Two would-be soldiers, he thought, drained by the silence and repugnant reality of death. Then the comfort began to turn into something else. They both became aware of the change and he didn't know if Kate would want it or if he was ready for it. Maybe she sensed his uncertainty. They stepped apart.

'I knew it would be bad,' he said. 'I didn't think it would be that bad.'

'At least we know. Nothing else can compare.'

They got back in the car and Reaper headed for the harbour.

They drove down the steep road to the front and Reaper paused at the bottom to make sure nothing was coming along the Foreshore Road. Old habits. He drove across and onto the West Pier, fishing boats in the harbour to the left, a few cars in the parking zone to the right, some of them occupied. Perhaps victims who had chosen to come here to die, either of the virus or a suicidal dose of drugs, whilst staring out at the view of the crescent bay.

He stopped the car and they got out. Fishing boats swayed at their moorings and the gulls swooped and screeched. The water sparkled in the sun and the air was free of the aroma of burgers, fried onions, fish and death. This had been a happy feeding ground for the gulls when fishermen, anglers and leisure sailors had used the harbour and tourists had used the resort. Now they had to fend for themselves.

The Harbour Office and Port Control were located on this, the main and broader of the three stone piers. Between the fingers of the other two were the pleasure craft, still at rest. Perhaps forever at rest. In the far corner were the tower of the helter-skelter and the Ferris wheel of the small Luna Park amusements. Rising behind the harbour, the steep hillsides of the headland were ringed by the walls of Scarborough Castle. The bay that spread to their left, as they faced the shore, was lined with deserted shops, restaurants, pubs and amusement arcades facing an empty beach. The clifftops above were filled with hotels, their sightless eyes staring out to sea.

Reaper and Kate still carried their carbines as they stretched their legs in the sun. The more they all got used to handling the guns the better. They were ten minutes early. He had been to the town three times on holiday as a child with his parents, who had an affinity for the place despite living so far away. He had resisted doing the same when he had his own family, but his choice of the Haven one summer had been influenced by its close proximity, and they had visited and enjoyed its typical English seaside robustness. He looked along the Foreshore and tried to pick out the fish and chip shop they had visited. He was brought back to the present by the arrival of Sandra and Jenny in the red Astra van. He was grateful. He had avoided sweet memories for such a long time that he didn't know how he might react if once more confronted by them.

The back of the van was full. The girls climbed out.

'Any problems?' he asked.

'No problems,' said Sandra. 'We met a couple of people. They were wary but okay.'

Jenny said, 'They seemed disorientated.'

'They are waiting for the Yanks to arrive,' said Sandra. 'No, really! They think America is still okay and that before long they'll send troops to clear everything up.'

He took the holdall from the back of the MPV and put it on the low harbour wall.

'Two flasks of coffee, black, no sugar,' he said, taking them out of the bag and placing them on the wall, along with plastic mugs. He also took out a tin of coffee whitener and a plastic container of sugar. 'There's also bottles of fruit juice and Lucozade. And the menu for today is cheese, corned beef and salmon spread.' He lifted out handfuls of baguettes, individually wrapped in kitchen foil.

'When did you do all this?' asked Kate.

'I baked the bread during the night. Made up the sandwiches first thing. We could have had fish and chips but . . .'

The poor joke hung in the air for a second.

'But these are better,' said Sandra. 'Which are which?'

'Do you know,' he said. 'I haven't a clue.'

They unwrapped the sandwiches, took their choice, poured coffee and had a picnic. Kate and Jenny sat on the harbour wall and Sandra opened the passenger door of the Astra and perched sideways on the seat with her feet on the ground. They exchanged information about where they had been and what they had done, although Reaper left out the details of the hospital. It was enough to tell them they had found no doctor.

As they were finishing, a Range Rover appeared from a street leading onto the harbour side over to the right.

''We've got company,' Reaper said. They put down the coffee mugs and the girls swiftly got to their feet. 'Stay behind the cars,' he said. 'Don't threaten with the guns, but be alert.'

He walked forward between the two vehicles until he was clear of them. He glanced back as the Range Rover approached slowly along the Sandside road. Sandra was closest to the sea wall, Kate directly behind him and Jenny to the beach side of their vehicles. At least they looked the part: all dressed alike;

the baseball caps aggressive beaks upon their heads; the carbines cradled in their arms; their trigger fingers in the correct position alongside the finger guards of the guns. All looked determined and capable. He hoped that if whoever was approaching wanted trouble, looks would not be deceiving.

The Range Rover turned onto the pier and stopped twenty yards away. A woman was driving and a man was in the passenger seat. They both got out and held their hands high before they approached. The man was about fifty, tall athletic build, craggy good looks. He was wearing jeans and an open neck blue shirt. The woman was in her thirties, black, big eyes behind big glasses, with a striking angular face. She wore shorts that displayed long smooth legs, and a T-shirt that hugged small breasts.

Reaper looked past them at the Range Rover.

'It's just the two of us,' the man said, and Reaper nodded, but he looked back along the Foreshore and the Sandside. He saw no one else. 'You're careful,' said the man.

'You have to be,' said Reaper. 'Why don't you put your hands down?'

'I'm Richard Ferguson.' He offered his hand and Reaper shook it.

The woman said, 'Greta Malone,' and he shook hers too.

'I'm Reaper,' he said.

'Unusual name,' she said.

He tipped his head to indicate the girls. 'Sandra, Kate and Jenny.'

The two new arrivals lifted hands in acknowledgement.

'You seem to be well organised,' Ferguson said. His voice was cultured.

'We are.'

'We have a group in the castle.'

Reaper glanced up at the ramparts on the headland. 'Good spot,' he said.

'Are you part of a group?'

'Yes. We've taken over farms inland.'

'That's brilliant,' said Ferguson. 'A new start.'

'We intend to try.'

'So do we. There are eight of us in the castle and we know there are more in town, but people are still in shock. Give them time and they'll join us.'

'What then?' asked Reaper. 'Will you stay there?'

'We could for a while. The supermarkets are well stocked, there's some arable land where we could grow things. Nothing ambitious. Allotments, that sort of thing. And there is, of course, fishing. If we did stay, we might redevelop the fishing industry and trade with inland communities like yours.'

'That's a long term plan,' Reaper said.

'Nothing is decided yet,' Ferguson said. 'But it could be one way forward.'

Greta Malone said, 'Richard has plans for regeneration.'

Ferguson snorted. 'I'm a physicist, which isn't exactly the best qualification, but I want us to use what we have and what we can sustain. I mean, everything went when we lost electricity. Communication, internet, gas services, the water supplies. Everything relied on electric power. One switch failed, it triggered more, and before you knew it, we had lost the lot. I want to use the technology we were developing then that can help us now. We don't have the expertise to build and run power stations, but we can put solar panels on roofs and use wind power.'

'I like your ideas,' said Reaper. 'Count us in.'

Greta had been looking at the girls. 'Are you some kind of military force?' she said.

'Something like that,' Reaper said, 'Some of our people have suffered. We want to make sure they don't suffer again.'

'There was a wild group in town,' Ferguson said. 'Then another lot moved in and left bodies all over the Imperial Hotel.' He shook his head. 'You would think there'd been enough death already, wouldn't you? But no, it carries on.'

Greta had been watching Reaper's reaction and she said, 'That was you.'

'Yes. That was us. That was Sandra and me.'

Greta glanced past him at the slim shape of the

youngest girl of the three behind him, the one who looked her steadily in the eye, and then back to Reaper.

'Just the two of you?' she said.

He nodded.

Ferguson also looked at Sandra before switching his gaze back to Reaper, as if assessing them and the carnage they had left at the Imperial.

'There were six bodies,' he said, as if disputing the odds.

'They were all bad guys,' Reaper said.

'You killed all six?' Ferguson said.

'They had to be dealt with.'

'Dealt with?'

Reaper sensed Ferguson did not approve and so chose his words with provocation in mind.

'They needed to be put down.'

'Put down?' The physicist shook his head, as if horrified. 'Who made you judge and jury?'

'Somebody had to be.'

'Why? They might just have gone away when they got bored. People like that have a short term attention span.'

'People like that?' said Reaper. 'Did you know them?'

'Of course not. We've heard rumours since. They were wild.'

'Wild?' Jenny's voice was tense with emotion. 'Do you know what they did?'

Ferguson shrugged as if what they did would have

179

been no concern to him, as long as they stayed away from his group at the castle.

'They took three schoolgirls,' Jenny said. 'They killed one. What would you have done? Let them go somewhere else when they got bored, to rape and kill again?'

The academic was surprised by Jenny's vociferous attack. 'I don't know what I would have done. Tried to negotiate, talk to them.'

Sandra said, 'There's no police any more. No courts, no prisons.' She paused. 'They needed killing or they would have done it again. We killed them.' The statement was cold and impassive. Coming from a teenage girl, it had all the more impact.

Ferguson could think of no reply. He shook his head in despair and said, 'Why does it have to be like this after all we've gone through?'

Greta said, 'Richard is an idealist.' She smiled in an effort to lighten a sombre mood that could turn hostile. 'He's an old hippy at heart.'

Reaper said, 'How do you feel about it?'

'I think they needed stopping.'

Ferguson glanced at Greta, clearly surprised by her response, and then seemed to take fresh stock of the situation. He looked at the three determined women behind Reaper and perhaps he guessed the reasons behind their determination. He nodded reluctantly.

'You're probably right.' He looked back at Reaper.

'I'm sorry, but I abhor violence. I believe in *jaw, jaw, rather than war, war.*'

'Churchill also said *we'll fight them on the beaches*, said Reaper. 'And we'll fight them anywhere.'

'I just find it so frustrating. After all that's happened.'

'Me, too,' said Reaper, offering the meagrest of olive branches.

Greta accepted it and asked, 'How many in your group?'

'A dozen plus and getting bigger every day.'

'I expect it will take a long time for people to organise,' she said.

'Our people were escaping the cities,' he said. 'They weren't nice places to be. When people get over the shock, they'll organise. They'll come to you and they'll come to us and other groups will form. There'll be a future.'

Ferguson said, 'I believe that to be true.'

Greta said, 'What are you doing in Scarborough?'

'Scouting. Getting supplies. Looking for a doctor.'

'Do you need a doctor?' she asked.

'We will do, eventually.'

Ferguson said, 'We've got a doctor.'

'You have? That's great.'

'You're looking at her. Dr Malone.'

'*Dr* Malone?'

'That's right,' she said. 'I was at Scarborough General.'

'We were there this morning,' he said.

Their eyes met and her look became a little glazed. 'At the end, there was nothing I could do,' she said. 'We could see that.'

Ferguson, glad to have moved on from their abrasive conversation of a few moments ago, said, 'Would you like to visit the castle? You'd be welcome.'

'Not this time,' said Reaper. 'But thanks for the invitation. We will visit, and we hope you'll visit us.'

Ferguson held out his hand again and they shook.

'This is our first alliance of mutual cooperation,' he said.

Reaper nodded and Ferguson went on to shake the hands of Kate and Jenny who had moved forward while they had been talking. Sandra had stayed back in guard position and Reaper, when he glanced behind, saw she was still watching the Sandside and the Foreshore roads.

Greta shook his hand and said, 'He gets intense but he's a good man. Till we meet again.'

'We'll be back,' said Reaper.

They watched the couple get back in the Range Rover and drive off the pier and back the way they had come. First there had been only their group, and now here was another. As Ferguson had said, the first alliance.

Sandra took the lead in the Astra van while Jenny directed her to Rutford School, four miles out of town. They drove through high gates, up a sloping drive between trees, and came out before an impressive Victorian building: a large frontage with an added west wing and more modern single-storey structures to the east connected by covered walkways. Over to the left was a separate clutch of houses and beyond them a sports pavilion and games fields.

Half a dozen cars and a minibus were parked on the gravel. They stopped their cars, got out and took stock of their surroundings. The place was as quiet as the grave, Reaper thought grimly, aware that that was what it had become.

'I'll go inside,' said Reaper. 'Kate, you stay by the cars. Sandra, you and Jenny take a look at the classrooms round the back. They look like science labs. Look through the windows but don't go in. Call out and see if anyone answers. Do it carefully. This place probably had an army cadet unit. If anyone is alive, they might have a gun.'

Sandra and Jenny moved off and Kate said, 'Why are you leaving me outside? I saw what was in the hospital. This can't be worse.'

'It can,' he said. 'It's kids.'

'I can handle it.'

They exchanged a look.

Reaper said, 'I know you can handle it, Kate, but I also want somebody out front.'

The look continued until she nodded her head. 'Okay,' she said.

'Stay behind the cars,' he said. 'Use them as cover.'

She nodded and he went up the steps, paused to pull on a surgical mask, and entered the school. He was in a large hall, corridors running off it, offices, and a wide wooden staircase leading to upper floors. He lifted the mask for a second and tested the air. It was musty but did not have the rich aroma of death. He replaced the mask and explored. This was a ground floor administrative centre plus classrooms. He toured them. All were clear. He went upstairs to investigate more classrooms.

Reaper looked out of a window at the back and spotted Sandra and Jenny working their way carefully around the outer classroom buildings. He heard them shout, asking if anyone was there. He returned to the ground floor and found an entrance into the west wing from one of the corridors. He lifted the mask again: the smell was here.

The bodies of the former students of Rutford School lay in shared rooms and small dormitories. Most lay in bed. As always, the flies were in attendance but he was almost used to them by now. Two young boys, aged perhaps eleven, were in the same bed together for comfort and to share the journey into the terrifying unknown. He found the bodies of four masters in different dorms and that of a clergyman who seemed to have collapsed across the bed of a youth whilst kneeling by its side, a prayer book still clasped in his hand. Maybe this is what it had been like at St Hilda's? Those who could still cope, caring for those who couldn't, until they, too, crawled into bed, collapsed into armchairs or fell to the floor, still trying to do their human duty for their fellows. Four bodies occupied the beds of the small infirmary. They had been there some time. The matron, a large motherly figure, lay slumped in a chair, still watching her charges with eyes that writhed with maggots.

He went back into the corridors and pulled off the mask and damn the smell. He shouted, 'Anyone? Anyone?' but knew there would be no answer in this public school charnel house. He clattered downstairs, took a side door and walked into the fresh air. He stood for a moment to regain his senses and then walked round to the front of the house. Kate stiffened at his appearance and raised a hand when she realised it was him. He joined her by the cars and she said, 'Was it bad?'

He nodded but avoided her gaze, staring instead towards the houses and the sports pavilion.

'Here's Sandra and Jenny,' Kate said.

'Nothing!' called Sandra. 'A few bodies, that's all!'

Jenny asked Reaper, 'What was it like? Inside?'

He knew she would have experienced the death of her own school but somehow, it seemed more acceptable to have been part of it, helping others, putting them to bed and then quietly closing a door. But he had opened the doors and the dead had been waiting.

'It was very . . .' he grasped for a word that might be adequate '. . . organised. They had cared for each other. It was very peaceful.' It had been awful, but what was the point in telling her that, when she probably guessed anyway. Her face closed on her own memories. 'Let's check the houses,' he said.

They spread out and walked towards the houses that he guessed had belonged to senior masters. He noted that Sandra periodically turned and walked backwards for a few paces at a time, to keep a watch to the rear. There were three houses, all Victorian, one detached.

He looked to Jenny and said, 'You try giving a call. If there is anybody left, they might respond to a woman's voice.'

'Hello!' called Jenny. 'Is there anybody there?'

'Sounds like we're holding a séance,' murmured Sandra, and she smiled at Jenny.

The young woman grinned back, not taking offence, glad of a reason to grin.

'Reaper!' said Kate, with urgency.

Two boys had emerged from the sports pavilion, one tall, one small. They were holding hands and their posture was uncertain. Jenny put the carbine on the ground and walked towards them.

'It's all right,' she said. 'We're friends. We've come to help.'

Reaper and the two girls stayed where they were

and watched Jenny get closer to them, her voice dropping to a level where they could no longer hear what she was saying. She reached the boys and spoke intently to them, then gathered the small boy in her arms. He was still hesitant, but then he put his arms around her in a tight clasp. The taller boy visibly relaxed and accepted an embrace. They broke apart and Jenny turned and shouted, 'They haven't eaten for two days. They're starving.'

The trio walked towards them and, as they got closer, it was apparent they had been living rough for a long time. The taller boy offered his hand to Reaper and said, 'James Marshall. Thank you for coming, sir.'

Reaper shook his hand, 'I'm Reaper. That's Sandra and Kate.'

'This is Tom Mason.'

Tom looked about eight. He was doing his best to sniff back tears. He held out his hand and Reaper shook it.

'I'm pleased to meet you, Tom.'

'Thank you, sir. Please, sir. We're hungry.'

'There's food in the car,' Kate said, taking the little boy's hand and leading the way.

Jenny picked up her carbine and said, 'They've been staying in the pavilion for two weeks.'

Reaper didn't blame them. It was a better option than the school of death.

*

The two boys ate and drank, revealing details about themselves and how they'd been living. James Marshall was fourteen and a little reserved but, once his hunger had been appeased, Tom, the younger lad, was quite happy to accept a cuddle from Jenny. Reaper asked James if the school had an army cadet unit. The boy confirmed that it did and led the way to the single-storey brick building that had been its HQ. Inside, Reaper found a dozen .22 rifles and 500 rounds of ammunition, and four semi automatic Cadet GP rifles. James had been in the cadets.

'They're ex British Army,' he said. 'But they've been modified. They only fire single shots but they're self loading.'

Their ammunition was the same as that used in the police carbines. There was not a great amount but there was also plenty of blank ammunition, which could be used in practice.

Reaper drove the MPV to the school armoury and loaded the weapons and ammunition into the back. Then they left for the settlement, James and Tom travelling with him and Kate.

Chapter 10

EACH DAY JAMIE HINCHLIFFE WENT OUT looking for other survivors in the countryside and nearby villages. His forays brought in more men, women and children – and cats and dogs – and he made contact with two much smaller groups that had formed in distant hamlets and which were already attempting to become self-sufficient communities by working the land and caring for animals.

Caroline, who had been a keen rider, was volunteered by Jenny to look after the horses in the hope that it might coax her out of her introversion. Helen, under gentle pressure, agreed to look after the children, with the view to starting a school with rudimentary lessons.

Pete had acquired an extra long wheelbase van and made trips for supplies that could be stockpiled that included tinned foodstuffs, clothing, bedding and household goods. He brought tools and workbenches from a B&Q and, on other trips, trail bikes for cross country forays, and two quad bikes. Reaper commented that when the oil ran out, real bikes might be useful and, on his next trip, he brought a load of mountain bikes, including some for the children. He also brought back a shiny red Harley Davidson X1200.

'I always wanted one of these,' he said. 'What a way for your dream to come true.'

Reaper had been practising daily on his own with the throwing knives and was reminded of the man with the crossbow who had attacked him and Sandra at the supermarket. It was another item to mention to Pete and, pretty soon, they had a stock of crossbows and bolts, longbows and arrows and a couple of target butts.

'You've just added another string to your bow,' Sandra said to Reaper, when she saw them.

He laughed.

'All we've got to do now is learn how to use them.'

Reaper and Sandra organised escorts for other foraging parties who wanted to visit Scarborough. They took Jamie and the Reverend Nick to visit Ferguson and Dr Malone at the castle and met their small band. They were living in both the Master Gunner's House, which had been a tea room before the pandemic, and two large caravans that were parked alongside.

It was a good defensive site but, Reaper thought, limited in its potential. Ferguson, a physicist from the University of York, and the Reverend Nick had an immediate rapport because of their shared pacifism, although Reaper sensed Dr Greta Malone was getting a little tired of Ferguson's belief in the painless attainment of a utopian future of equality and mutual respect.

Reaper and Sandra visited the resort of Filey, further down the coast. Sandra drove the MPV along a narrow street of shops towards the sea front. She slowed because of a lorry that had been abandoned across the road ahead. When a bullet hit the tarmac ahead of them, they realised this was a barricade, rather than an accident. Sandra reversed swiftly and parked round a corner. Reaper judged the shot to have been a warning. He got out and shouted that they just wanted to talk but another shot chipped the brickwork above his head and a man replied, 'Go away and leave us alone!' When their further efforts to make contact brought the same results, they did as the man had suggested and drove away.

They diverted down a parallel street and saw that side roads had also been blocked off by cars and vans left broadside to stop vehicular progress. Whoever was behind the barricades was serious, so they didn't push the issue. If they wanted to remain isolated that was their business. Maybe they would feel differently when the supermarket stocks began to run out.

The diversions they had had to take led them onto a crescent of tall white Victorian buildings that stared grandly out to sea, with landscaped grassland tumbling down to the promenade below and the wide expanse of Filey Bay. This was an old-fashioned seaside town that looked as if it had been proud of the fact: the sort of town where families had come on holiday for generations.

'This is a nice place,' said Sandra. 'Genteel.'

'Time for lunch?' Reaper suggested, and she stopped at the south end of the crescent near the White Lodge Hotel, the nose of the car facing the sea, and they got out. The day was overcast but warm and they could smell the brine. The ever-present gulls swooped at their unexpected arrival.

'I wish one of those chip shops we passed was open,' Sandra said. 'But I'll settle for one of your sandwiches instead.'

They rested against the car bonnet as they ate and drank coffee, occasionally taking a look behind them to ensure their safety. The gulls became even more interested in them because of the food and, when they finished and threw the last of their crumbs and bits of sandwich onto the grass, the turf was swarmed by birds.

'It's strange how things turn out,' Sandra said. 'Here

I am, humping a gun, sidekick to the Reaper.' She smiled. 'A regular Starsky and Hutch. Or is that Laurel and Hardy?'

'You know your old stuff.'

'I told you, mum was a fan.' She sighed. 'And all I wanted to do was go to uni.'

Reaper looked at her in surprise.

'University?'

'Don't sound so shocked. At first, I was going to go to the local FE college. I'd gone into it. I could have taken a foundation course. Improved my education. Things were hard round where I lived and I didn't want that kind of life. I'd messed around when I was younger, but my mum had pulled me round and I had a job. We planned it together. A foundation course and then, maybe, uni.'

She said it as if it equated with entering the kingdom of heaven.

'Your mum must have been special.'

'She was. I miss her.' she said, still looking out to sea. 'I never had a dad. He left when I was little. I never knew him.' She looked at Reaper with a smile. 'Now I've got you.'

'Everybody needs somebody. How are you getting on with Jamie?'

'Okay.' She sounded unsure. 'I know it's not been long but I really like him and I think he likes me. It's just that . . . what happened.'

'You don't know how you'll react if you go to the next stage.'

'That's part of it.'

'And you don't know how he'll react if you tell him.'

'What do I do, Reaper?'

'It's your decision . . . but it's hard to live with a lie.'

'So I should tell him?'

'He's a good man. I think he'll understand. If he doesn't, I'll kick his ass.'

'Ass?' She laughed. 'Don't you mean his arse?'

'I thought we were Starsky and Hutch?'

They sat in comfortable silence, enjoying the moment with only nature's sounds on the breeze.

'What about you, Reaper? What about you and Kate?'

'Is it that obvious?'

'Pretty much. Are you going to make a move?'

'I don't know. I carry a lot of baggage. I don't know if I should. I don't know if I deserve to.'

'Deserve to?'

Sandra was young but he was at ease with her and felt she partly understood him. She'd been through a lot. Why not tell her? At least some of it.

'My life ended a long time ago. My daughter was raped and committed suicide. I found her hanging from the hook behind her bedroom door.' Sandra's hand shot up to her mouth. 'Yes . . . just like Stacey.'

Mum and dad, I'm sorry, she said in the note. *I love you.* Emily had left a diary that explained in simple terms why a fourteen-year-old would want to end her life. She couldn't continue to carry the guilt, depression and disgrace of being raped and beaten and then having her character maligned in court by her abuser's barrister. Death was preferable.

'During the trial,' he said, 'the local newspaper printed the details. Of course, she wasn't named, but her friends knew. She was not spared. They used all the lies the bastard told. I complained and the editor said the verdict would vindicate her; it would tell the public who had told the truth. But the lies were printed, just the same. The judge even suggested she might have partly provoked the attack.' From a pocket of his Kevlar vest, he took a small head-and-shoulders photograph of his daughter, which he gave to Sandra. 'She was only fourteen.'

Sandra looked at the picture for a long time before she said, 'She was lovely.'

She handed it back and he replaced it in the pocket. He sat back on the car, his right hand resting on the car bonnet. Sandra touched his hand and he took her fingers in his and he smiled sadly at her, to let her know it was all right, even though it never would be. They held hands and he looked back out at the grey ocean.

'Then my wife got cancer. She was already suffering

from a broken heart, but the doctors said they were not connected. Margaret died six months ago.'

In her illness and grief she had turned to religion. The grief turned to anger, and he was the only target. She had been demanding and he had grown to resent her. The resentment made his love for his lost daughter all the more powerful.

'We hadn't had a happy marriage. It wasn't one of those hearts and flowers affairs. The best thing about it was Emily. When she went, the reason for living seemed to go, too.'

'What happened to the bloke?'

'He went to prison. Not for long. Then he was out and living it large as if nothing had happened. He was a nine-carat bastard. The thing is, I was a copper. Just an ordinary bobby. I enjoyed my job. Enjoyed helping people. I took a firearms course because my superior thought I had the right temperament, but I didn't like it. It wasn't for me. I was happy being a bobby with my own patch. I knew the people and I believed in the system. Then the system let me down. It let my daughter down. And that bastard was back on the streets.' He looked into Sandra's eyes. 'I stopped being a copper when my daughter died. There was no point. I no longer believed. Then, by chance, I saw him in the street and decided that justice needed to be done. I killed him.

'It was no big decision. I had no reason to live and

didn't care if I died. I wanted him dead and didn't mind going to prison for it.' He shook his head. 'I even planned on suicide by police. Point a gun and have them shoot me. But they didn't. I got arrested and then the pandemic went into overdrive and I was last man standing in the police station. I'm a murderer, love.'

Sandra moved into his arms and they held each other; the man with no reason to live and his new daughter.

They moved apart and she said, 'You're no murderer. You did what had to be done for your daughter. And you did it for me. I'm lucky you were last man standing. I'm lucky you found me. Those people back there are lucky you found them. The rules have changed. You said so yourself. We're making them up as we go along.'

He smiled. 'When this superbug thing happened, I thought it was God's way of providing me with a purpose. A strange theory to have, because I don't think I believe in God. I thought I had been left alive to protect others, give others a chance. The chance Emily didn't have. An act of atonement, if you like, for not saving her. For not loving my wife. For committing murder. And if I'm here to atone, should I be allowed to have feelings that I gave up long ago?'

'Of course, you should. You deserve feelings, too, Reaper. You'd be less of a man without them. And besides . . . you have nothing to atone for in my book.'

He looked into her eyes and said, 'How old are you?

You're beginning to sound like a wise old woman.'

'Listen,' she said, punching him on the arm. 'I could have gone to university. I could have been a contender!'

It lightened the mood and, picking up their carbines from the bonnet of the car, they got back in the vehicle. Sandra had reversed into the road and begun to follow its curve away from the sea front, when two men came out of the White Lodge Hotel. She stopped, and they watched the men come hesitantly down the steps from the entrance.

'Keep the engine running,' Reaper said. 'And your eyes open.'

Sandra's carbine was in the back of the car, so she took her Glock from its holster and lay it in her lap. Reaper got out of the car, cradling the carbine. The men stopped partway across the car park. They held their arms away from their bodies, their hands open, no weapons in sight. One was fortyish and overweight and his chins wobbled. The other was late twenties, medium height and lean build, black wavy hair and even white teeth.

'Hi!' the younger man said, and the pair came closer. The fat man was sweating with nerves. 'We haven't seen anybody for days. Are you the rescue squad?'

'Are you alone?' asked Reaper.

'Yes, just the two of us.' They stopped a few yards away. 'I'm Jason Houseman. This is Milo Montague. Milo was a financial advisor. I was in property.' He shrugged and gleamed another smile. Reaper guessed he was the sort of bloke who had never been short of girlfriends. 'We're both redundant now. But what about you? We were watching you from the hotel. Are you police? Military?'

Reaper said, 'There are barricades down the other end of town. Do you know anything about them?'

'You mean Crackpot Charlie. That's Charlie Miller. He was a butcher but now he fancies himself as some kind of prophet. He's gathered himself a new family, if you know what I mean. A couple of nubile girls and some other misfits and they've tried to turn the place into a fort.'

'Were you with them?'

'I didn't fit in so I left. I told you. He's crackers. I think he's got a thing for the girls.'

'Are you both from Filey?'

'I lived here,' the fat man said. 'Had a flat on The Crescent.'

'I had a house at Flixton, a few miles away,' said Houseman.

'Family?'

'Divorced,' said the fat man.

'One of life's bachelors,' said Houseman.

'Are you armed?'

Houseman said, 'Good God, no.'

Reaper had reservations about the pair; maybe it was the smile, maybe he was jealous of another good looking younger man. The windows in the car had been down and he knew Sandra had been listening. He backed up to the car and leaned down to speak through the window.

'What do you think?'

'Not a lot, but if we are here to kick-start civilisation maybe we should offer them the chance. It takes all sorts.'

Which is what Reaper had been thinking himself. He straightened and faced the two men.

'We have a community. It's inland. Anybody who is willing to work is welcome. If you come along and don't like it, you can leave. If you like it, you can stay.'

'And you are?' asked Jason Houseman.

'We're the law. I'm Reaper. That's Sandra.'

Houseman crouched to stare through the window and gave her a white smile.

'We'd like very much to come along,' said Milo Montague.

'Do you have a car?'

'Of course. Doesn't everybody?' he said.

'Then follow us.'

He got back in the MPV and they waited until the two men went into the hotel and re-emerged a few minutes later. Montague was pulling a suitcase on wheels and Houseman was carrying a leather holdall. They put the bags in the back of a Range Rover and drove it out of the car park.

'Home?' said Sandra.

'Home,' said Reaper.

Because it was home now and, according to Sandra, he was allowed feelings. But did he want them?

As the weeks went by and the population of the Haven – or simply Haven as it was increasingly called – grew, the community took on self-imposed rules and disciplines. The Reverend Nick, Jean and Ashley acted as welcoming committee and billeting officers, explaining to all newcomers that they had to work. There were too few of them to put up with malingerers or those looking for an easy life. It didn't matter what religion anyone professed, they would work hard six days a week and rest on the seventh, which just happened to be Sunday, when Nick would hold a non-denominational service for those who wished to attend.

Ashley and Kate suggested this arrangement might be enhanced if the pub was reopened one night a week, on a Saturday, and a social evening held in its dining room. This was enthusiastically agreed. Kate also moved into the flat above the pub.

Reaper's armed force continued to train with their weapons, practising loading, combat positions, stance and firing with blanks, and always cleaning their equipment after use.

James Marshall, despite being only fourteen, proved an excellent shot and opted to continue his military training. He was a mature boy, tall and rangy with a mass of curly hair, but had yet to grow into his body. After a week, Reaper had no qualms in issuing him with side arm and carbine, and he began to partner Pete. On the second trip, he returned with the same combat uniform worn by Reaper and the girls. Pete, who preferred civvies to military service, made a joke about it. But the little army was taking on an identity.

Archery proved popular as a sport and a dozen men and women practised regularly on the butts they created. The crossbow was the more deadly close quarter weapon but took longer to load than the longbow, which was the more popular weapon. Reaper and Sandra took part in the practice shoots and Sandra became very proficient.

In Bridlington, Reaper and Sandra met a group who had settled into the Royal Yorkshire Yacht Club. This distinctive white building was built on a sharp corner, and had the appearance of a liner from an earlier age, that had been beached on land. Its prow pointed purposefully towards the harbour across the road. Prominent among its two dozen people were Bob Stainthorpe, a former Yacht Club member, and Nagus Shipley, the skipper of one of the small fishing smacks in the harbour. Nagus had already re-started fishing to augment the group's tinned diet. After being initially suspicious, they welcomed Reaper and Sandra and saw the sense in forging alliances. They served them fish and chips and, when they left, they had a box of cod in the back of the car, which meant that they were soon driving with the windows open.

'I'll put up with it,' said Sandra. 'I never thought I'd taste proper fish and chips again.'

Reaper kept one worry to himself: the Territorial Army base in Scarborough, home to members of the 4th Battalion of the Yorkshire Regiment (TA), had been raided and all weapons had gone, although some ammunition had been left behind. He had searched the offices and discovered that most of the local service personnel had actually been in Canada on manoeuvres but, whatever weapons had been left, were now missing. Should he worry unduly? It could be another group like their own, wanting only protection. But the niggle at the back of his mind was that it could be a gang like Jerome's, only better organised and with more ambition. He asked Ferguson and Dr Malone at the Castle about any other groups, but they had heard nothing.

Reaper teamed up with Kate for a trip to Scarborough and they called at The Alma to find Shaggy and see if he had any new intelligence. The visit was an experience but elicited no useful information. The middle aged woman Reaper had first seen sitting on the pavement drinking wine was sleeping on a bench seat. He got the impression she slept from one hangover to the next.

'That's Dolores,' said Shaggy. 'She looked after her invalid mum all her life until it happened. Suddenly she was free.' He shrugged and glanced at the thin, elderly chap with long white hair and straggly beard, who wore a black cloak. On closer inspection, the cloak was velvet and embroidered with magical symbols. 'Ernie's not really a follower of wicca. He got the cloak from The Futurist – the theatre? There was a magic act on. Ernie was stage doorman.'

A middle-aged man, in a respectable but grubby suit, sat alone in a corner reading a newspaper, sipping whisky and water. Shaggy inclined his head in his direction. 'Mr Windsor. Solicitor. He comes in every day, lunchtime and teatime. Reads the newspaper. Same newspaper. Keeps to a routine. Then goes home to the furniture shop across the road. He sleeps in a bed in the side window. He doesn't talk about his family. He had a wife and two daughters.'

A girl in her twenties, who had a wide-eyed lost look and was carrying a holdall on a strap across her shoulders, came nervously to Shaggy and touched his arm.

'This is Elaine,' Shaggy said. Elaine smiled without focusing on either Reaper or Kate, and nodded her head. 'Can you get me another packet of those Jalapeño crisps, sweetheart?' Shaggy said and, nodding, she moved away. 'She lost her baby,' he whispered. 'It was two months old.' He took another sip from a bottle of tequila and pulled a face. 'It makes you wonder if it's worth it, man. Know what I mean? Maybe I should find a gun and blow my head off.' He smiled at Reaper. 'You could lend me one, man. Have it back after.'

'I won't do that, Shaggy.'

'Didn't think you would.' He pushed the tequila bottle to the far side of the table. 'God but I'm getting tired.'

Kate said, 'Of life?'

'Of this. And if this is life . . .?'

Reaper said, 'Maybe it's time to stop drinking, Shaggy.'

'Nothing else to do. All the weed is gone and I never did trust pills.'

'What did you do?' Reaper said. 'Before?'

'Not a lot, man.'

Kate said, 'You must have done something.'

Elaine came back with the crisps, dropped them on the table, sat next to Shaggy and said, 'Rock star. Shaggy was a rock star.'

'A rock star?' said Kate.

Shaggy pulled a face but patted Elaine's hand in thanks for the crisps.

'I was in bands. We supported Quo once. And Dr Hook. Supported lots of bands. But never headlined – except in pub gigs. But that was then, man. I haven't played for three years. Lost the urge. And now . . .' he tried to laugh but the humour fizzled out, 'now there's no one left to friggin listen.'

Kate said, 'Why don't you come back with us? You and Elaine.'

'Become a farmer?' He shook his head as if it was about as farfetched as him being a rock star. 'Besides, who'd look after this crew?'

Reaper looked round the room.

'How did you meet?' he said.

'They just drifted in here and liked the ambience.'

Reaper said, 'There's a group at the castle. They'd help you.'

'I heard about them. But who'd want to look after a bunch of loonies? Maybe the madness will wear off, eventually. Maybe they'll just drift away. Maybe.'

'If you're waiting for them to leave, you could be waiting a long time,' said Kate.

'I'm in no rush. I've got nowhere else to go.' He leaned towards Elaine and said, 'Sweetheart. Would you get me a can of lemonade?'

The girl got up and went towards the bar, happy to have a purpose.

Reaper said, 'When the time comes, remember you'll be welcome with us.'

'Yeah, man. When the time comes. When Elaine gets a little better. That bag she carries? Her baby's in there. I think we'll wait awhile.'

They shook hands with Shaggy and waved to Elaine as she came back with the lemonade but she didn't notice them.

'We'll be back in a week,' Reaper said.

'We'll be here,' said Shaggy.

Chapter 11

SANDRA WORE THE DRESS THAT REAPER had given
her for the first Saturday night social. He had come
to regard her as friend, comrade, confidante and surrogate daughter, and had forgotten she was also a young
and pretty girl.

'You look stunning,' he told her.

'It was your choice.'

'I don't mean the dress. You are stunning.'

Reaper still wore his usual combat trousers and
T-shirt, although he had discarded the Kevlar vest and
weapons. He had left his sidearms on a top shelf
behind the bar. Pete was standing guard in the mobile
home outpost on the other side of the hill, Reaper
would relieve him in a couple of hours. The whole

community was turning out for the evening and the crowd had spilled outside onto patio tables and benches. Music was coming from the dining room, sounds of the sixties on a battery operated disc player. Before the night was out, he guessed people would be dancing and maybe forging tentative relationships enhanced by alcohol and hope.

'Do I get a dance later?' she said.

'You'll get lots of dances,' he said, glancing over her head. 'Most of them with this chap. Good evening, Jamie.'

'Reaper.' Jamie Hinchliffe was freshly scrubbed in pressed jeans and an open-neck blue shirt. His eyes were locked on Sandra. 'God, Sandra, You look wonderful.'

He took both her hands in his own and kissed her on the cheek, making her blush.

'I'll see you later,' Reaper said, and eased himself into the crowd.

Kate and Ashley were behind the bar. Reaper commandeered the solitary high stool and leaned with his back against the wall in the corner, watching the people, all of them still suffering in one way or another, still grieving, but beginning to maybe have faith in a future. He marvelled at the normality of what was happening this evening, to the strains of the Beatles, the Searchers and the Stones. Kate was wearing a fitted blouse, black skirt and an enigmatic smile.

'You look like the Mona Lisa,' he said, as she poured a can of Tetley bitter into a pint glass for him. 'What's so amusing?'

'You? Without a gun?' He shrugged. Since the happening, he had always worn one or slept with one to hand. 'You look naked,' she said.

He widened his eyes. 'What a terrible thought!'

'Oh, I don't know,' she said, and moved away to serve someone else.

He continued to survey the room, seeing how, even in such a short time, people had begun to change. Lugubrious Gavin Price nodding his head in agreement as he listened patiently to the always garrulous Jean Megson, wearing yet another low cut blouse to its best advantage. Milo Montague, looking a lot fitter than when Reaper had first seen him, relaxed in Judith's company, and Jason Houseman doing his best to charm the former schoolgirls Caroline and Helen. Reaper wondered if Houseman's gleaming smile was powered by batteries. Jenny joined the group and he couldn't tell whether it was because she was attracted to Houseman or because she wanted to protect the girls.

Outside, the children were playing under the watchful eyes of others of the company and he noticed that strangers were present, people he had not seen before, who had come from the surrounding villages and farm communities. Reaper was pleased at this coming together, this melding of different folk from different backgrounds in a new beginning, but felt separate from it, like the spectre at the feast. People smiled at him, but didn't seem particularly keen to be in his company. They appreciated his reputation for violence, but wanted no part of it. He was, he supposed, a necessary evil, and the thought made him smile.

'Now you're smiling,' Kate said.

He looked into her eyes. 'Why not? I like the company.'

Reaper only had the one beer and left after an hour. The social was good, but it was not for him. He asked Ashley for his sidearms and, as he was strapping them on, Kate came over. 'You're leaving already?'

'This is more Pete's scene. Him and Ruth and Emma.'

'You'll miss the pie and peas. Jean's special recipe.'

'I'll get some next time. Goodnight, Kate.'

She nodded goodbye, still smiling her enigmatic smile.

Reaper walked up the hill, the sounds of music, conversation and laughter fading behind him. At the top he looked back. The light was still strong but a lamp glowed through one of the pub windows. It was a scene that would have pulled at his heart if he had been sentimental, but he wasn't. He was the man alone, the man with the reputation for death. He strode over the hill to relieve Pete.

*

The night was warm and he sat outside on a folding camp chair, the handguns still strapped around his waist and a carbine propped against the side of the motor home. It was close to midnight and a moon showed an empty countryside. No sounds, no lights. He heard a twig crack.

He grabbed the carbine and ran silently to the side of the van. He glanced round it and saw a figure coming carefully down the hill towards him carrying something that could be a club. He waited another few moments, judging the approach, moved out of the cover of the van, pointed the carbine and saw the red dot of the sights appear on the shadow in front of him.

'Stop right there,' he said.

The figure stopped and said, 'Not a very friendly welcome.'

'Kate?'

'I bring gifts.'

She held up what he now saw was a bottle of wine.

He lowered the carbine, feeling foolish, and she came closer and he saw her in the moonlight, smiling. She put her arms around his neck, bottle still in hand, and kissed him on the mouth, her soft body pressing against his. For a moment he didn't react. He was surprised, even shocked. She broke away and looked at him quizzically.

'That's not particularly welcoming either,' she said.

She went into the van and put the bottle of wine in the sink. He followed and she took the carbine from him and put it on the table. 'Why don't we try again?'

This time he did not hesitate. His arms went around her and he thrilled at her closeness, her softness and the taste of her mouth. His breathing was becoming laboured and he was aware of his arousal and he stepped away.

'I don't know,' he said.

'I do,' Kate said.

'You don't know about me.'

'You can tell me later. Or not. But right now, I know all I need to know. And I know you need me.'

'I don't know.'

'You need someone, Reaper. And I'm here and I need you.' She moved back into his arms, they kissed again, and his confused emotions broke apart and he was touching, feeling, reaching. They moved to the bed at the back of the van, falling upon it and upon each other.

Much later, they lay naked together in the shadows. The initial sex had been fierce and fast. Then they had rested and made love; slowly with patience and discovery, before drifting into a half-sleep where he kept touching her to reassure himself it had not been a dream.

'Did you have this planned?' he said.

'Yes.'

'That was why you were smiling?'

'Yes.'

'You're a special woman, Kate.'

'If I hadn't made a move, you never would have.'

'I'm glad you did, but I still don't know if it was the right move.'

'Reaper, I'm attracted to you and I know you are attracted to me. We're not children and neither of us should have any illusions. This . . .' and by the way she moved her head he knew she meant Haven, 'could end tomorrow. Life is precarious. We both know that. So what's so wrong about it?'

'Nothing. Absolutely nothing. It's just me. I never thought this would happen again.'

'This?'

'Making love. Attraction. Feeling foolish when I'm with you. In the past, I made promises to myself and I don't know if I deserve this – *you*. I carry a history.'

'It's not just a history you carry. It's guilt. And you think too much. Every moment is precious. We should enjoy the moments we can.'

'You're probably right but it's been a damn long time since I had a precious moment.' He leant over and kissed her. 'I suppose I'm out of practice.'

Kate slept a little and Reaper got up and dressed and watched her sleep. Watched the curves of her body, the rise of a breast as she breathed, the slightly parted lips that still seemed to hold a secret smile, her clear pale skin, her long legs, the curling hair like burnished copper beyond. He wanted her again but he resisted. She was right. He felt guilty but not despondent. The guilt would always be with him but he now realised there was also room for love. He put on the Kevlar vest, strapped on all his weapons and, as the early dawn began to lighten the sky, he brewed fresh coffee. The smell, and his movements, roused her.

She lay on her back and propped herself on one elbow, uncaring of her nakedness. That smile again.

'I can't tempt you?' she said, knowing the moment had passed.

'Always. But right now I'm resisting temptation. It will make me stronger.' He thumped the Kevlar vest like Tarzan. 'And it will make next time all the sweeter.'

'Good,' she said. 'Bring on the next time.'

He smiled and poured coffee. 'You're a wanton woman.'

'That's true. I want you, Reaper.'

He looked up and their eyes met. Her expression was serious. So was his, but could she read the flickering doubts he still had?

He poured the coffee, added milk to one of the mugs and handed it to her. Their fingers touched as she took it. He stroked her hair and looked guiltlessly at her nakedness.

'I want you, too, Kate.'

'That's good,' she said and moved her head against his hand.

When she was dressed, he walked her back over the hill. They did not hold hands and he cradled the carbine. The sun was blazing light horizontally across the land, birds were singing and the world was coming to life.

'We never did drink the wine,' she said.

'I'll save it for next time.'

'You still know nothing about me.'

'You'll tell me when you're ready. And maybe I'll tell you about me.'

He had been so obsessed with his own past that he only now realised he knew nothing about Kate's.

They walked down the hill, the village peaceful ahead of them. No drunken bodies lay by the side of the road or on the benches outside the pub. The social evening had apparently ended with decorum. The Reverend Nick stepped out of the manor house onto the steps and stretched his arms behind him in the morning air. He stopped mid-stretch when he saw them together and smiled.

'Good morning,' he said.

'Yes, it is,' said Reaper, and Kate smiled.

Reaper kissed her, she went into the pub and he walked back over the hill.

Jason Houseman volunteered for the defence force, but Reaper told him he would have to go onto a waiting list. Houseman was not pleased. Reaper suspected he thought driving around the countryside was preferable to working in the fields or the barns. Milo, on the other hand, seemed to take to the rural life. He shed excess weight and had an air of contentment. His previous career may have given him a fine salary and an apartment facing the sea, but it hadn't included job satisfaction.

Pete Mack and James Marshall returned from a scavenging and scouting trip to the town of Driffield in the south with three more new people. Manjit was a Sikh lady in her late thirties who had been a lecturer in chemistry at the University of Bradford. Her husband had also been a lecturer and had died in the pandemic. She had gone onto the campus looking for students out of a sense of duty. That was where she had found Cheryl, a twenty-year-old psychology student. Cheryl had lived with her family in the city and, when they died, she had gravitated to the campus looking for fellow students. They had met Arif, an eighteen-year-old Muslim youth when he ran into the building they were staying in. He claimed he had been attempting to evade three white men who had been hunting him. He suggested the men's animosity towards him had been racially motivated.

When Reaper spoke with Arif, he found him streetwise and hip, a young gangsta in a hoodie and black leather jacket who used a lot of hand movements with pointed fingers to articulate his speech. He was sharp and had quick eyes. Reaper liked him. The three men who had chased him might have been racists but, having talked to Arif, it was just as likely that he had pissed them off. He was carrying a Beretta 9mm handgun and had a Mac-10 submachine gun in the Transit in which the party were travelling. The van also contained 10,000 rounds of 9mm ammunition which would fit either weapon. It was also compatible with the Glock handguns they had at Haven.

'Where did you get the guns and the ammunition?' Reaper asked.

'I knew a man, right?' His hands worked, fingers pointing. 'A man in the business, the drugs business, know what I mean? I knew him, right, but I didn't work for him. I wouldn't work any shit like that. But I knew him. Where he lived and that. And when every-thing went tits up, I thought he wouldn't mind, right, if I called round and collected a few things like. Him being dead and that, right?'

'Right,' said Reaper. 'Do you know how to fire the guns?'

Arif gave him a look of incredulity as if he had asked if he knew which end was up.

'What you think?'

'Right,' said Reaper.

When Arif saw the girls and James all dressed like Reaper and carrying guns, he went straight back to Reaper and volunteered to serve.

'Look. I've got my own gun, right. Although like one of those Glocks might be an improvement on the Beretta. Know what I mean? That's an old gun, right. It might jam in a jam. Get it? But I'm cool to keep the machinegun. Right? And where do I get the uniform?'

Reaper delayed making a decision for four days but took him out on trips and came to like him even more. He had a lot of front, but behind the flash he was a young boy who had survived a hard background even before the pandemic. Manjit and Cheryl both spoke highly on his behalf. He had tried being Mr Cool at first and had made a pass at both of them but had apologised after Manjit had beaten him about the head and told him that some rules never change, even after an apocalypse. Since then he had been considerate, protective and cunning. They had been together four weeks and had got here without mishap.

Finally Reaper allowed him to join, and issued him with the body armour and kit, minus the carbine. The set of combat trousers and T-shirt he had got for Helen in Scarborough fitted Arif, because he was a slight youth, although Reaper didn't tell him they had belonged to a girl. He could replenish the kit, as they all did, on their trips to town.

The appointment was welcomed by the others in the growing troop, who quickly took to Arif, but it did not go down well with Jason Houseman.

'Why him and not me?' he asked bluntly, after trekking over the hill to confront Reaper as he sat at the table in the mobile home.

'He was more suited,' Reaper said.

'He's a Paki! You give a gun to a Paki and not to me?'

Reaper stood up and slapped Houseman hard across the face. 'Leave,' he said.

Houseman was flushed, Reaper's hand mark visible on his flesh. He clearly burned with rage, and for a moment Reaper thought he might strike back, but he saw the cowardice in Houseman's eyes. If he were to strike back it would be from behind when no one was looking. Houseman tried to control himself.

'Look, I apologise. I didn't mean anything by what I said. It was heat of the moment.'

'I want you to leave.'

'Leave?'

The glint of cowardice and fear in again. Clearly Houseman didn't know if Reaper meant the van or Haven itself.

'Get out of my van. Go back to work.'

Reaper saw the relief in his face.

'Yes . . . yes, of course. And look . . . what I said . . . I didn't mean anything by it. There's no point telling anyone else . . . is there?'

'Just leave,' Reaper said, wearily, and Houseman left.

Reaper took a deep breath and marvelled at the human race. A pandemic had wiped out almost all of it but still left prejudice and racism behind. He would have to watch Houseman. Maybe he should go to Filey and talk to Crackpot Charlie Miller and find out why Houseman had left. Or would Milo know?

Milo didn't know. The two men had met after Houseman had left Charlie Miller's enclave. The next time he went to Filey, Reaper was determined to have a proper talk with Miller rather than exchanging shouts across a barricade. But he had a lot to do before then. He wanted to travel to nearby military camps. There were many RAF camps within reach, as well as the army base at Catterick, where there might be organised groups of airmen and soldiers. Perhaps someone with the training to organise the restructuring that was happening on a community basis. If not, he could always look for more guns and ammunition, even if only to put it beyond the reach of any local despot.

He wondered if he was becoming obsessed about weaponry? He wouldn't be surprised. He had become obsessed about many things in the last three years. Thank God Kate had made the first move in what had become a continued relationship that everyone now knew about. If she hadn't, he might have developed another obsession. He smiled at the thought he might one day have to approach the Reverend Nick and ask him to marry them. He might be dubious about God but he did believe in order.

He and Kate exchanged stories. He was as honest with her as he had been with Sandra. He showed her the photograph he had kept of Emily. She listened and made few comments. Her sympathy and sorrow for what had happened to his daughter was genuine and unforced. Her understanding of his actions was unspoken but obvious. He listened, in turn, to her story.

'Nothing very dramatic,' she said. 'A marriage that didn't work, a divorce and getting on with life.'

She hadn't been bruised by marriage. They had both been too young, she said; she had only been eighteen, for goodness sake – a mother at nineteen. Neither of them had expected parenthood to be so demanding and their relationship had floundered.

'Not surprising, really. It had been based on Saturday nights in the Blue Lagoon and lots of sex.'

She said it without embarrassment and when he widened his eyes, she added, 'What? You weren't mad for it at eighteen?'

The marriage had ended when their daughter Amy was four. Her ex-husband became a weekend father every fortnight, and he helped with the finances.

'When Amy was ten, he died. Car crash. I felt I should have been sadder, but I wasn't. I was devastated when my dad died of cancer the year before, but this was different. It didn't compare.'

Kate and Amy had moved in with her widowed mother.

'It gave my mum a new lease of life. A kid to look after. I was working in an office and hated it but, with my mum helping with Amy, I looked for something else. I worked in a local bar in the evenings. It was a safe way to have a social life with no commitment. I was one side of the bar, they were the other.'

'You must have had offers,' said Reaper.

'Plenty of offers. I had a couple of boyfriends, no one serious. Then I applied for the job as manager of The White Swan and was surprised when I got it. It was a nice pub, in an old part of town and had a great crowd of regulars.' She smiled and said, 'The sort of bar where everyone knows your name.'

'Like the TV show?' he said.

'Exactly like that,' she said with a smile. 'I met someone. Thought this time it might be serious, but it didn't work out. My choice.' She took a breath and changed tack. 'When Amy reached eighteen, she inherited money left by her dad and set off trekking the world, like teenagers do. Did. She met a bloke in Australia and settled there. He seemed good for her and she seemed happy. Then it happened. The pandemic hit Australia before it reached here. The bloke was called Sean. He phoned me to say she'd died. We cried on the phone together, I don't know how long. Soon after, everybody started dying. My mum died.'

Kate took another deep breath, perhaps to keep the memories under control.

'I don't know what I would have done if Ash hadn't shown up. Jane turned up first. We were frightened. Didn't know what was happening, didn't know what to do. Then Ash turned up and looked after us.'

Reaper continued to live in the mobile home. He went out every day, if only to patrol the lanes and villages and drive as far as the outskirts of Hull or past York along the deserted highways to see if anything was moving on the road from Leeds. Another project he had in mind was visiting Humberside, where he was sure there was an oil refinery. A tanker-load of fuel would help the settlement.

The other members of his special forces went out as and when they were required, for particular missions or to escort members of the growing community who wanted specific items. They also acted as escorts if a group wanted to visit the town or coast on Sundays for recreation and a change of scenery.

On another fine summer day, when he and Arif were due to go out, Reaper walked over the hill and down into the village. He called into the pub where Kate greeted him with a kiss and gave him breakfast. They were baking their own bread now and had moved pigs onto a neighbouring farm. He had bacon and eggs and fresh bread and tea. They had come a long way in a short time.

Arif stopped the MPV outside and put his head round the door.

'I'm out here, right Reaper?'

'Right.'

Kate smiled at Reaper, enigmatic again.

As he was finishing the food, Jamie Hinchliffe came in.

'Morning, Reaper. Got a minute?'

'Of course.' Jamie sat down opposite and Kate left the bar. 'What is it?' he said, sipping the last of the tea.

'It's Sandra and I,' he said. 'I want to get straight to the point about this, Reaper. I mean . . . you know we have been seeing each other . . .'

'I noticed.'

'And, well . . . our relationship has become . . . intimate.' His face flushed as he continued his mission to get straight to the point.

'Intimate?'

'Yes.'

Reaper picked up the carbine from the chair next to him and slipped the strap over his head.

'We are, of course, both consenting adults and we both have great affection for each other.'

'I should hope so.' Reaper checked the mechanism of the gun.

'So I thought it only right that I inform you of our intentions and ask your permission.'

'Ask my permission?'

'Yes.'

'For what? You mean you want *my* permission to move in together?'

'Good God, no! To get married!'

Reaper was stunned. 'Married?'

'Yes.'

The silence lengthened because Reaper didn't know what to say.

'Do you give your permission?'

'What would you do if I didn't?'

'We'd still get married.' Jamie had transcended nervous and had now reached stubborn.

'Good for you.' He put his hand across the table and Jamie shook it in surprise. 'Of course you have my permission. Who put you up to this? Did Sandra tell you to ask me?'

'Of course not. But it is the form, sir – I mean, Reaper.

'Of course it is, Jamie. And I thank you for the consideration.' He got up. 'Now, where is she?'

'I'm here,' she said, stepping into the room.

They embraced and he gave her a big squeeze and a kiss and whispered into her ear, 'Asking my permission?' and she giggled.

'Congratulations,' he said. 'I know you'll both be very happy.'

'Will next Sunday be okay?' she said.

'For what?'

'The wedding?'

And when he thought about it, there was absolutely no reason at all for a long engagement. Why not Sunday?

'Sounds great.'

He hugged her again and shook Jamie's hand again and felt moisture at the back of his eyes.

'Reaper?' she said. He had moved to the door, eager to be away. He paused and looked back.

'You need anything?' he said.

'I thought I'd go into Scarborough tomorrow and choose a dress with Kate.'

He nodded. 'I'll ride shotgun,' he said.

Chapter 12

THEY WENT INTO TOWN IN TWO CARS. Reaper and Kate in the MPV and Sandra and Jenny in the Astra van. They hadn't encountered trouble for some weeks but they were still alert in case of danger. Reaper drove to the Alma Inn. He hadn't seen Shaggy in a while and wondered whether he was ready yet to join the growing group at Haven. Sandra and Jenny went to a vintage fashion shop on Northgate that Jenny recommended and they promised to meet up outside the Brunswick Centre in half an hour. The day was wet and squally and they all wore their weatherproofs.

He stopped across the road from the Alma and hesitated before getting out. A body lay on the pavement outside the pub.

'Stay behind the car and keep me covered,' he said.

Kate obeyed without question, leaning against the rear of the MPV, her carbine pointing across the road. Reaper held his carbine at the ready and took a long look at the buildings opposite. If someone had collapsed and died outside the pub, Shaggy would have moved the body.

He crossed the road and nobody shot him. He sensed the pub was empty, abandoned. He crouched next to the body and saw it was that of Mr Windsor, the solicitor, who had blocked his grief by maintaining a routine of silent visits to the hostelry, as he probably had done before the pandemic. Now he had joined his family in death. He had been shot.

Reaper stood up and went to the pub door, took a breath, and went in quickly. He had been right; it had been abandoned, although two of its recent residents were still there. Dolores, the middle aged woman, was crumpled in the corner of a bench seat. Ernie, the stage doorman from the town's theatre, was face down on the floor, arms wide, the black velvet cloak spread like wings. They were both dead, and had not been dead very long.

'Shaggy,' he shouted. 'Elaine.'

No one answered and he left the place to run back across the street in a sudden panic. People with guns who shot harmless people for no reason were on the loose, and so were Sandra and Jenny, blithely choosing frocks whilst unaware of the danger.

'Three dead,' he called to Kate. 'We need to tell the others.'

They got back in the car and he drove onto Northgate but the Astra was not where he expected it to be. A smashed window was the obvious reason; the shop they had been going to visit had been vandalised and partly burnt out. He changed direction for the Brunswick Centre, the sense of dread increasing.

The Astra was on the opposite side of the road from the Brunswick Centre and the girls were in the act of getting out of the vehicle. Reaper braked to a halt and jumped out, relieved at having found them safe. He and Kate approached and they met the group on the pavement. They sensed something was wrong from the way both Reaper and Kate were holding their guns and scanning the buildings.

'There's been trouble,' he called. 'Three shot dead at the Alma.'

'Shaggy?' asked Sandra.

'Shaggy's not there.'

All four were now on high alert. The perpetrators could have left Scarborough and taken their killing spree on down the coast. Reaper wondered if the community in the Castle were okay? They would check on their safety later.

The girls were behind the cars and Reaper was still

standing in the gap between them, when two things happened: Shaggy appeared from a side street, out of breath from running. 'Reaper!' he shouted, as a shot rang out; Reaper felt a thump in the middle of his back that threw him face down onto the concrete.

Disorientated by the impact, he was vaguely aware of Sandra taking charge and barking orders, and Shaggy pulling him into cover. Sandra fired two shots at a target across the road and shouted, 'Jenny, cover left! Kate, cover right! *Kate!*' Her voice cut through Kate's concern as she hovered over Reaper, and the red haired woman did as she was told.

'Shit, Reaper! Are you all right?' said Shaggy.

'I'm okay.' He was getting his breath back and thanking God the shooter hadn't attempted a head shot. He tapped his chest with his fist. 'Armoured vest.'

'I saw you at the Alma, but I was upstairs across the road and couldn't get to you before you drove off. They came yesterday. Called themselves Muldane's Army. They're bastards, Reaper. They shot them in cold blood.'

'How many?'

'Four of them. They all have guns.'

Two shots sent chips flying from the concrete and Sandra fired two shots in return.

'Stay alert,' she said, in a calm voice.

Jenny and Kate remained crouched behind the cars, but facing outwards to cover their flanks.

A man shouted from across the road.

'Hey girls! Put down your guns! There's no point us shooting each other. *Make love, not war.*'

Someone laughed a dirty laugh, and added, 'Yeah. Let's make *lurv*, baby!' in a joke Barry White drawl.

'You can become Muldane's volunteers if you treat us nice!'

'Yeah. You can volunteer for anything we want!'

Sandra said, 'They're on the first floor. The window is open. Stay alert! The chat's probably diversion.'

Reaper may have been wrong, but he thought the girls had stiffened almost imperceptibly at the sexual references. They knew all about men without morals or restraint.

Jenny fired, two, three shots and Reaper glanced down the street. Sandra had been right. A man had tried running across the road to get behind them. He now lay on the ground, wounded and scrabbling to complete the crossing.

'One down,' Jenny said.

'Is he still moving?' Sandra said.

'Yes.'

'Finish him.'

Jenny took careful aim, fired twice more and the man moved no longer.

'Bitches!' said a male voice from across the road, and a face emerged pointing a rifle in their direction. Reaper saw the red dot from Sandra's sight touch the man's forehead and, before the man could fire, Sandra had, and his head jerked back. The man's gun fired aimlessly into the sky as his finger spasmed on the trigger.

'Fuck!' someone said. Something was knocked over and a door slammed.

'Keep your positions!' ordered Sandra and the two girls did as they were told.

Reaper had fully recovered, but at this moment was redundant and very proud of the way the women had reacted and continued to act. They heard a car engine revving through its gears and getting louder from the top of the street and a Range Rover suddenly appeared, driving along Northgate. Kate immediately opened fire and got three shots away, obviously with good effect, as they heard the car crash. Reaper pushed his carbine into Shaggy's hands and began to run.

As he ran, he pulled a Glock from its holster and racked the slide. He didn't hesitate at the corner, but went straight around. The Range Rover had piled into an abandoned lorry. The front was mangled and the driver trapped. If he'd had a passenger, he was gone. The driver was conscious but had no visible weapon in his hands, and there was no sign of anyone else on the street.

Reaper slowed to a walk alongside the vehicle. One of Kate's shots had put the driver's side window through. Maybe that had caused him to lose control.

He cocked the gun and placed the muzzle against the man's head. The man stopped moaning and trying to free himself. He raised his hands in surrender.

'How many of you?'

'Four.'

'Where's the fourth?'

'He did a runner. The bastard did a runner.'

'What is Muldane's Army?'

'Major Muldane. He's building an army.'

'And Muldane's volunteers?'

'The volunteers? Well, they're the women.'

'How many men are in his army?'

'Thirty, forty.' The longer the conversation was going on, the more comfortable the man was becoming. 'Look, you'd be welcome. Well looked after. We've got drones to do the work, and the volunteer women, well . . . for other things, if you know what I mean?'

'I know what you mean. Drones?'

'Yeh. Blokes who do the work. Non-military types. You'd be all right. One of the soldiers. Officer material.'

Reaper scanned the inside of the car and saw no weapons. A car started in a street not far away and drove off without coming into sight.

'Bastard!' breathed the man, in a last curse at his former comrade-in-arms.

'Where's Muldane?'

'Whitby. He owns the town. He's got a sweet set-up.

Look, you really would be welcome. What do you say?'

'I don't think so,' said Reaper. He pulled the trigger and the interior of the Range Rover got an instant re-spray.

When he turned round, Shaggy was on the other side of the street, holding the carbine nervously, watching him. Reaper holstered the handgun and walked to him. He took the carbine and said, 'Thanks, Shaggy.'

'I didn't do anything.'

'You tried to warn us. That's enough. How's Elaine?'

They began to walk back to the girls.

'A lot better. Me, too. I don't drink as much anymore, man.' There was a pause and he said, 'We buried the baby.' Reaper stopped walking as Shaggy explained what had happened. 'I persuaded her it would be best. We took her to a church and I dug a grave, made a cross. It helped. She's not completely okay, but she's better.'

'That's good. You're a good man, Shaggy.'

'Just don't tell anybody, okay?'

They rejoined the girls who were still taking precautions by staying in cover, but Reaper accepted what the man had said. He told the girls and Shaggy what he knew, and then they scouted across the road. They found a dead man in an upstairs office that was filled with champagne bottles. His weapons were gone. The man Jenny had shot running across the road had a Beretta in his hand, which they took.

'They were mad trying to take us down,' Sandra said.

'They were possibly drunk, and they didn't want to take you down. Just me,' said Reaper. 'With the capes on, maybe they didn't appreciate what we were carrying. Maybe they thought that once I was dead, you girls would squeal and give up.'

Sandra growled.

'I know,' he said. 'Fat chance. You were brilliant.'

'What about this Major Muldane?' Jenny said.

'Let's hope he stays in Whitby.'

They checked on Ferguson and Dr Malone and the group at the castle. They had heard shots the day before and had been careful not to light any fires that might have given away their position.

'We stayed put and hoped whoever it was would move on,' said Ferguson.

Reaper said, 'There's strength in numbers. You might want to reconsider joining us.'

'I think we'll stay on our own for now,' he said. 'If any here want to join you, they're free to do so. But I think we've made progress. There are twenty-four of us now, and it would be a shame to abandon what we've started. We need diversification, after all.'

Reaper nodded and looked at Dr Malone but she

simply shrugged. Her loyalty, for now, remained with her own group.

Shaggy and Elaine returned to Haven with them. Their luggage included two guitar cases and an amp. He had started playing music again. Sandra didn't choose a dress. The entire group's mood was sombre – the girls perhaps reflecting on what they had done, the men they had killed, and all too aware that the threat of Muldane's Army would one day have to be faced.

The wedding went ahead on Sunday, under a blue sky. Everyone sensed it was a special occasion, not just for Sandra and Jamie but because it was the first wedding at Haven; the first of the new beginning.

Almost everyone attended from the extended community, as well as a group from Scarborough Castle. Only the two guards that Reaper insisted stay on duty at the mobile home were absent. The threat from up the coast made him take extra care. Two guards with trail bikes, brought in by Pete, were positioned in the trees on the hill overlooking the gates. The sign outside that had said *The Haven* had been removed. There were no indications that the estate was occupied and a casual driver might go past without suspecting what was inside.

Sandra had gone to Bridlington, further down the coast and another twenty miles away from Whitby, this time with Kate, on a swift trip to find a dress. Reaper had been ostensibly happy to watch them go but, as soon as they were out of sight, he had headed for the town on a motorbike by an alternative route and had been their friendly stalker – just in case. They never knew he had been there.

She wore a simple knee-length white silk dress, high heels and a radiant smile. Jamie wore a tan linen suit and white shirt, but without the formality of a tie. Pete Mack was his best man. Reaper gave the bride away and for once was without any weapons. He wore a dark blue shirt and slacks. He felt uncomfortable in normal clothes, but this was a special occasion.

The Reverend Nick conducted a short but moving service in the dining room before a makeshift altar – a table covered in a white cloth, upon which was a cross taken from a deserted church. Shaggy had been an active participant, too. Pete had brought an upright piano and the rock musician played *The Wedding March* as Sandra walked down the aisle on Reaper's arm. In the past, it would normally have been played after the ceremony, but they were breaking new ground anyway, so who cared? After the ceremony, Shaggy played and sang the Beatles' song *All You Need Is Love* and everyone joined in. Sandra and Jamie couldn't stop laughing and smiling as they walked out arm in arm. Even Reaper grinned.

Drinks were served at the pub while the dining room

in the manor house was swiftly converted back to its original purpose, and a buffet, organised and supervised by Jean, was laid out. Kate sat with Reaper on the top table. While the usual speeches were made, there were untypical variations, inevitably making reference to all that had happened. It was a memorable day, but Reaper was glad to be able to change back into fatigues by escaping to the bedroom above the pub he shared with Kate when he was not on duty in the mobile home.

Recorded music was playing, couples were dancing, people were drinking, the day was waning. The happy pair had disappeared to consummate their vows. Reaper was relaxed and content. Nevertheless, he was about to arm himself and go over the hill to relieve Pete and Arif, when there was a scream from the barn. Heads turned, many in the crowd probably dismissed it as youthful exuberance from the younger elements, but the tone of the cry alerted Reaper. Seven-year-old Emma stumbled into view, paused, to adjust her clothes, and then ran, shouting for Ruth between her sobs. Ruth, who had become her surrogate mother, broke from the crowd in wide-eyed panic, dropping a glass. The girl rushed into her arms.

Reaper ran past them to the barn. The main door was round the corner. It was closed, but the smaller access door was open. He went through it and found Ashley pinning a flushed Jason Houseman against the wall, with one big hand around his throat. Houseman's trousers were unfastened. Ashley was bristling with fury and from the colour of Houseman's face, was on the brink of strangling him. Reaper was inclined to let him.

'The bastard,' Ashley said. 'He was . . .'

'I know,' said Reaper. 'I saw Emma. She's okay, Ash.'

The Reverend Nick joined them.

'Let him go, Ashley. You're choking him.'

Ashley took a deep breath and let him go. Houseman fell to the floor, gasped for breath and fumbled to fasten his trousers.

'You're lucky Pete's not here,' Reaper said. 'He'd rip your head off.'

'There's been a mistake,' Houseman whined. 'You've got it wrong! I was having a pee. I didn't know the little girl was there.'

Ashley kicked him and he doubled over.

'You lying scumbag!' Ash said. 'I saw you.'

Nick stepped in between them. He looked desperately into the angry man's face.

'Are you sure there was no mistake?'

'There was no mistake. Ask Emma.'

Reaper said, 'We don't need to. But we do need to get rid of this piece of rubbish.'

'What? You'll take his word instead of mine?'

Now Reaper kicked Houseman hard in the ribs and Nick didn't know where to stand to protect him.

'Look, this can't be solved by kicking him from pillar to post.'

'And how *can* it be solved, Reverend?' asked Reaper.

Others had now gathered at the door and the mood was becoming ugly.

'*Banishment*,' said Nick. 'We kick him out, right now. So he can do no more harm.'

'Until he finds another child,' said Reaper.

He and the cleric exchanged stares. Nick read Reaper's intention in his eyes.

'No, Reaper,' he said. 'We have not yet descended to the level of beasts.'

'It seems some of us have,' Reaper said.

'We banish him. Now. And I'll escort him from Haven myself.'

Reaper knew he could sway the crowd but he didn't want to turn a group of honest citizens into a lynch mob. They had to believe in a better tomorrow. He would have preferred to deal with Houseman on his own, quietly, well away from Haven, with a bullet in the back of his head. Perhaps he still could.

'Okay, Reverend. Get him out of here. Right now.'

He turned and walked away back to the pub, where he armed himself, watched by Kate who, like everyone else, now knew what had happened.

'What are you going to do?' she said.

'You know what I'm going to do.'

He slung the carbine over his shoulder and began

to run up the hill. Pete Mack came riding a trail bike towards him. He braked, the engine growling vigorously beneath him.

'Is it true?'

'It's true, but Ash stopped it before much happened.'

'I'll kill the bastard.'

'That's my job, Pete. Nick says he should be banished. That's okay by me. Just give me the bike. I'll follow him and make sure the banishment is permanent.'

Pete hesitated.

'Come on. Ruth and Emma need you now. I'll take care of it. Just don't tell Nick where I've gone.'

Pete got off the bike and Reaper got astride it, revved the engine, engaged gear and turned it back up and over the hill. He cruised into the shadows of the trees by the mobile home command post. James Marshall was with Arif. He had run to alert Pete. Arif was full of questions that Reaper answered briefly. The young men were as outraged as Pete and Ash, and as convinced as to the course of action that should be taken.

'Go open the gate, Arif,' Reaper said. 'And when he's through, I'll follow.'

Arif rode the other trail bike down to the gate and did as he was instructed. He waited, sitting astride the bike. About fifteen minutes later, the Range Rover that Houseman had arrived in, came over the hill, its lights on in the gloom. It drove straight through the gates and turned left. Reaper let out the clutch and followed. Arif tipped a finger to his baseball cap in salute as he went past. Reaper kept his lights switched off.

The vehicle turned left again onto the main road to Scarborough and Reaper judged they were by now far enough away for justice to be dispensed. He put on the bike lights, flashed them at the Range Rover, and accelerated past. He waved his left arm like a traffic cop and slowed to a stop. The car stopped behind him and he got off the machine and walked back, his right hand on the butt of a Glock. The car door opened and Nick got out.

'Don't argue, Nick. This has to be,' Reaper said, and then realised no one else was in the car. 'Where is he?'

'I sent him out the back way, past Inglewood Farm,' said Nick. 'I knew you'd be waiting.'

Reaper said nothing. He bit back his anger at the meddling cleric. He turned away without another word and got back on the bike, started the engine and turned it round to race back as fast as it would go, to try to pick up Houseman's trail.

He hurtled past the entrance to Haven, round to the rear access of the property. He had the choice of three routes. He took the first, but after five miles of hurtling along lanes, he gave up. He found a hill and drove across a field to its crest and looked out over the plain for a sign of car lights. There were none. If

Houseman had any sense he would have anticipated pursuit and gone as fast as he could, to get as far away as possible. By now he would be safe from retribution.

Chapter 13

REAPER WAS STILL ANGRY THE NEXT DAY: angry at
Houseman's attempted assault and escape; and angry
at himself because he had not returned to Filey to
make a further attempt to talk to Crackpot Charlie
Miller to discover what he knew about Houseman.
Now was the time to rectify the omission.

Sandra drove slowly down the main street of the
town towards the sea front. She stopped the MPV
when they reached the side road into which they had
turned previously, after the warning shot had been
fired. Ahead of them, the road was still blocked by
the lorry parked broadside. Reaper got out of the car,
wearing his sidearms. Both his and Sandra's carbines
were in the back of the car beneath a blanket. From

the car, he took a pole on which was attached a white pillow case. He held this above his head. So far, no one had shot at him.

'Charlie!' he called. 'Charlie Miller!'

He waved the homemade flag. The lorry blockade, he saw, had been augmented with a car at one end and fridges and washing machines at the other.

'Who wants him?' The voice was male and gruff.

'My name is Reaper. I'm from a community called Haven. We're in the country, about twenty miles away. It's a good community. Men, women, children. We're farming the land.'

'You don't look like a farmer.'

'Me and Sandra,' he nodded to the car, 'we look after them. Protection.'

'What do you want?'

'To make contact. Organise trade. There are groups in Scarborough and Bridlington.'

'I know. We fish together.'

'Then perhaps they mentioned us?'

'Perhaps they did.'

'Can we talk face to face?' There was a long pause. At least the request was being considered. 'I need to warn you about a group in Whitby.'

'Warn us?'

'They're violent.'

'We can be violent.'

'And I want to ask you about Jason Houseman.'

'Houseman?' The anger spit from his voice. 'You know Houseman?'

'We took him in. But yesterday he assaulted a little girl. We banished him. We thought he might try to come back here.'

'He won't come back here.' Another pause. 'Walk forward. Keep your hands up.'

Reaper did as he was told. Sandra stayed in the car. He walked slowly, his hands high, the flag still held in his right fist. One of the refrigerators was wheeled away to provide a gap in the barricade. Reaper had to bend from the waist to get through. The washing machine was on rollers and had been pulled aside by a young man with goldfish eyes that gave him a permanently surprised expression. A stocky middle-aged man pointed a shotgun at him. Reaper stood upright and lay his flag on top of the washing machine.

Twenty yards away, the street turned right. A cafe faced up the street and, inside it, a group of people stared out at him. On top of the building, another figure pointed a rifle in his direction. He glanced to his right and saw another man on a lookout post behind the cab of the lorry, pointing a rifle down the street towards where Sandra waited.

Reaper held out his right hand.

'I'm Reaper,' he said.

'I'm Miller.' The man didn't take his hand but at least he lowered the shotgun so that he carried it at waist height, its barrel pointing at the ground. 'What do you want?'

'We're in regular contact with the group at Scarborough Castle. Ferguson and Dr Malone?'

Miller's eyes showed interest.

'Didn't you know they had a doctor?'

'No, we didn't.'

'And we trade with the group at Bridlington at the Royal Yorkshire Yacht Club. Bob Stainthorpe and Nagus Shipley.'

'I know Nagus.'

'Bob and Nagus gave us fish and chips.'

Miller stared at him for a while longer and nodded. 'Aye. Well, you'll have to make do with coffee this time.' He offered his own hand at last and they shook.

'What about Sandra?' Reaper said.

'Invite the lass in.'

Miller was a man of few words but Reaper had made the breakthrough. He went back to the gap and called Sandra to join him.

They went to the cafe, which was clean, orderly and still operating. The coffee was brewed on a large camping stove and served at one of the tables by a young woman who introduced herself as Sharon and who also placed before them a plate of biscuits and sliced cake. She was blonde and in her early twenties, a pleasant girl who smiled at Reaper and Sandra as if delighted that her group had at last extended its horizons. The other men, women and children remained in a cluster near the counter and listened intently to Reaper as he explained what they were doing at Haven, and the progress that was being made at Scarborough and Bridlington.

In return, Miller gave an outline of how they had come together.

'I had a butcher's shop. Lived above it. Me and my son. He died.' He indicated the others with a tilt of the head. 'Everybody lost people. Same as everywhere. Nobody knew what to do at first but this is a close community. The wagon blocking the street was left there a day or two before it all went bad and no one bothered to move it. Afterwards, I came here, to this cafe. I always used to come here. It was easier than cooking. Me and my lad, we lived alone. Anyway, others drifted in and we sort of waited for someone to come and rescue us. Like a lot did, I suppose. Then we realised no one was coming and so we got organised. We cleared the houses of bodies down this end of town. We gave them a burial at sea. Said the words, did it respectful. And we never did bother to move the wagon. Glad we didn't when the low-life came.'

'They were smashing windows and looking for trouble. We heard a woman screaming one night and then they came here, for us. But we were ready and they got more than they bargained for. We beat them off. Killed one, hurt a couple. They went away and they haven't been back. So we made the barricade better, front and sides. And we still have access to the sea. There's another lot starting over at the golf club down at the south end of town. But I suppose we've been a bit wary of leaving the barricades. Maybe it's time to take them down. Maybe it's time to trade.'

'How many of you?' asked Reaper.

'Twenty seven.'

'How many at the golf club?'

'Thirty, forty.' He grunted and almost smiled. 'I think I might have put some off from joining us. I'm told I have a forceful personality.'

Reaper grinned. 'Forceful personalities can be useful.'

'In their time and place. But it sounds as if people are getting back on their feet, or trying to. Maybe it's time to take down the barricades.'

'Maybe not. There's a bloke in Whitby who is building an army. "Muldane's Army". Have you heard of him?'

'No.'

'We ran into four of them the other day. They had come down to Scarborough on a scouting expedition. One of them got away.'

Miller caught his eye. 'Meaning three of them didn't?'

'That's right. But this Muldane has as many as forty armed men. They seem to take other groups prisoner and make them work for them.' He glanced at the people straining to catch every word and lowered his voice. 'The young women are used for recreation.'

Miller sat up straighter and stiffened his shoulders. He nodded his understanding.

'It's always been the same, hasn't it?' Miller said. 'Throughout history. The beast is always lying fallow in man. Remove the rules and certain men allow the devil to rise. The beast is now risen and will not be denied.'

Reaper thought Miller a little poetic but he had the right idea.

Miller continued. 'Before the plague we were living in Sodom and Gomorrah. I was not surprised when we suffered the apocalypse. And now, it seems, the Lamb will have to face the Beast in Armageddon.' Seeing Reaper's expression at this outburt, Miller smiled for the first time, almost self-consciously. 'I was a part-time preacher as well as a butcher.'

Reaper could not think of anything to add to that summation, so drank his coffee. After a couple of minutes, Sandra broke the silence, 'Great cake!'

Sandra joined the group at the counter and left the two men to talk about trade. Miller's group had three fishermen among them who were training others in the way of the sea, and their catches were plentiful. They had hens and a couple of pigs and had also planted allotments, but were not growing fruit and vegetables on anything like the grand scale as Haven. They agreed that trade and the interaction of the groups would be of benefit and, perhaps, in the future, they might devise a mutual defence treaty in case Muldane and his army decided to sweep down from Whitby and conquer new people.

Miller said, 'You mentioned Houseman. What did he do?'

Reaper said, 'The day we first came here, we stopped to eat on The Crescent. Houseman came out of The White Lodge Hotel with another bloke. Milo Montague?' Miller shook his head to say he didn't know him. 'They came with us to Haven. Montague has fitted in well. He's a good worker and is well-liked. But Houseman? I never did like blokes who smiled that much.'

'He'll never smile again if I get my hands on him.'

'We kicked him out yesterday. He was found assaulting a seven-year-old. Thank God he was found in time, but the intent was clear enough.'

'You kicked him out?' he said, as if slightly incredulous.

'We have a clergyman among us. He does not have your fire and brimstone. He . . . means well. And he tries to act as our conscience.' Reaper hesitated. 'Well, maybe my conscience. I would have removed Houseman permanently but our cleric demanded banishment. I went along with it and waited at the front gate. I was still going to remove him, but the vicar let him go by the back door.'

'He is slime of the worst kind,' Miller said, in a low but angry voice. 'A child molester, a paedophile, a beast who has already sold his soul to the devil. He committed a similar crime here. A ten-year-old girl. And then he ran before God's justice could be imposed.'

'You would have shot him?'

'I would have burned him alive to give him a fore-taste of the fires of hell.'

Reaper believed him.

When they left Charlie Miller's enclave, the girl, Sharon, went with them to introduce them to the Golf Club settlement.

'Do you reckon it's like this all over the country?' she asked, as they drove along the empty and deserted West Avenue.

'I think it must be,' said Sandra. 'People getting together in groups, like you and Mr Miller and us at Haven.'

'Haven sounds better than this,' she said.

'Haven is hard work,' Reaper said. 'We're agricul-tural. Every settlement will be different. The grass isn't always greener.'

He could foresee a problem if some of Charlie Miller's lot suddenly decided they wanted to move to Haven. Miller might not take kindly to a sudden shift in popu-lation or a loss of congregation; Reaper felt sure he held services every Sunday. The former butcher was someone he would rather have as a friend and ally, than an enemy. Eventually, it would be inevitable that people would move about from one new village to another, to find a role more suited to their skills or because of relationships. He just didn't want Sharon to start a trend quite so soon.

They drove straight up to the front of Filey Golf Club. There was no guard, no one keeping a lookout. Sharon led them into the foyer of the clubhouse and shouted 'Hello'. A man and woman emerged from a room and looked at them in surprise.

Sharon said, 'Barry, Veronica. There was no one on the door so we came straight in.'

Barry was a small elderly man in corduroy trousers, a V-neck red jumper and a bow tie. He wore glasses on a cord around his neck. Veronica was about fifty, wearing a twinset and pearls. They could have stepped out of the wings from a middle England stage comedy. Reaper had to restrain himself from enquiring, *anyone for tennis?* He wondered, did they even know there had been a pandemic?

'That's all right, Sharon,' Barry said. 'We were working on the rotas.'

The two of them viewed their guests with slight alarm, probably at the sight of the guns they wore. Thank God they had left their carbines locked in the boot.

'This is Reaper and Sandra,' Sharon said. 'They're

from an inland settlement. Haven.'

'We've heard of you,' said Barry, holding out his hand. 'I'm Barry Upson and this is Veronica Glass.' They all shook hands. 'We do the admin. Veronica, because she's bloody good at it and me, because I'm bloody useless at anything else.'

'Everybody else is out at the moment,' said Veronica. 'We're turning part of the course into allotments. Greenhouses and everything.'

'The greenhouses are essential because of the coastal winds,' said Barry.

'We're digging, planting, erecting,' said Veronica. 'It's all go.'

'The children are at school, we have two boats out fishing and teams out on requisition work,' said Barry. 'That's a polite way of saying looting.' He smiled. 'I used to work at the Town Hall. We had a euphemism for everything.'

'Don't you have anybody on guard?' Sandra asked.

'What's the point?' said Barry. 'We have no guns and don't want any. We would hope that if anyone turns up, we can help them, or we can help each other. If someone wants to cause trouble we can only hope our numbers might deter them. We have thirty eight on the roll: eighteen men, thirteen women and seven children under the age of sixteen. Four boys and three girls.'

Reaper acknowledged that Barry was definitely an ex-civil servant.

'Anyway,' said Veronica. 'We're forgetting our manners. How about a nice cup of tea?'

They exchanged experiences over a cup of tea and laid the foundations for future cooperation. Barry was wistful about the way they were digging up the nine-hole academy golf course. He had been a senior member at the club and had many happy memories of games played, stories swapped in the bar, and the time he almost got a hole in one.

'But everything has changed,' he said. ''I'm lucky. I was a widower. But some have had a bloody *awful* time.' He shrugged. 'So what if we dig up the academy course? If it works, in a year or two, we may dig up the rest. In the meantime, I still go out on a Sunday for a few holes.'

After leaving, they dropped Sharon back at Miller's blockade and set off to return to Haven.

'The Golf Club seems well organised,' Reaper said. 'They should do well.'

'If no armed gang turns up to eat their food and take their women,' Sandra said.

'We are at the rebirth of a nation,' Reaper said. 'Hell, the rebirth of a brave new world. We can hope people like Barry and Veronica make it . . . but I have a feeling that only the strong will survive.'

'So we'd better be strong,' said Sandra.

*

Reaper asked for volunteers for a defence corps; a militia that would be called upon in the event of attack. The Reverend Nick was not in support of the idea, but neither did he oppose it. Haven had eight armed personnel, including Reaper and Sandra, but Reaper thought it better if they had more, as well as a plan of defence. The community was now run by a committee that included Nick, Pete, Jamie, Ashley and Judith, the elegant vet. They called a general meeting and Reaper made his pleas for volunteers. Ten agreed to join, including Ashley.

'Times change,' he said. 'Needs must.'

Reaper and Sandra trained the other recruits in the basics with handguns and carbines, for an hour a day for the next week. He put Ashley in charge of the new force and the quiet man reluctantly accepted. The militia's weapons would be stored in the manor house armoury and they would only collect them when it was deemed necessary.

Henceforth, Haven would have a permanent guard in the mobile home in the trees above the front gate of the estate, and another in a cottage at the rear entrance near Inglewood Farm. If a large group of strangers approached, they could warn the village and a reception committee could be prepared, with armed personnel discreetly positioned out of sight. If a threat or attack was perceived, the alert would send everyone within the area into the manor house, which would become their main defensive position. Guns would be issued to those trained in their use, and Asps, pepper gas and Tazer guns would be available for those who felt able to use them. The house had interior wooden shutters on the ground floor, which were reinforced under the supervision of Ashley and Gavin Price. Gun slots were added so that defenders could return fire, although the main defensive position would be on the upper floors.

'I don't think this will ever be needed,' Nick told Reaper, on the last day of training.

'I sincerely hope it will not,' he replied. 'But we have a good thing here. We all know that and so will any intruders. Other communities are growing in other parts of the county, probably all over the country. But there will still be those who don't want to work. Who will be content to live off supermarkets until they're fed up with tinned food. Then we will look a very attractive proposition. Someone just might decide to march in here with an armed gang and take over. Take the produce, the fruits of our work, and the women.'

'You don't know that, Reaper.'

'I know that men can behave far worse than animals, Reverend. I've seen it, you've seen the results of it. These people deserve better than that.'

'There are bound to be shifts in power, you know, as the communities grow?' Nick said. 'Alliances? Maybe regional governments.'

'If you're suggesting I may be worried about losing whatever power I have here, you're wrong. I don't want any kind of power.'

'Apart from that of life and death?'

'As I said, I don't want any kind of power. But I do want to protect the people here and make sure that, if Haven comes under threat, at least we will have a chance of holding our own and persuading any attacker that it might be better to move on and find easier prey.'

'I believe you, Reaper,' Nick said earnestly, 'I just hope you're wrong about the dangers. After all that's happened, I would like to think that man might try to make a fresh start without the violence.'

'So would I. But let's just be prepared for the alternative.'

Chapter 14

THOUGH THE POSSIBLE THREAT FROM WHITBY seemed to be quickly forgotten by most of the settlement, it continued to play on Reaper's mind. A week later, he decided to scout the town out. The manor house had brochures and maps from its days as a holiday destination. He studied the maps of the area and the photographs of the fishing town. He had never been there, so he listened to Jamie's descriptions and also learned something of its history.

This was where Captain Cook had served a naval apprenticeship with a local company that sailed coastal vessels. It was also where Bram Stoker had stayed whilst researching his novel, *Dracula*. Stoker had the vampire reaching England on a crewless ship driven into Whitby harbour by a storm. He based his drama on a real event: a vessel carrying occupied coffins had floundered off the coast in the late 1800s and the dreadful cargo was washed up on the beach. Reaper wondered if Muldane had added any more corpses lately.

Whitby was a town split by the River Esk as it ran into the sea. It was built on both sides of the estuary on high cliffs, with the red-roofed houses tumbling down the steep hillsides to sea level. On the East Cliff was St Mary's Church and graveyard, where Dracula was supposed to have taken refuge, and the ruins of the 7th century Whitby Abbey. A hundred and ninety-nine steep steps led down from the church to feed into narrow Church Street, the start of the 'old town' that clustered at the water's edge.

The West Cliff opposite had Victorian hotels and boarding houses and tight streets that led down to the main shopping area of Baxtergate, where franchise stores from national chains occupied old buildings. The two halves of the town were connected by a bridge across the Esk that divided the harbour into inner and outer basins. Reaper studied the map.

'The old town can be sealed,' he said. 'A guard where the road from the bridge meets Church Street, and another at the top of the steps by the church.'

Jamie agreed. 'The streets are very narrow and the only other way in or out would be via the harbour wall itself.'

The two concrete arms of the harbour stretched out into the North Sea, reaching towards each other to almost touch, like the fingers of a Michelangelo painting, but leaving a small gap for the safe passage of fishing vessels.

Beyond the abbey on the east side was open country and farmland. The west side had been developed with suburban housing. That was the way he would approach.

He went alone on a trail bike at two in the morning. One man would have a better chance to enter and leave the town unobserved, he told Sandra. He didn't say that he didn't want to take a woman with him because of the consequences if she was captured. Sandra and Ashley would be in charge in his absence. The night was overcast and he took the country roads across the North Yorkshire Moors rather than the coastal highway, which he suspected would be watched. He arrived on the modern outskirts of Whitby at three thirty with no lights on the bike.

He was among roads of semi-detached housing, as bland and commonplace as anywhere else in the country. He cruised silently down the slope towards the town, hardly touching the engine. The bike's momentum carried him and, when he needed power, he used it softly as he wended his way through back streets to avoid main roads. He left the bike in the drive of a house in Argyle Road, not far from the

Royal Hotel. Just another abandoned vehicle that would provoke no interest.

His route was fixed in his mind. He walked across a playing field, past more abandoned cars in a municipal car park, and found himself at a modern building that was the Registry of Births, Marriages and Deaths. He slipped into the town proper, past a big church, and down a road lined with impressive old houses that had been converted into private hotels. He was silent and careful, pausing frequently to listen from the shadows.

Reaper had no idea where the man Muldane might create a headquarters for an army of occupation. If he had been in charge, he would have chosen an elevated position as protection against attack or intruders. But what had Muldane chosen? The streets remained silent, filled only with ghosts and abandoned cars. The road ended at a terrace of steep landscaped gardens.

The harbour was below him and the moon obligingly came out and he could see the two arms of the harbour and, up on the far cliff opposite, the church and the ruins of the Abbey. No wonder Stoker had set his novel here; the vista was certainly Gothic – no doubt about that. Reaper saw lights across the water in the old town.

He let himself into a tall hotel with views over the harbour. He went upstairs, using his torch carefully. Some of the rooms would contain bodies but he hoped they would be confined to owner and staff and by now the advanced process of decay had started to take the edge from the sickly sweet smell of death. Surely holidaymakers would have gone home, if they had come at all, considering the panic that had swept the country when the pandemic happened.

The room he chose was empty. A good view. He opened the window to let the fresh night air sweep away the mustiness, and moved an easy chair to the window. He had brought a pack with coffee, bottled water and sandwiches. He had a base. He stared at the old town through binoculars. The glow of a fire seemed to be coming from the market place. A torch was lit high on the hill, he guessed it was at the top of the 199 steps that led down from the church. He needed a closer look.

Reaper left his carbine in the room. He went out of the hotel and slipped back into the night. He snuck down grassy embankments, along alleys, ginnels and lanes, until he reached the waterfront. No one was about; no patrols were on the streets.

He came out on the harbour near The Pier Inn. No guards, no signs that anyone was inside. He went carefully along the Pier Road towards the old town. The clouds were breaking up and he could see movement at the bridge – one shape, maybe two; the flash of an electric torch, the glow of a cigarette. But the buildings seemed to be abandoned. He went back inland through an alley, climbed a hill and reached shops on a higher level. He went back down another steep winding lane past a church and was at the end of Baxtergate, the shopping street that led to the harbour bridge.

A few yards away it joined with Bagdale, one of the main roads into town, but he could see no guards there, either. Muldane was either slapdash or very confident. Reaper went up Baxtergate, pausing every few yards, listening to the night sounds but hearing nothing unusual. He went through another ginnel that gave him a view of the inner harbour, the railway station and a roundabout where two main roads met. All remained silent and he wondered if he dared move his base closer.

Reaper familiarised himself with this side of the town and went back to the hotel on the West Cliff. He retrieved his pack and carbine and returned to the shadows of Baxtergate. He was aware there was a guard nearby, on or near the bridge. The closest building was a bank. Any looter worth the name would opt for an off-licence rather than a bank with a sealed safe full of redundant money, so he guessed it should be empty. The door was open, the wood splintered around the lock. Maybe looters had tried it anyway.

Inside was silent and dark. There were no tell-tale smells of habitation, no snores. He waited until his eyes adjusted. The banking interior was normal but doors had been broken open. He went through into offices and explored until he found a staircase. He climbed, aware that any creaks he made could be fatal. He went up to the top floor and found an office that overlooked the harbour. This couldn't be better. Venetian blinds hung at the windows and he eased one strip of plastic apart to provide him with a view. A car blocked the bridge and a man sat inside it. He could see the glow of his cigarette.

He checked for an escape route in case he was discovered. A fire escape was accessible through a window at the side of the building. That would have to do. He eased the window open a few inches, unpacked his bag and put his food and drink on the desk. He moved a swivel chair to the window and had a cup of coffee.

Reaper dozed off but was awakened before dawn by the sound of feet marching across the bridge. Two unarmed men and an unarmed woman followed by three men with guns. The guard in the car got out and stretched.

'About bloody time,' he said.

One of the armed men stopped by the car, opened the door and recoiled in pretend horror.

'You could have left the windows open. It smells like a shithouse.'

'Fuck off,' replied the guard, now relieved of his duty. He walked off across the bridge towards the old town.

The rest of the group turned right onto the harbour side. He heard doors opening and closing. They had entered a building.

A little later, as it got light, using his binoculars, he watched another group cross a wooden jetty on the far side of the harbour. Three unarmed men and two armed. The two armed men were dressed in black; sweaters and trousers. He realised the other armed guards had also been dressed in black. All five climbed down into a fishing boat. The engine started, they cast off and it set off onto the calm sea.

It was another hour before people started moving and he caught the aroma of baking bread. That must have been the early morning party he had watched crossing the bridge on their way to work. Now that the sun was up, he could see more clearly. There was a second guard on the far side of the bridge at the end of Church Street. They had blocked off the old town and he surmised that this would be where the so-called drones and volunteers were being kept.

Six armed men left Church Street. They split into two parties and climbed into two Transit vans. Both drove across the bridge, waiting while the guard moved the car blocking it, and headed out of town. Reaper ate a sandwich, had a cup of coffee, and kept watching. About nine, the bakers reappeared carrying black plastic bin bags that he presumed were full of bread. The woman was missing. Still working? But with no guard in the bakery. He watched them cross the bridge.

Reaper picked up the carbine and left the bank. He was pretty sure this side of town was unoccupied but he still took care, slipping through the back streets to the rear of the buildings that fronted the harbour. He let his nose guide him like a Bisto kid. He followed the aroma of baking. He climbed a wall into a yard. The back door was open; after all, baking is a hot business. He stepped into a preparation room and came to face to face with the missing woman. She was small and rotund and in her middle years. She had been rolling pastry but now stopped and looked at him with surprise. Perhaps she thought he was just another guard. Then she realised he wasn't and she dropped the rolling pin, glanced behind him to see if he was alone and then at the door that led to the front of the shop.

He raised one hand to calm her.

'I'm not with them,' he said.

'Please,' she said. 'I don't want any trouble.'

'All I want is information.'

She had already started shaking her head before he made the request. 'If they see you, they'll kill me as well. Please go. Leave me alone.' The woman was terrified.

'No one will see me. No one will know I've been. I want to help you. Not now, in the future. Is Muldane in charge?'

Her gaze kept going back to the door that led to the shop but she nodded.

'How many men does he have?'

She shrugged. 'They're the New Order. He said so. Please leave. They don't need an excuse.'

Reaper nodded to reassure her. 'I'll go. But I'll be back.'

As he backed towards the door, she picked up a small cob of fresh bread and threw it to him.

'I'm sorry,' she said.

He smiled and nodded and kissed the bread in acknowledgement and left. He retraced his steps to the top floor room in the bank. The bread was warm and tasted delicious. The woman's gift was in lieu of words she hadn't been able to utter because of her fear that the guard would return and discover her visitor. Such fear. What had she experienced already under Muldane's New Order? And who the hell was Muldane? Apart from a bloke who enjoyed making up names to explain his actions. *New Order*, *drones*, *volunteers*. Was he mad, dangerous, or both?

The fishing boat returned and was unloaded by three more citizen drones. Up on the hill by the church, half a dozen more carried down sacks and baskets, presumably of vegetables or meat. He guessed they were tending the fields beyond the abbey. The two men guarding them, again dressed in black, waited at the top of the steps and chatted with the man posted there, until their charges returned. They led them off again, probably to a waiting van or truck.

Muldane had a small productive empire. The town had shops and supermarkets, fish from the sea and excellent farming country nearby. Maybe he wouldn't be interested in other, more democratic communities and wouldn't be a threat for a long while. Maybe Reaper didn't have to get involved. Except that Reaper felt guilty leaving such a man in control and polluting other people's lives. And he would have to do something eventually, because eventually Muldane would decide to expand his empire. It was ever thus, even with civilisation surviving by its fingertips.

Some time later, a small van drove across the bridge from the old town and stopped outside the bakery. Soon after, it returned the way it had come, presumably loaded with the cakes the baker had been making. She followed, on foot. Late afternoon, the two Transits returned and he watched male drones carry boxes from them into the old town. An ordinary day seemed to be drawing to a conclusion, when people started walking onto the east harbour wall.

The civilian drones, men and women, were being herded along by armed men. Children were among them, small children. And then came a group comprised only of women and he felt an emptiness in his stomach as he realised these must be what had been described as 'Muldane's volunteers'. These were the younger and more attractive women, some hardly into adolescence. His eyes dampened as he stared through the binoculars. While the drones wore nondescript clothing, the girls and women wore dresses and tight jeans and high heels and make up. Muldane had created a brothel for his men.

Down the steps came another ten 'civilians', eight men and two women, presumably from the outlying farms they were helping to run. With them were six armed guards. Reaper reckoned there were close to fifty adult civilians in total at the harbour plus eight young children, another twenty women who would be classed as 'volunteers', and at least twenty-eight armed men keeping them in order. Add the guards at the bridge, the end of Church Street and one still at the top of the 199 steps, plus maybe others in posts on the main roads leading to the town, and that was an army approaching forty.

The prisoners were gathered on the facing harbour wall. Some of the women and girls of the volunteers moved among the others to find companions, friends. When they did, some held each other and cried. Some of the women didn't move at all, didn't seek anyone. They remained alone in the midst of the crowd. Over them all, hung an air of defeat, of subjugation.

An open-topped Land Rover came from the old town and crossed the bridge, followed by a BMW four-by-four. The guard at the bridge stood at an approximation of attention as they went by. A man in an army uniform sat in the passenger seat of the Land Rover. It could only be Muldane. Reaper fixed him in the binoculars. A portly man, aged about forty, with a trimmed moustache. His uniform had a crown on the epaulette, signifying a Major in the British Army. He did not appear a figure to inspire terror. Reaper switched his gaze to the driver, who looked like either a career thug or a career soldier. A powerful man dressed in black. Muscles bulging though his T-shirt. Across his chest hung a bandoleer.

The Land Rover and the BMW turned right along Pier Road. Reaper sensed something out of the ordinary was about to happen. From his location, he lost sight of the two vehicles on Pier Road, which curved inland beyond the buildings in his sightline. They came into view again where the road curved back. They stopped at the west harbour wall.

Muldane got out of the Land Rover. He stretched and strutted a few paces with a swagger stick tucked beneath his arm. He wore a service revolver in a holster on his belt. His driver remained a close companion. A fearsome and powerful figure with a shaven head, carried a sub-machine gun in addition to his holstered sidearm. Four more black-clad men, got out of the BMW, each had the same muscular build and professional bearing and all wore holstered pistols. They pulled a fifth passenger from the BMW – a male civilian who had his hands either tied or cuffed behind his back.

The party marched onto the concrete wall, Muldane in front, as if about to inspect troops, his sergeant at his side. He stopped and the four men in black knocked their prisoner to his knees. Muldane and his party faced the captives clustered across the narrow stretch of water on the other side of the harbour. The man in the major's uniform was making a speech, but Reaper was too far away to hear what was said.

The day was hot, the sun silvered the calm sea, and the horizon smudged into a pale blue sky. Gulls wheeled and swooped for a closer look. On a day like this in late June, the town would normally have been full of people; shoppers in Baxtergate, tourists climbing the 199 steps to visit the legends and the history outlined in ruins on the cliff top. Others would be crowding the cobbles and quaint shops of Church Street and the old town or visiting the Dracula museum. But that was then and this was now.

Two of the guards dragged the man forward until he knelt on the harbour side. Muldane took the revolver from his holster and shot him in the back of the head. The body tumbled into the sea. The gulls screamed and arced away from the gunshot.

Muldane turned on his heel and his party marched back to their vehicles. Across the water, the captives had watched the proceedings almost without reaction.

Only one or two had seemed shocked. The show over, they were being marched back to where they had come from. Reaper didn't know what offence the dead man had committed, but he guessed it hadn't been criminal. 'Muldane's Army' were the criminals: thieves, murderers and rapists. Maybe the dead man had shown dissent, complained about brutality, or attempted to escape. No wonder the baker had been terrified. When the rule of law was no more, any madman could impose tyranny on a whim.

Reaper waited for night to descend. He ate and drank and watched. Buildings in the old town were lit by lanterns. Street illumination was provided by a car's headlights that shone down Church Street. When they dimmed, they could fit a new battery. He listened to the sounds of revelry get louder as more drink was consumed, the forced hilarity of women, the occasional scream and yelp of pain, the macho laughter of beasts at play.

He had seen all he needed to see. He packed his bag and left the building, slipping through the silent streets of West Cliff, back to his motorcycle and the ride home.

Chapter 15

REAPER HAD NOT LIKED WHAT HE HAD witnessed in Whitby, but did not see how he could change it. Such a change would require direct action – a war, and Muldane had a black-clad army of forty or more well-armed men who raped and killed without compunction. To stand any chance of removing Muldane from power, he would not only have to mobilise and arm all the able-bodied citizens of Haven, but would need to persuade members of other peaceful settlements to join them in the fight. He knew he would find sympathy, but few would be eager to join such a crusade and, to be honest, he did not want to put the lives of his friends in such danger.

There would come a time when Muldane, or someone

like him, would move against them and then there would be no choice but to fight. He would concentrate on training and preparation for when that happened. In the meantime, he would make everyone aware of the danger and, perhaps, as they grew stronger, they would become confident enough to take the fight to the enemy and liberate those he enslaved.

As he drove back through the night, he thought again about the Royal Air Force bases along the East Coast flatlands, and the army base at Catterick. They held the possibility of both hope and danger. An officer commanding even a small group of trained soldiers could be a force for good or evil. Is that where Muldane had come from?

Fiefdoms and robber barons were inevitable. But an officer with trained troops might restore order, or impose it. The trouble was, having achieved power, the officer might be reluctant to relinquish it. History taught that.

How swiftly civilisation had crumbled, reflected Reaper.

He reported all he had witnessed and his fears for the future to the ad hoc committee at Haven. Even the Reverend Nick took it seriously, and they all agreed to maintain training, periodically review their defences and to inform all neighbouring groups with whom they had contact.

Their community, that now included two farms and

a nearby village, numbered 176. New arrivals were now infrequent. The first wave of settlers had been looking for somewhere else – anywhere else – in the belief that it had to be better than what they had left behind. A few travellers still passed through on the main roads, but they were itinerants who were unlikely to ever settle down; some were too emotionally scarred to start a new life, others preferred to drift rather than face the new reality.

Haven also had close contacts with the groups in Scarborough, Filey and Bridlington, and looser arrangements with those in Malton, Pickering and Driffield. Through them, they were aware of others in more distant areas. There were also smaller groups, sometimes consisting only of a handful of folk in villages or on farms, who preferred independence while accepting mutual cooperation.

On his travels, Pete had requisitioned a thousand-litre mobile fuel bowser with an electric pump. He and Gavin now made regular trips to petrol stations to fill up with petrol and diesel for their expanding settlement. The Haven farm had a fixed diesel bowser, and the manor house a diesel generator. An extra petrol bowser was brought to Haven and both were kept topped up, the first for farm and domestic use, and the second to supply their small fleet of vehicles. The mobile bowsers were also used to stock up the underground tanks of Taylor's Garage in the nearby village.

There was a great deal of fuel still available with so few survivors but, eventually, it would run out. As they travelled greater distances to drain the tanks of vehicles and filling stations, they would inevitably come into territorial conflict with other groups. But that was a problem for the future. The time would come when everybody might have to revert to horse drawn transport and, with that in mind, the farm had a growing stock of ponies and shire horses.

They had also collected books for teaching, trade and engineering, as well as a fiction section. One of the rooms in the manor house had become a library. Before long, they would have to start civilisation from almost scratch. Ferguson at Scarborough had agreed to help them install solar panels and erect a windmill at Haven, as first ventures into harnessing the power of nature.

A week after his Whitby excursion, Reaper undertook another mission beyond their usual parameters of travel and salvage: to Catterick army camp. He and Sandra went north in the MPV through Pickering and Thirsk. They had contacts in Pickering but did not stop. They knew there was a group at Thirsk but bypassed the town. An awful lot of the countryside was empty. Animals lay dead in fields, vehicles abandoned in villages and on highways. They also passed though areas where crops and livestock were obviously being tended, but they did not stop to look for people and neither did people attempt to stop them.

The towns closest to the army camp were Northallerton, five or six miles to the southeast, and Richmond, two or three miles to the northwest. Reaper figured they were the ones that might have benefited or suffered most from any military presence that still existed. Sandra and he approached the market town of Northallerton along the Thirsk Road. A pole resting on oil drums provided a flimsy barrier or checkpoint at the bottom of the High Street, where other roads met at a roundabout. Sandra was driving and stopped before the roundabout, Reaper got out of the vehicle and walked towards the pole with his hands raised. He stopped ten feet short of it. A woman came out of a white painted building on the right. She was middle aged and wearing a tracksuit. She carried no weapons, which made Reaper feel slightly overdressed.

'Hello?' she said, in a breezy and welcoming way.

He lowered his arms and said, 'Hello. We're passing through, if that's all right?'

'Of course.' She motioned towards the pole. 'It's just a formality to give us warning of visitors. It's become quieter now but, at the beginning, there were one or two incidents until we got properly organised.'

Reaper looked at the pole.

'It doesn't seem very substantial.'

'It isn't.' She smiled. 'But I have a colleague in the building behind me who has a rifle trained on you, and a young chap with an anti-tank gun across the street.'

Reaper nodded.

'That's substantial enough,' he said.

'Our market day is Friday so you haven't come to trade. Or . . . have you?'

'Not this time, but maybe in the future. We're on a scouting trip. We're from a place near Scarborough. Haven. Population about two hundred. We're doing okay, growing crops, keeping animals.'

'It's good farming country there,' she said.

He looked around but could see neither the man with the rifle or the one with the anti-tank gun.

'This trip is outside our usual territory. We have contact with groups in our area, but don't usually go any further than Pickering in this direction.'

'There's not much point. I suppose everywhere is pretty much the same. Struggling to make a new start. Become self-sufficient.'

'That's the ideal. But not everybody is doing it. Do you know about the man called Muldane in Whitby?'

'No.'

'He has a private army and lives off plunder. He takes captives, uses them as slave labour and sex workers. You should be aware of him. Before long he'll want to expand.'

'Thanks for the warning. But you haven't travelled all this way to tell us that, have you?'

'No. We came because of the army camp. We thought there might be martial law or some kind of local government.'

The woman smiled again. 'You'd better come in.'

Reaper waved Sandra forward in the car and helped the woman lift off the pole so she could drive through.

'Come on. I'll go with you,' she said, and held her hand out for Reaper to shake. 'I'm Mavis Wilburn.'

'Reaper. That's Sandra.'

They drove into Northallerton along a wide handsome street with a large pedestrianised area designed for markets. The town was neat and tidy. Abandoned vehicles had been moved. No bodies were in evidence. Mavis directed them to stop outside the Black Bull, then led them inside. Reaper still didn't know if she had had the cover she claimed at the barrier. They went into a lounge area while she went behind the bar and lit the gas flames of a camping stove, shook a kettle to confirm it contained water and placed it to boil.

'Tea or coffee?'

'Coffee.' Sandra and Reaper said it together. Reaper added, 'Please.'

'Please, sit down,' she said. 'There's only me here at the moment. We take turns at being the welcoming committee. There's a school in the back.' She indicated the rear of the building with a nod of her head. 'Six children. We have people working in allotments and on the golf course, which we cultivated.' She smiled. 'We really have returned to a rural economy. We keep some livestock, too, although not enough. We rely on trade with a farm a few miles away that is functioning quite well. We have a small engineering shed that we operate with generators. They've been making ploughshares and farm implements for when the petrol runs out.'

'That's enterprising,' said Reaper. 'Something we haven't done. Something we'd be interested in.'

'We manage. But it's been a struggle.' She smiled. 'But you wanted to know about Catterick.'

'That's right.'

'Catterick Garrison, the biggest military garrison in Europe with more than 9,000 soldiers. signals, mechanical engineers, artillery, mechanised brigade, infantry, guards, is entirely gone.'

'Gone?' Reaper was surprised.

'The most senior officer who survived was Colonel Owen. We believe he had about a hundred men gathered under his command when the plague ended.' Reaper noted her use of the term plague. Every district probably had its own terminology for what had happened. 'There were some other survivors, but many just upped and left. You can't really call them deserters, can you? I mean, after what happened. There were about fifty wives and dependants – sons, daughters, infants. The colonel visited us. He said he had been in touch with the Ministry of Defence. A new government was being formed at Windsor under Prince Harry.' She shrugged. 'Anyway, that's where forces were being concentrated for a new beginning. The plan, Colonel Owen said, was to regenerate from Windsor with legal authority.'

'So we may already have a government in Windsor?' Reaper said.

'Maybe. Who knows? Catterick camp covered a wide area. Catterick village itself is in the middle of it, as well as several other villages. The colonel visited them all, as well as Richmond, speaking to those who were left. He offered transportation, welfare and medical care for all who wanted to go south with him. Many went. On the face of it, it wasn't a bad offer. A safe environment and a new start. They went in a convoy of trucks. Soldiers, dependants, locals. They took guns and equipment. What armaments they couldn't take, they destroyed. The explosions went on for two days.' She looked at Reaper. 'Was it the guns you came for?'

'We came to see if there was law and order here but, if guns had been available, we'd have taken them.'

The kettle whistled and Mavis made coffee. Sandra got up to help, added whitener to her own mug, and left Reaper's black.

They sat and sipped in silence.

Mavis said, 'Thinking of going south?'

'No,' Reaper said. 'We're good as we are. Although

it might be worth travelling down there to make contact. Find out what's what. Strange though, that we've not heard any radio broadcast. We keep a listening watch.'

'So what now?'

'We'll come to your next market.'

'That's good,' she said. 'But don't go getting your hopes up. It's not a huge market, but it is a chance for people to meet, exchange news and advice, as well as buy ploughshares.'

'Are there people in Richmond?'

'Yes. There is a small community of sorts, but it's a bit . . . odd. The leader is a chap called Arthur Dobson. He hasn't come out and said it yet, but it seems he thinks he's a reincarnation of King Arthur. Do you know the legend?'

'Which one?'

'King Arthur and his knights are supposed to sleep beneath Richmond Castle, waiting to be called again in time of England's greatest need.'

'Maybe someone should call him.'

'Arthur keeps hinting they already have. He's a benign chap, really. He was a librarian, local historian and chairman of the Civic Society. Maybe what happened turned his mind. It didn't do a lot of good to mine. Anyway, he's a big chap and he's taken to wearing a sword and they have meetings at a round table. But, give him his due, he has combined the different groups that formed in the area afterwards, into one community. They are about fifty of them. And he seems to be a good administrator, so they are putting up with him.'

'Who knows. Maybe he *is* King Arthur.'

'Stranger things have happened.'

'Haven't they just,' said Sandra.

They left Northallerton and drove unopposed into the environs of Catterick Garrison. Most of the barracks remained standing, although military buildings, trucks, tanks and other vehicles had been demolished by explosives. Three large holes in the ground, surrounded by debris and broken concrete, suggested where munitions might have been disposed of.

'Where now?' said Sandra.

It was noon and, while one mission was over, they had time to pursue another. Reaper took a map from the glove compartment.

'Let's check out RAF Lemington.'

They drove to the A1 and turned south. An hour later, they turned left and followed the sign for the camp. The flatlands made it ideal country for airfields and aerodromes. Many had been sited here during the Second World War. Since then, a couple had been converted into commercial airports and some had survived to remain operational with the RAF.

The village of Lemington seemed deserted; thirty or forty houses, some substantial, a row of cottages, a village store and the White Horse pub. They continued without stopping for another five miles, the road running through fields, until they could see the main gate of the camp ahead. The road they were travelling along formed the trunk of a T-junction. The other road, that crossed it to form the bar, ran parallel to the camp fence. Where the two highways met was a roundabout. At the other side was the entrance to the camp. A scrub of woodland was to their right.

Sandra stopped the car. A Range Rover had been abandoned on this side of the roundabout and a white van partially blocked the left hand curve. The perimeter fence of the camp was six-foot high chain link attached to concrete posts. Razor wire ran along the top. The gate was closed. The entrance was marked by two short stretches of three-foot high wall. Inside was a gatehouse and a checkpoint with the barrier down. The gatehouse was half brick and half glass.

Sandra took the right hand curve of the roundabout slowly to negotiate past the abandoned vehicles. They were only part way round, when someone opened fire from the gatehouse. A three-round burst shattered the windscreen. She screamed and braked, slammed the car into reverse and tried to retreat. More shots: into the engine and then to take out the tyres. The car slew sideways.

'Out!' shouted Reaper, throwing himself into the back of the vehicle and pushing open the back door. Sandra did the same with her door and they both fell out onto the road. The car was broadside in the road and now both curves of the roundabout were blocked. More three-round bursts hit the car and glass showered around them. He glanced at Sandra who met his gaze. She was shaking from being under fire but keeping a grip on herself.

'I'll make for the van.' he said. 'When I start, you make for the trees.'

She nodded. He hoped he had calculated correctly and that the person firing at them might soon need to change magazines. He got up and ran. A three-round burst hit the tarmac by the rear of the car and then he was haring across the grass of the roundabout, and the gun fell silent. New magazine.

He got behind the van and looked across at the trees beyond their now shattered MPV. From their cover, Sandra waved to him, attracting gunfire. Reaper took the opportunity to run again, keeping low, across the road to the perimeter fence. Before he got there, he heard Sandra returning fire with three, single-spaced shots that broke windows, which would at least give their opponent something to think about.

For a few seconds he lay in the grass and got his breath back. They had been fired on with three round bursts, which meant a military weapon. Police carbines were modified so they only fired single shots. Military were fully automatic. Was the camp being defended? Or had it been looted? The military, he reasoned, would not fire at ordinary citizens without warning. Unless they were a rogue element.

The camp entrance was fifty feet away. The gate-house was on the far side and he was now protected from sight by the three-foot wall. He crawled until he was midway between two of the concrete posts that held the fence and tugged at the base of the chain link. It lifted slightly and the ground was uneven. He pulled the Bowie knife from his right boot, and began digging into a depression in the turf. The ground was soft because it had rained recently. He heard Sandra main-taining occasional fire, which brought more bursts from the gatehouse.

He paused when he heard the noise of an engine. An open military Land Rover inside the camp was driving fast towards the gatehouse. He shuffled side-ways and lay flat, taking advantage of the slight rise in the land before it met the fence. Two men in uniform leapt from the Land Rover and ran inside the building. Reaper resumed digging, desperate to get inside and give Sandra support.

At last he had moved enough turf and loose earth to push beneath the fence on his back, head first. The wire snagged on his vest and equipment a couple of times, but he made it through. He leapt to his feet and ran until he was behind the wall. The gunfire was following a pattern, the two sides taking turns to fire. He peered round the corner of the wall near the barrier pole. People were shouting inside the guard house. He cocked both Glock handguns, replaced them in their holsters and then moved silently across the road until he was by the open door.

'You daft bastard!' someone shouted.

'Fuck!' yelled someone else, and this time, an extended burst of gunfire was aimed across the road and into the woods where Sandra lay hidden.

Reaper lay the carbine on the ground and took out both handguns. As another burst was fired, he took a deep breath and stepped inside, guns levelled. The uniformed man to his left turned at the sound of his entry. He was tall and skinny, with a round head like a Belisha beacon, eyes big behind glasses, and a mouth that had dropped open in shock. Reaper shot him in the face, at the same time sending a bullet into the back of the figure leaning against a steel filing cabinet, firing out of a window. The third man began to turn but Reaper shot him before he managed it: two shots, one from each gun; head and back.

He took a deep breath. The three bodies lay sprawled inelegantly on the floor, blood pooling, gunsmoke the dominant smell for the moment. He took a step forward, careful not to stand in the blood, the guns still ready in his hands, but they were all dead.

'Sandra!' he shouted. 'Are you okay?' He stepped to the windows, two of which had been opened, the others had been shattered by Sandra's return fire. 'It's clear!'

She stood up and left the cover of the trees and waved. He waved back, an immense feeling of relief sweeping over him. What would he have done if she had been hurt or killed?

He went outside. The main gate was secured with a padlock and chain. Reaper fired at the lock three times before it burst open. He put his guns in the holsters and opened the gate. Sandra came into his arms and hugged him, then pushed herself away self-consciously.

'That was a bit hairy,' she said.

He nodded and turned to stare into the camp to see if anyone else might be coming, but the place seemed deserted. Sandra looked towards the gatehouse.

'Three dead,' he said. 'All in uniform.'

They both stared at the camp. A housing complex for service families was to the immediate left, ordinary detached and semi-detached houses with gardens that could have been a Barrett estate. Military buildings were further on. A control tower in the distance dead ahead, the airfield and hangars and more single-storey buildings to the right. A giant transport plane, big enough to carry tanks, sat abandoned on the far side of the runway. A sign near the gatehouse informed visitors that this was the home of 11 Fighter Squadron. Sadly, not any more.

'Who were they?' Sandra asked.

'They wore uniform and had military weapons, but . . . I don't know . . . Rag, Tag and Bobtail? Looters? Muldane's Army?'

They exchanged a look.

'Are there any more of them?' Sandra said.

'We'd better find out. We'll use the Land Rover. Hang on, I'll get their weapons.'

He went back into the guardhouse. The three men had been armed with L85 rifles and Browning 9mm automatic pistols. He began unstrapping the belts containing the handguns and realised Sandra had joined him. He was continually amazed at how such a young girl had steeled herself to function under fire, and to accept death and the casualties of battle. Her courage filled him with pride and he knew, without doubt, that he would die for her. She picked up the rifles and took them outside. He got the last of the belts and noticed the half empty bottle of bourbon and the glass that were on a desk. Thank God the idiot who had opened fire had been too pissed to shoot straight.

Reaper went outside and put the belts and guns in the back of the Land Rover, along with the rifles.

'Do you want to drive?' he said.

Sandra got behind the wheel, adjusted the seat, and turned the vehicle round and drove along the concrete road. Fifty yards away, a truck was parked with its rear facing the gatehouse. Sandbags were stacked in the back of the truck around a machine gun. Arc lamps were fixed to the top of the truck. Maybe this was a night-time guard post. Sandra drove past and stopped at a junction. The road ahead ran alongside the runway and led to the control tower. He pointed left.

'Let's try there.'

They went slowly, Reaper holding the carbine upright and at the ready. The residential housing was off another road to the left, open-plan frontages with gardens at the rear. They kept driving towards a large, handsome red brick building that looked like a small country mansion, with a wide gravel parking area out front. Sandra stopped at the side and they approached carefully, ducking below windows, as they made their way to the open front door. More sandbags and another machine gun nest, also unmanned. From inside, they could hear music playing.

Reaper took a quick look round the doorpost then pulled his head back. No one in sight. He stepped around the sandbags and into an entrance hall, carbine at the ready, Sandra behind him. Offices to the right, a wide staircase ahead and an open door to the left from where the music came: Elton John. A sign above it said *Officer's Mess*. Reaper prepared himself in case he saw another scene like the one he had witnessed in the Imperial Hotel in Scarborough. He exchanged a nod with Sandra and they both stepped through the door, giving each other space and covering the occupants inside.

The room was large and richly carpeted, comfortable furniture, a bar to the right. A black youth in uniform lay slumped over a table, a can of lager in his hand. A young woman in a summer dress lay on a couch, knees up in a foetal position, asleep, the dress carelessly showing her legs. Two children played on the carpet, a boy about six, a girl about nine. They stopped what they were doing and stared at them with a wide-eyed gaze. A blonde-haired woman in her forties was sprawled in an armchair. She opened her eyes and blinked to focus.

'It's okay,' Sandra said. 'You're safe now.'

'Safe?' the woman said.

'Safe,' Sandra said. 'No one will hurt you anymore.'

'Who the hell are you?' she said. 'Where's Corp? And Billy and Tommy?'

Sandra glanced at Reaper who felt his stomach lurch into emptiness. Either this was an extreme case of Stockholm Syndrome or they had jumped to a massively wrong conclusion.

'I said who the hell are you?' The woman spoke with an upper class voice that rang with authority. 'And where are Corp and the boys?'

Her rising tones had awakened the sleeping girl and the slumped airman. The girl sat up and rubbed her face, the airman squinted in an attempt to focus his thoughts. They both looked to be about seventeen.

'What's going on?' the airman said.

Reaper said, 'We were fired on. We returned fire.'

'Where are they?' said the airman. 'Where are the lads?'

Reaper saw no point in prevarication.

'They're dead.'

'They're *dead*?' said the airman, incredulous at such a concept. The girl burst into tears. The woman got to her feet.

'What the hell have you done?' she said.

'We were fired on,' Reaper said.

'They were warning shots!' she said. 'We never shoot to kill.'

'They came bloody close to my head,' Sandra said. 'They didn't feel like warning shots when I was in the trees.'

'You've killed them?' the woman said.

'Oh my God, what a fuck up!' said the airman, then looked at the woman in a reflex action and said, 'Sorry ma'am.'

'That's quite all right, Clifford. You are perfectly correct.' She was bristling with rage. 'It is a complete fuck up. Now. You. Explain yourselves.'

Reaper realised he was still pointing the carbine. He shifted its position and held it in the crook of his arm.

'It seems there has been a misunderstanding. As I

said, we were fired on, without warning, and felt we were in danger. No one attempted to shout to us or warn us off. They just opened fire. When we got into the guardhouse, I found a bottle of bourbon. I suspect whoever started that fire-fight had been drinking fairly heavily. But once the bullets started, we felt we had no option but to fight back.'

'You could have gone away,' the woman said.

'We were under fire. Our car had been shot to pieces. If we had run away, we would had have been in open sight of our attacker.'

'He wouldn't have shot you.'

'We couldn't know that. We saw our only way of surviving as fighting back.'

'And you killed them,' she said, all the anger suddenly leaving her. She sank back into the armchair.

Reaper kept his voice low. 'I'm sorry but there was no communication. No shouted warning, no explanation. Just bullets.'

'Three young men,' she said. 'Three good young men.'

The airman at the table suddenly threw the can that he still gripped at the bar behind him.

'Bastard!' he said, not at them it seemed but at the situation. He dropped his head into his hands and burst into tears.

'Who *are* you?' the woman said. Her tone was almost conversational.

'My name's Reaper. This is Sandra. We're from a

community near Scarborough. About two hundred of us. They're good people. We were on a scouting mission. We went to Catterick first. Thought there might be a military government of some kind but it was deserted.'

The woman gave a tired and dispirited laugh.

'So we tried here on the way back.'

'Why here?'

'The same reason.' He caught her look and knew he should be honest. 'And to see if there were any weapons or ammunition.'

'Weapons. To kill more people?'

'We had some bad experiences at the beginning. Rape and killing. And there's a bloke at Whitby who has set himself up as a warlord. He takes women as sex slaves. We need to be able to defend ourselves.'

The woman finally nodded, as if accepting what had happened. Her eyes glazed and she looked away, perhaps remembering the three young airmen. Reaper knew none could have been older than their early twenties.

'I'm sorry,' he said. 'Sandra and I escaped from a city. Law and order had broken down. Those who were left were taking what they wanted. Including women. We have seen terrible things, experienced terrible things. We have been conditioned to react the way we do.'

Her eyes refocused and she looked at them again, first at Reaper and then at Sandra.

'How old are you?' she asked Sandra.
'Eighteen.'
The woman shook her head slowly in despair.
'Emily,' she said, 'stop crying and make some tea.'

Chapter 16

THE WOMAN WAS CASSANDRA CAIRNCROSS, THE wife of a Squadron Leader. Her husband and most of the people on the base had died from the virus. The most senior surviving airman had been Flight Sergeant Harry Babbington. He had arranged for the service personnel to don plastic coveralls and face masks and search all the buildings on the airfield. Bodies had been removed and placed together in a hangar at the far end of the camp, which had been primed with aircraft fuel and an explosive device. He had moved the survivors into one accommodation block near the officers' mess. He had, it seemed, done a good job.

'We never intended to stay here,' Cassandra told them. 'The plan was to move out in strength and find others. Before we went, we would set the funeral pyre. Then we got a Morse code radio message. It said an emergency government was being formed in Windsor. Prince Harry had survived and people from Whitehall and the Services were gathering in Windsor Castle. Flight Sergeant Babbington held a meeting and told everyone what was happening. A vote was taken. Everyone wanted to go.' She smiled. 'Prince Harry. It was like a clarion call. The Flight Sergeant had twenty-seven service men and women, nine women civilians and six children.'

She turned her head and looked at the boy and girl who were playing on the carpet.

'And then these two became ill. Everyone was worried at first, thought the virus might have returned, but it turned out to be only a childhood thing. Some sickness and diarrhoea. Anyway, Emily and I volunteered to stay behind with them. Corporal White and three airmen volunteered to stay with us. We were to follow the main party to Windsor when they were better. They left in a convoy of trucks and took whatever equipment they could.'

'The children look fine now,' said Reaper.

'They are. Bursting with health. Have been for three weeks.'

'So why didn't you follow?' asked Reaper.

'Another radio message. Very brief. It said: *Returning. Stay where you are. Imperative, stay where you are.*'

Reaper thought before he spoke. 'This was Morse code?'

'Yes. Morse code may be basic but it is the most reliable radio communication when others fail. The RAF teaches it as a fail safe for pilots and air traffic control. Presumably, the other services make it a requirement in their signal corps.'

'But so far no one has returned?'

'That is correct. We have been getting anxious. Particularly as we have had five visits in the last eight days, one of them last night. That is why Clifford was sleeping. That is probably why Tommy was drinking. Nerves were shredding, Mr Reaper.'

He nodded and said, 'Just Reaper. It makes sense now, the fire pattern he put down. You are right, it was meant to deter. Not kill. But we didn't know that. And perhaps he panicked because we returned fire. Had that happened before?'

'A shotgun was fired at us once. And last night, someone had a pistol and a rifle. But bursts from the machine gun we have mounted as secondary defence, deterred any entry.' A tired tip of her head indicated a mental shrug. 'It is a big perimeter. There are easier access points. But we thought if we made a show of strength at the main gate, it would make any attacker think we were defending in force and send them away. Until now, it had worked.'

'But after last night, everyone was on edge?'

'That is correct.'

'I'm sorry. We're sorry.'

She shook her head. 'Not your fault. An accident waiting to happen. Friendly fire. Casualties of war. A fucking cock up.'

Reaper let the silence settle. It was Sandra who eventually broke it.

'What will you do now? You can't just wait. No one may come, except the people from last night. They may try to get in somewhere else. It would be best if you came with us to Haven.'

Cassandra smiled sadly. 'What beautiful irony. You kill us to save us.'

'Things sometimes happen that way,' said Reaper.

Leading Aircraftman Clifford Smith insisted his comrades should be buried. He didn't want them to go to the hangar with the other bodies. Reaper agreed. Besides, he could guess that opening the hangar would not be pleasant after all this time. He volunteered to help with the task.

'Body bags.' said Clifford.

'What?'

'We have body bags in the bunker.'

'What bunker?'

'The nuclear bunker. It was built in the sixties. It's used for unusual storage.'

Body bags would qualify, thought Reaper.

They drove in the open Land Rover to the far side of the field along a perimeter road that followed the contours of the fence. The bunker was a rectangular lump in the turf about three feet high. Air ducts and a door were the only visible parts. Clifford used a key to open a set of doors, went down steps and opened another set of doors that were air-locked. He switched on lights that were as grey as the interior. They were in a complex of low ceilinged rooms: lavatory and shower block, steel bunk beds, steel tables, steel cupboards; a command position and store rooms. And a lot of missiles.

'What are these, Clifford?'

'It's the stuff for the planes,' he said, wincing at his name. 'I'm usually known as Smiffy.'

'Except by Mrs Cairncross and your mum. Right?'

'Right.'

'Okay, Smiffy. Now explain. The stuff for the planes?'

'There are eight Eurofighter Typhoons in the hangars and no one to fly them. The Flight Sergeant thought it best to store their armaments somewhere safe.' He glanced around at the ordnance, as if ticking them off from a list in his head. 'Air-to-air missiles, cruise missiles, anti-radar missiles, Paveway III guided bombs, ammo for the machineguns.'

'It's a lot of stuff,' said Reaper.

Smiffy nodded and led the way to a storeroom at

the back that held tins of paint, cardboard coffins and body bags.

'This place may be obsolete,' Smiffy said, 'but it could still save your life in a nuclear attack. Unless it took a direct hit, of course.'

'Of course.'

They collected three body bags and Smiffy carefully locked the doors behind him as they left. Reaper was amazed at the amount of armaments he had just seen. A nuclear bunker was probably the best place for it. Smiffy turned the Land Rover. As they were heading back, Reaper pointed to a yellow JCB digger that was parked next to the transport plane, that he now noticed had US insignia.

'We should use the JCB,' he said.

Smiffy nodded and changed direction.

Reaper said, 'The Flight Sergeant took everything useful?'

'That's right. He left us well supplied, though. Two heavy and three light machine guns and plenty of ammo. Anything he couldn't take, he spiked.'

'What's in the transport plane?'

'The Hercules? Hummers for the Middle East. It was refuelling.'

'What vehicles have you got?'

'Three other Land Rovers, the truck out front and six other trucks. But four of them are in for service or repairs. Then there's the civilian cars, as well.'

Smiffy volunteered to drive the JCB, which was a relief, because Reaper hadn't a clue how. He drove the Land Rover to the guardhouse, parked and waited for the airman. The young man was no longer chatty. He gulped at having to face what was inside. Reaper guessed Smiffy had never been in action. He may have seen plenty of dead bodies after the plague, but none that had been the victims of close range gunfire. He stood in front of him to stop him entering.

'Look . . . what happened. I'm sorry. I'm really sorry.' The young man nodded and his Adam's apple bobbled as he gulped. Reaper put a hand on his shoulder. 'You start digging. I'll put them in the bags and then we'll move them. Okay?'

'No,' he said, in a rush of determination. 'I want to do it. They were my mates.'

Reaper nodded, stepped aside and let him go first. Inside the door, Smiffy stopped, he gasped and burst into tears once more, turned and went back outside. Reaper went in and bagged the bodies. It was difficult work on his own but the dead don't complain at being manhandled like sacks of potatoes. Reaper was a realist. He would give them as much dignity as he could, but bagging them was an awkward business. Besides, he was more concerned with the living.

By the time he finished, he could hear the noise of the JCB digging the grave. He dragged the bodies away from the blood towards the door then went outside.

The clouds were breaking, the sun coming through like a searchlight, the day was getting warmer and he realised he was sweating badly enough to be able to smell himself. Clifford switched off the JCB, climbed down and walked to Reaper. The hole he had dug was about three feet deep and six or seven feet square.

'I'm sorry,' Smiffy said.

'We're all sorry. Come on.'

He led Smiffy back inside the guardhouse, and together they carried the bodies of his former comrades out into the sunshine, laying them in a row at the edge of the communal grave. They paused a moment, in reflection, but Reaper felt that too much reflection might be bad for the youngster.

'Okay?' he said, stepping down into the freshly dug earth.

Smiffy nodded and climbed down to join him. Together they lifted the bodies and lay them side-by-side in the ground. Afterwards, Smiffy used the JCB to push the earth back, creating a mound on top of the grave, a mound of newly turned earth that stood out on the green sward that stretched all the way to the runway.

They loaded all the supplies that had been left, plus the machine guns and other weapons and ammunition, into the back of the lorry. It was agreed that Smiffy would drive the lorry with Reaper as his passenger.

Cassandra Cairncross would drive her own car, a Mitsubishi four-by-four, with Sandra as her guide and Emily and the two children in the back. Before leaving, Cassandra left a message in an envelope addressed to Flight Sergeant Babbington pinned to the notice board in the Officers' Mess. It explained where they had gone. The Mitsubishi would lead and the lorry follow, and they did not intend to stop until they reached Haven. But first, they had to say their goodbyes.

Smiffy had disappeared for half an hour while they were loading and had made a cross in one of the workshops, bolting together two pieces of metal that had come from an aircraft's mainframe. Reaper thought it highly appropriate.

The group stood on the grass by the grave and watched while Clifford thrust the cross into the earth. When it was secure, the young man stepped back, brushed any dirt from his uniform, and stood to attention. Reaper wondered whether he should say anything, as the silence lengthened on a sweet summer afternoon, but Cassandra Cairncross took the responsibility.

'Lord, look after these three young men, James Billings, Billy Bentley and Tommy Shaw. They were good young men and always did their duty, even unto death. We will remember them but please, Lord, you take care of them.'

They bowed their heads in silence for a moment

and Leading Aircraftman Clifford Smith saluted, as rigid as the iron cross he had driven into the grave. After long seconds, Reaper said, 'Amen to that. Now, one last duty.'

He and Smiffy got into the Land Rover and drove across the field and onto the runway. The transport plane was on their right, the control tower on their left and the tarmac, that had usually accepted Typhoon fighter planes, now whistled to the tyres of their creaking vehicle as they headed for the far hangar.

Smiffy directed Reaper to stop the Land Rover beside a hut next to the hangar.

'It's a five-minute fuse,' he said.

He jumped down, went into the hut and returned a few seconds later. He climbed back into the Land Rover and nodded to Reaper who checked his watch and then drove back the way they had come. It might be a five-minute fuse but even explosives experts made mistakes and Reaper drove as fast as possible back to where the Mitsubishi and the truck were parked near the fresh grave.

The group waited, Sandra armed as usual and keeping an eye out for possible danger that might be lurking beyond the perimeter fence, while Cassandra, Emily and the children stood holding hands in a line waiting for the last act. They were so calm that Reaper felt obliged to slow his mad dash to a speed more commensurate with a mass cremation. He stopped the vehicle and Smiffy went to join the women and children. Reaper joined Sandra, both pretending to watch for danger. They exchanged a look and he saw the sympathy in Sandra's eyes and felt the moisture in his own. What a fucking cock up, the lady had said. *His* cock up.

He looked at his watch.

'It's about due,' he said, and he and Sandra turned to face the hangar, slightly apart from the group that had legitimate reasons for grief. After all, their loved ones were in that hangar and had been waiting for their funeral rites. This time, no one said anything.

The explosion was small and a little disappointing. No windows were shattered, no pieces of hangar were blown off. But it had obviously been designed to act as a combustible and, as the fire within took a grip, they saw the power of the blaze. Flames came through the roof and black smoke rose in acrid clouds.

'Let's go,' he said, wanting to move the mourners before the smell of burning bodies drifted across the airfield.

They boarded their vehicles, Cassandra taking one last look and mouthing a farewell before she got behind the wheel, and then they were off on their journey to Haven.

The new arrivals were welcomed and Reaper and Sandra made their reports to Nick, Ashley, Pete Mack,

Kate and Judith in the dining room of the manor house. Cassandra Cairncross sat in on the debriefing. Sandra told of the new contacts made at Northallerton, the possibility that King Arthur had been reborn in Richmond and how they had found Catterick Camp deserted after soldiers and villagers had answered a radio call and left for Windsor.

Reaper then took up the story and told how he and Sandra had come under attack. He gave the details of his own counter-attack baldly and succinctly, and explained how they had gone on to discover the truth in the Officers' Mess. He made no excuses and did not try to mitigate what might be seen as an excess of zeal in shooting the three men dead. Sandra added a few brief comments when he had finished, stressing how they had both believed themselves to be under an attack that could prove deadly, and the group lapsed into a momentary silence, before Cassandra asked if she was allowed to speak. When she was invited to contribute she was also succinct.

'What happened was no one's fault. The times have conditioned us all. We were determined to keep people out, because we feared their motives. We did not attempt negotiation because we felt ourselves to be in a vulnerable position. Reaper and Sandra believed they were in danger and they have been conditioned by past experience to react in a swift and certain way. That resulted in the three deaths. It was no one's fault. It was the fault of the times we live in.'

Nick murmured something conciliatory and Ashley moved the conversation on by asking what they thought might be happening in Windsor. The group talked around the possibilities for a while without getting anywhere.

'Speculation won't help,' Pete said. 'At some point, we'll have to go and find out.'

'But not tonight,' Nick said. 'It's time we all got some sleep.'

Judith took Cassandra to the room in the manor house where Emily and the children had been placed. For tonight, the group would stay together. Tomorrow, new arrangements would be made that would be more suitable to individual needs. Smiffy had already shed his uniform and was bunking down in a spare room in one of the houses with two other men.

Reaper left the meeting with Kate and they stood outside the pub. The night had become overcast and there was a promise of rain. Kate, wearing a T-shirt and jeans, shivered.

'You should go inside,' he said.

She hooked her arm through his.

'What about you?' she said.

'I don't know about me.'

'It wasn't your fault.'

'I know. People have said.'

'But you don't believe them?'

'I'd be lousy company tonight.'

'What makes you think you're good company any other time?' He managed a smile as she thumped him. 'Go on,' she said. 'Stay strong and silent. I'll be waiting when you need me.

He kissed her gently. 'I'll always need you.'

'But not tonight,' she said, and went into the pub.

Reaper walked slowly up the hill, letting the dark swallow him. Clouds and no moon. He didn't look back from the crest but continued down the other side to the mobile home that had become their guard post. Arif was on duty.

'Hey, Reaper, man. I heard there was action.'

'Three dead. I killed them,' he said, deadpan. 'They didn't need to die.'

Arif immediately sensed his mood and left Reaper alone to sit in the camp chair outside. The young man went inside and brewed coffee. He took a mug of it out to Reaper.

'If you want something in it, there's whisky,' he said. He shrugged. 'I don't myself, but . . .'

'No thanks. The coffee is good.' Reaper raised the mug in a salute to him. 'Thanks, Arif.'

'No problem.' He stared out at the night. 'Look, as long as you're out here, I'll catch some zeds, right?' Reaper nodded his agreement. 'I'll take that top bunk, right? I mean, probably too high for an old man like you, anyway.'

'Careful, Arif.'

'Whatever. Night, Reaper.'

'Night.'

Reaper let the night envelop him. He wondered what the hell had happened at Windsor. Survivors from at least two military camps had apparently gone there and the only word back was: *Imperative. Stay where you are* – which implied that Windsor, or some location on the way, was extremely unhealthy.

Was Windsor under siege?

That was a crazy idea. There weren't enough survivors to mount a siege. But maybe there was a conflict. Didn't anyone ever learn? Another nagging thought came to the surface. What if the appeal to military units was a con trick perpetrated by someone who wanted to acquire whatever weapons they might possess? Prince Harry? As Cassandra Cairncross had said, his name had been a clarion call. Order in the midst of chaos. A rallying point behind the banners of one of the most popular royals. But it wasn't necessarily true. Someone down south might simply be empire building; attracting units into an ambush, disarming them, killing any officers who might resist, coercing the rest to join or go the same way. It would be a hell of a way to raise an army. It was a worrying thought. At least Windsor was a long way away and, if this empire builder was based in the south, it would be the south he would first wish to pacify. He probably thought the north had already reverted to wicker and woad.

Reaper would try other military bases and forge new alliances for that time in the future when conflict arose. War was not a popular concept for those who had escaped to Haven but the possibility had to be faced and proper preparations would reduce casualties. Which brought him to the crisis of conscience he had felt building all day.

Three young men had died. He had killed three servicemen who had been doing nothing but try to protect the women and children they had been told to protect by their commanding officer. He had made assumptions that had been wrong and three lives had been snuffed out. But had he been wrong? Should he have done it differently? Could he have done it differently? Would it have been better to simply go away and leave the area?

Why hadn't leaving been an option? He could tell himself that he had feared there might be women and children at risk, that they might have been captive like the schoolgirls in Scarborough. He could tell himself he was protecting Sandra. But they could have run away. Retreated, found another car and returned home. The truth was, Reaper hadn't wanted to retreat. He had wanted the conflict: wanted to test himself, to prove how deadly he had become. Had he become immured to normal sense and sensibilities? He preferred to believe he had simply reacted. He had been faced with gunshots, the possibility of death. And, in this new order, he had eliminated the opposition. He had done nothing wrong.

But he was still racked with sorrow at taking three young lives. He wondered, if the situation arose again, would he be able to react as clinically as he should?

Chapter 17

AS THE POPULATION OF HAVEN HAD GROWN, volunteer squads had cleared bodies from the homes in the surrounding villages. The buildings had been cleaned and disinfected and occupied by new arrivals. Among their community they now had carpenters, bricklayers, mechanics, an engineer, a plumber, academics, a nurse, teachers, working and professional men and women, even a journalist, whom Reaper avoided in case his prejudices surfaced. One of their unlikeliest success stories was Ronnie Ronaldo from Castleford, which he swore was his real name. He was a chap who confessed he had avoided work for the last fifteen years, yet had become their best ever scavenger. He had led them to an Asda warehouse that had enough stock to service the north of England. For Ronnie to discover his vocation, all it had taken was a plague.

They were in contact with eight other communities, none as big as their own, but all wishing to maintain peaceful and mutually beneficial relationships. The Haven committee was still mainly made up of first arrivals, but they knew it would not be long before they would have to hold elections to create a democratic council. Reaper was pleased that such progress had happened in a relatively short time. Nevertheless, he worried about maintaining the peace, and the possibility of what might be happening in Windsor. As Pete had said, there would come a time when someone would have to take a trip south to find out what was going on. Reaper knew it would be him. First, though, he would try another airforce base, this time in the flatlands of Lincolnshire.

He went the next day. He waited until the others had gone off to their allotted duties. He wanted no arguments about going alone. It had been his ruling that missions should involve at least two people; that everyone should have a back-up. But he was still brooding about the three dead servicemen and knew he would be a poor companion for a field trip. Reaper found Smiffy and asked him where the nearest RAF station was located across the Humber. Smiffy knew of a camp near Brigg because he had once visited the place, but was unsure if it was the closest. Nevertheless,

Reaper was happy enough to have a destination and, if he saw signs for any other along the way, he could always divert. He told Arif of his intentions, overrode the young man's objections, and took the Astra van.

Reaper bypassed Driffield and Beverly on his way to the Humber Bridge. He was used to empty roads with only the occasional crashed car or abandoned vehicle to disrupt his speed, but he slowed as he approached the suspension bridge that crossed the mouth of the estuary. It was a glorious feat of engineering, a beautiful creation, almost a mile long, that had been designed to support a daily load of traffic in each direction, and last for more than a hundred years. It would last a lot longer now, with no traffic at all. Reaper slowed as he went through the tollgates and drove at a sedate pace across the wide expanse of water. Was it his imagination? Perhaps the sun was playing tricks on the surface, but the water seemed clearer, as if the world was healing now that man-made pollution had almost ceased.

He saw no signs of habitation on his journey. Some areas, he had discovered, were like that. The few people who had survived had moved on from sparse rural areas, to come together with others to form small groups. Even Brigg seemed deserted, although he knew only too well that residents might prefer to remain hidden.

The camp was easy to find and was deserted.

Buildings and hangars were ruins and the remains still bore the marks of the fires that had destroyed them. Had these airmen also gone south? There was no one to ask. He drove in past a gatehouse that was poignantly similar to the one he had stormed, and followed the road to destroyed barracks and office blocks. The Officers' Mess was one of the few buildings left intact. Reaper got out of the van to explore it and went inside cautiously, his carbine at the ready. There were no messages on the notice board, no relevant entries in the log in the office. The bar was strangely untouched, neat and tidy. Chairs set around tables that were clear of any clutter, tall stools waiting at attention at the bar.

He put the carbine on the polished bar top, went behind it and took a can of Boddington's Bitter from what had once been a cold shelf. He flipped the ring-pull and poured the beer into a pint glass. He took a beermat from a pile near the till, placed the mat on the bar and the glass on the mat. He had food in the van but couldn't be bothered to eat. He sat on a high stool, his back against the bar, and faced the empty room. He raised his glass and drank.

'Absent friends,' he said.

He meant Jimmy, Billy and Tommy.

They had been survivors, young decent men that the world needed, with demanding futures ahead of them. Not anymore. He got another can and drank that, too. Then a third. Then decided he was being a prick and drinking alone was doing no one any good. He should still be making a contribution, even though this trip had failed to find anyone. He had a thought: one of those that he had kept at the back of his mind for future consideration. As he was on the south side of the Humber, he could check out Immingham and the docklands near Grimsby. He would look for the oil refinery there. It would be useful to make contact with whoever held it, because he knew an oil refinery would not be standing empty and unguarded.

In the van, he checked the map. The road ran straight into Grimsby. South of the port was the holiday resort of Cleethorpes. He would head across country and visit Cleethorpes first. When displaced and confused people had gone looking for somewhere to settle, they might easily have chosen a resort rather than a working port. Holiday memories and the seaside were more attractive than the urban sprawl of Grimsby, whose very name might be a deterrent. After visiting Cleethorpes, he would take the road straight up the coast through Grimsby and Immingham to the Humber Bridge. He would be back late, but that didn't matter. Kate would understand.

Reaper drove through small villages and hamlets that had no sign of habitation, and looped off the main road into the Lincolnshire Wolds. He stopped to relieve himself and to check the map. He was no longer sure of where he was, but reckoned if he kept going in the same direction, he would eventually reach the coast and the main road. It was almost six and he hadn't made the progress he had hoped.

He went through Waltham, joined the A16 and turned off at the sign for Cleethorpes along the A1098. This would bring him to the coast, south of the resort. He would take a quick drive through the town and be on his way. He went past Peak's Top Farm Guest House, past a Tesco store, round the roundabout and along a wide highway through a housing area. At the end of this road was the sea. It was liberating to leave the buildings behind and emerge to face the endless freedom of an ocean that held the promise of distant foreign shores. He wondered if there was someone on the coast of mainland Europe looking at England wondering what was happening here. Dismissing the thought, Reaper turned towards the town centre.

The ocean was calming, the promenade deserted. Ahead was a distinctive block of flats in red brick, with white facings and balconies. It was modern, but its refined lines evoked an earlier and more elegant age. He could imagine Hercule Poirot stepping out from one of the apartments to take the air.

The shot shattered his reverie along with the windscreen.

Reaper pulled the wheel to his left, mounted the pavement and braked, but couldn't stop the van from ramming into a low wall that fronted the gardens of a row of terraced houses. Another shot, angled down again. 'Poirot' was shooting at him from the balcony of one of the flats. Reaper pushed open the nearside door and slid onto the tarmac, pulling the carbine with him. He crawled backwards, keeping the vehicle as cover. Another two shots smashed glass and pinged through metal.

No warning, just shots. Not a great welcome to the seaside. But had the shots been intended to kill? He had made the mistake of assuming that before, to devastating consequences. Had the beers he had drunk blunted his awareness? He was bleeding from a cut on the face but had no other wounds.

'Hey!' he shouted. 'Stop shooting!'

'Fuck off!' came the reply. Brief, and to the point. A young male voice. 'This is our town.'

'I'm just passing through.'

'Not anymore.'

Three more shots. The bullets were tearing through the bodywork of the car and coming uncomfortably close. He levelled the carbine, rested his back against what was left of the wall and leaned back so that he could see around the bonnet. The shooter was on a second floor balcony. Reaper fired, deliberately close but not to hit, and the youth ducked back.

'Let's talk!' shouted Reaper. 'There's no need for this. There's no reason!'

More shots hit the car, this time from across the road, from behind railings that protected the start of landscaped gardens that fronted the sea. Another voice shouted.

'Who needs a reason?'

'Better than the Waltzer!' the first voice shouted.

The car was being pinged with bullets from both directions. Reaper cursed. If this was their town, then it seemed as if the resort was in the hands of a gang of delinquents. Bollocks to this.

He rolled behind the rear wheel of the vehicle and pointed the carbine across the road. The youth who didn't need a reason rose with his rifle levelled. Reaper put two shots into him, sending him sprawling backwards.

'You bastard!' shouted the youth on the second floor. 'You're dead, mate! Dead!'

The youth kept firing, single shots but rapid fire. As the sound of the last one died, Reaper moved up to a crouch, already knowing his target's location. He aimed and fired once. The youth screamed and the weapon dropped to the balcony floor. Reaper was up and running up the road and round the corner to enter a neat square, a small car park opposite, shops at ground level beneath flats. He reached the residents' entrance, and ran in without hesitation, up the stairs to the second floor, along a carpeted corridor that muffled the sound of his steps and round a corner. He came face to face with a youth of about nineteen or twenty – young enough to have to contend with acne – who was wearing a stunned expression, jeans, a black shirt, cowboy boots and a leather Stetson. He looked stunned. He was bleeding from his left arm and it hung uselessly at his side. He was carrying a rifle in his right hand.

The wannabe cowboy said nothing, but came to a sudden stop, his eyes widening and his mouth open. Reaper already had the carbine raised and didn't hesitate. He shot him. Survival rules. Reaper went past the body and checked the flat the youth had just left. Two girls, scantily clad, were sprawled on settees: one in her twenties, the other younger, *much* younger. Their eyes were wide with a fear that had not been caused by his appearance. Their fear was perpetual, they had seen and been required to do too much. Reaper did not have time for a rescue mission against unknown odds, but their eyes never left his face. Their expressions were slack with abuse.

'Do you want to come with me?' he said, but neither reacted. 'If you want to come with me, you have to come now.'

Even Reaper realised it was not much of an offer. Frying pan to fire? They knew nothing about him except that he was an older man with blood on his face who killed people. The younger girl moved to the older girl who put her arms around her.

'I'll be back,' he said. *But God knows when.*

He retraced his steps down the corridor and kicked open the door into another flat that would provide a view down the promenade and into town.   It was a well-furnished sitting room with big windows: the sea to the right, the promenade and the town dead ahead. About two hundred yards away, four men were leisurely getting into a car as if they had just left a pub, presumably alerted by the gunfire. They probably intended to view the kill or join in the hunt. At least one of them was holding a rifle, another had what looked like an Uzi. Reaper could guess the sort of regime they ran but the odds were wrong for him to take them on and dispense justice. Weren't they? He glanced down into the square. A row of cars were in the parking bays and a BMW stood right outside the entrance to the flats. If he had to guess, that would belong to the Cowboy, and he didn't need it anymore.

Reaper went back to Cowboy, took his leather Stetson and patted his pockets, but found no keys. He took the stairs down, three at a time. The keys were in the ignition of the Beamer. He threw the carbine onto the passenger seat and started the car. He lowered the window and put the Stetson on his head. It might help confuse the opposition for a second or two. He took a Glock from its holster, racked the slide, lay it in his lap, and drove slowly onto the promenade.

The men were in a Jaguar, heading towards him.

Reaper picked up the Glock and let his elbow hang out of the window. The sea breeze was pleasant. The two cars got closer and, in the final seconds before they met, the Jaguar slowed, as if the occupants were expecting an explanation. He pointed the handgun and fired it point blank into the limousine, emptying the 17 shot magazine. The Jag slewed onto the nearside pavement and shuddered to a halt. Reaper stopped the BMW and got out, throwing the empty Glock into the car and taking out the second, cocking it as he stepped towards the crashed vehicle.

A man fell from the rear nearside door. He was large, middle-aged and wore a black leather overcoat, even though it was July. He was the man with the Uzi. Reaper let him stagger to his feet and look round with a dazed expression before he shot him twice. Head and chest. Reaper took three paces closer to the car to improve his line of sight. Three more shots. The occupants of the Jaguar no longer posed a threat. This time he felt no remorse, no doubts. These were thugs running a regime of which he could not approve. They needed to be removed.

He threw the Stetson into the road and hoped acne was not contagious. His mood of self-righteousness was abruptly disturbed by three shots from a handgun. He turned and saw three more men who had exited the same pub as the four who were now dead. They were unsteady on their feet and if their aim hadn't been off he could have been in serious trouble.

Reaper got back into the Beamer, put it into reverse and started to make his escape when a burst from a sub-machine gun perforated the engine. He turned the car sideways in the road for cover, grabbed his weapons and took to the side streets. Maybe he hadn't totally removed the bad guys but perhaps he had seeded the start of a revolution. Maybe he would keep his promise to the girls and come back and finish the job. If he did so, it would have to be with more support.

The side streets behind the coast road confused him and he guessed those chasing him would know the points of containment and his possible escape routes. Perhaps they would have done a better job but for the fact they had apparently been drinking for much of the day. Either that, or they were rank amateurs. Even so, it took him an hour to get clear of what he considered the danger area before he could start looking for another car. But then there was another problem. The folk of Cleethorpes had been very safety conscious; almost all the cars were locked and he didn't want to risk the noise of breaking glass.

He found an old Ford Fiesta left unlocked outside a guest house in Isaac's Hill. If he was going to hot-wire a vehicle, it had to be an older car. Newer models had more safety features that made it difficult. He found a flat-blade screwdriver in the glove compartment. He pushed it into the ignition and turned. Nothing. He glanced up and down the street and tried again, ready to pump the accelerator. On the fifth attempt it started. Thank God it had been a warm and dry summer.

Reaper drove out of Cleethorpes warily in case the gang who claimed to hold the town had outposts to the north as well as the south. He encountered no problem. Perhaps any guards had been summoned into the centre to search for him. As he approached Grimsby, he saw a second-hand car dealership. He left the Fiesta running, kicked in the door of the on-site office, and chose the keys for a two-year-old Honda Accord. The engine turned over but did not catch – the battery appeared nearly flat. He opened the bonnet, drove the Fiesta nose to nose, found jump leads and started it on the second attempt. He patted the Fiesta in thanks – it had served him well in a moment of crisis, but he really needed a faster and more powerful car to get home, and besides, the Fiesta needed fuel. The Honda had half a tank of petrol and Reaper knew it was enough.

Dusk was setting in and a close inspection of the docks and oil refineries could wait for another day. He drove steadily, alert for danger, and began to feel safer when the road became a dual carriageway. He burst out laughing as he passed a huge dockland area to his right. A short time earlier, he had been desperately looking for a car, now he was passing the massed ranks of thousands of imported new cars that were still waiting to be delivered. They would be waiting forever.

Back into the countryside Reaper felt safer still and increased his speed. Eventually, he turned onto the A15 and headed back to the Humber Bridge. Halfway across, he passed an abandoned Bentley. He speculated that maybe the driver had come here in both style and despair to take a final leap from the bridge.

He was tired but had shed his despondency and reclaimed his positivity. He stopped at a village store that had not been pillaged. He drank a can of Coke and ate some chocolate for the rush of energy he needed. Almost everybody would be asleep by the time he got back. The community had adopted the old custom of rising with the sun and going to bed with the dusk. God knows how that would work in the winter when daylight was often reduced to less than eight hours.

The day had been overcast and the night was the same. He continued driving, his mind turning to his arrival back at Haven. He would leave Kate undisturbed and stay in the mobile home. He smiled to himself and allowed another one of those possibilities that had recently begun to lurk in the back of his mind, to surface unchallenged. Maybe it was time.

Sandra had married. Two other couples had done the same, and more were living together, bound by commitment, if not the words of Reverend Nick. Maybe he should make it official and ask Kate to marry him? His smile got broader. This was a conclusion he could never have imagined a few months ago. Like Ronnie Ronaldo, it had taken a world catastrophe for him to find himself.

It was after ten thirty when he arrived at the gates of Haven. He stopped to remove the chain and push them open, closing them once he was through and replacing the chain. He stopped the car near the guard post. He could see the glow of lights from over the hill and was tempted to go straight to the village to propose to Kate. Although, on reflection, it would be better to wait until the cold clear light of day, when Kate would know he meant it. He got out and stretched. In any case, he should first check in with whoever was on guard duty.

Arif was sitting out front on the camp chair. Reaper walked towards him softly. The young man, who always prided himself on being alert, was asleep. Reaper would tease him at being caught off guard by an 'old man'. A few paces away, he sensed all was not right. It was the way Arif slouched, the tilt of his head. Reaper sensed the presence of death; he had been around it many times and could recognise its posture and its soft aroma. Reaper's carbine was slung carelessly on his shoulder and, as he reached for a firmer grip, a figure stepped into the doorway of the mobile home, pointing a Mac 10 sub-machine gun. Another figure came round the far corner of the guard post, a pistol levelled.

'Welcome home, Reaper,' said the man in the doorway. Jason Houseman. 'Put the gun down, there's a good chap. There's been a change of management.'

What the hell has happened? thought Reaper. Where were Kate and Sandra? Then his fears and anxieties were obliterated by a thump on the back of the head that brought bright pain and then total darkness.

Chapter 18

REAPER AWOKE UNDER BRIGHT LIGHTS in the middle of the village. He had been stripped of his weapons and the Kevlar vest. He lay on his back and his head hurt. Someone was kicking him.

'Get up!'

Houseman. He held Arif's sub-machine gun.

Reaper's wrists were held in front of him with plastic cuffs, police issue. Also wrapped around his wrists and the plastic was a length of rope, which someone tugged.

'Get up!'

Another kick.

He rolled onto all fours. The movement made him feel sick. Now he knew what people meant when they said their head was splitting. It felt as though his already had. He got to his feet unsteadily.

'Reaper!'

The cry was made in anguish and he recognised the voice as Sandra's. He straightened and screwed his eyes against the lights which were mounted on trucks. These were adding to the interior lights of the first floor of the manor house, which were blazing and illuminated the village square. Sandra had shouted from the pub and he looked in that direction. Sandra, Kate, Jenny and young James Marshall were standing outside, in their special forces blues, their hands cuffed behind them. They were being kept under guard by men dressed in black.

'So you're Reaper.'

He turned his head at the new voice and saw Muldane, the small, rotund man in the uniform of a major in the British Army, who he had last seen conducting an execution by Whitby harbour. Muldane walked towards him. The same well-muscled thug who had accompanied Muldane on that day, walked a pace behind.

To the left of the manor house a mass of people had been shepherded together – the inhabitants of Haven. Had any escaped? Two hadn't: he saw their bodies on the steps of the house. His heart lurched when he recognised Sandra's husband Jamie, sprawled on his back, arms and legs spread like a starfish. Milo Montague was alongside him. The former financial adviser, who had buckled down to farming to become slimmer and hugely popular, lay on his face, a clawhammer still clutched in his right hand – an indication that he had found his new life and friends worth fighting for, despite the odds.

Reaper squinted at the herded residents. They had been split into two groups, the men separate from the women and children. He recognised faces in the crowd, some bloodied, some wounded, probably by beatings rather than gunshots. All the men had their arms secured behind them, undoubtedly cuffed with those unforgiving and unyielding plastic bands. The way they were standing made him look more carefully. They were in pairs, shackled together at the ankle for extra security. With rope? More cuffs? The women were roped together differently; the rope tied around each waist.

Machine guns had been mounted on the backs of two lorries. One was at the base of the hill behind him, pointing into the square. The other was to the rear and side of the captives, keeping them under cover.

Muldane stopped in front of him.

'You don't look so tough,' he said, and struck Reaper across the face with the swagger stick he carried.

The pain was sharp and vicious, but it cleared Reaper's head.

'What do you want?' Reaper asked.

'Want?' said Muldane. 'I don't *want* anything. I've got what I want.' He indicated his meaning with a vague wave of the swagger stick at the people and the village. 'You're a bonus. A disappointment, but a bonus. I really thought you would pose more of a problem after everything Houseman told me.' He leaned back and pretended to give Reaper a closer scrutiny. 'But, if truth be told, you don't look much. Certainly not Grim Reaper? More like Dim Reaper.'

'What happens now?'

Muldane smiled and his chubby cheeks dimpled. 'I'll tell you what happens now. At midnight . . .' He looked at his watch. 'In just over an hour's time, we shall burn you at the stake.' The words were meant to shock and they did. 'You see, you have a reputation. A bullet in the back of the head isn't good enough. You deserve something more theatrical. An event where you can scream for a while so that your reputation dies with you.' The dimples got bigger. 'A little performance that will make the men see the wisdom in offering no resistance, and the women more willing to fulfil their duty as volunteers. For a short time, you'll be the star of the show. Now . . . that's something to look forward to, don't you think?'

'It's novel,' Reaper said, a lot more calmly than he felt.

'Then we will give the men the chance to join us as soldiers. Those who don't make the grade will become drones. Dangerous ones will be put down. The women will become volunteers and will be given to my men.

Your *special forces* . . .' he said it with a sneer ' . . . are being kept apart. They will receive special treatment. Even the boy – we have chaps of a certain proclivity within our ranks. But first, we shall put on our little show so that everyone can see you certainly aren't that special and that resistance is pointless.' He nodded in satisfaction. 'I'll see you in an hour.'

'I can hardly wait.'

Muldane snorted at him in derision, turned abruptly away, and walked towards the manor house.

His sergeant said, 'Take him to the barn.'

The rope was pulled and Reaper fell. He was kicked several times before he could regain his feet. Dragged to the barn by Houseman and two guards, they went in through the small access door. The barn was illuminated by a battery-powered lamp. Half the interior had been used for storing drums of petrol and Pete's Harley Davidson, shapeless beneath a sheet of canvas, but there was still enough room for them to throw the rope over a beam. The rope was pulled taut and his arms were stretched above his head. It was thrown over again to stop it slipping, the height adjusted so that he was on his toes, and the remaining length was tied off on the central supporting timber. The position was meant to render Reaper helpless and make him feel vulnerable. It succeeded.

Houseman stood in front of him, close enough to spit on. So Reaper did.

The man lost his grin and slapped Reaper across the face.

'A slap? Is that the best you can do?' Reaper taunted.

Houseman swung his fist, and pounded it into Reaper's body. Landing one blow seemed to rouse his animosity further and he continued swinging, throwing punches with both fists until Reaper hung from the rope and no longer attempted to stay on his toes.

'Muldane told you what's going to happen,' Houseman said, breathing heavily, 'but he left out the detail. Let me fill you in.' He stepped closer to Reaper so that he was almost whispering in his ear. 'The men we captured will be given the opportunity to join our army. There are two conditions before they are accepted. They either have to kill someone in cold blood, or rape a woman. We nominate the victim and a selection committee watches the deed take place. Neat, don't you think? It means that everyone in our ranks is equal. We have all committed the ultimate crimes, we have all made the same commitment.' He grinned. 'We truly are a band of brothers. Evil bastard brothers perhaps, but brothers none the less.'

'You'll get no takers,' Reaper murmured. 'No one will join you.'

Houseman laughed softly. 'Your faith in humanity is misplaced. We'll get takers, never fear. We always do. And do you know something? Once that threshold has been crossed, the men no longer hesitate to cross it again. They become serial killers, serial rapists. They lose their souls.' His grin was vicious. 'Oh yes, and your special forces? You know, those special forces you allowed a Paki to join but turned me down for? They will, as the Major says, get very *special* treatment. Gang rape before they all follow you into the flames of hell. Every man in the army will take a turn. By the end, they'll welcome the fire. If they're still alive.'

Reaper raised his face and locked eyes with Houseman. He couldn't help but rise to the bait.

'I should have killed you when I had the chance.'

'Yes, you should. Because my revenge will be very, very sweet. The Major has promised me the girl. Little Emma? Very understanding, the Major.'

Reaper attempted to spit again but Houseman saw the intention, stepped back and threw more blows into his body. Reaper swung like a punch bag. Houseman aimed a kick and Reaper managed to turn enough to avoid the boot's direct contact with his genitals, although he groaned loudly as if it had found its target.

'I'll see you soon, Reaper.'

Houseman left with one of the guards, leaving one behind. The man sat on a bail of straw and watched Reaper dangle from the rope. After a while, he walked behind him out of sight, and Reaper felt a sudden blow in his backside that caused him to swing further. He groaned. The guard walked to the front and stared at Reaper with a grin. He was in his fifties, thin as cancer, and had a front tooth missing.

'Just wanted to kick a legend up the arse,' he said, and laughed throatily.

He wandered back to the straw bale, took out a packet of cigarettes and put one in his mouth. Just as he went to light it, he looked at the stacked drums of petrol, thought better of it, and went outside. As soon as the small access door closed, Reaper grasped the rope and began to heave himself upwards. He did not have a great deal of play in the plastic cuffs, but he was able to climb the rope, hand over hand. Houseman's blows had hurt, but had not been harsh enough to cause any real damage. Reaper had faked greater pain and injury than he had felt. How long would the guard take? He climbed quicker, ignoring the pain in his wrists and in his shoulders.

Eventually, he could throw a leg up towards the beam and, at the second attempt, he straddled it. They had stripped him of almost all his weapons, but had somehow not noticed the throwing knife that lay between his shoulder blades from the slim silver chain around his neck. He tugged at the front of the chain and retrieved the knife in its sheath. The cuffs had cut into his circulation. His fingers were numb and felt three times their normal size, but he managed to palm the knife and run the razor-sharp blade over the plastic. It parted swiftly, giving him more scope to use the knife on the rope. A few deft cuts and he was free, just as the door opened and the guard stepped back inside.

The man closed the door behind him before turning. He stopped in surprise when he saw the empty space where his prisoner had been. He looked up and saw Reaper on the beam just as he threw the knife. It embedded itself in the man's forehead: three inches of steel straight into the brain. He fell without a sound, and a second later, Reaper dropped to the floor.

Among Reaper's earlier defensive preparations, he had hidden caches of arms in four different parts of the community. One was beneath the guard post where Arif had been killed, another was near the rear entrance to the estate, the third was in the pub and the fourth in the barn. The guard had been armed with a Lee Enfield rifle that must have been more than sixty years old, and a Webley army revolver. Muldane's army, Reaper recalled from his watch in Whitby, were equipped with a wide variety of arms. Perhaps some had already exchanged old for new from Haven's armoury.

He took the Webley and the lamp, and went behind the oil drums. He shifted two straw bales, prised up some boards and pulled out a bundle in a sack. Inside, wrapped in a greased cloth, was a loaded Glock, two spare magazines, and a Bowie knife that fitted comfortingly in the empty sheath strapped to his right leg.

There was also a set of throwing knives which he strapped to his left arm. He pushed the Glock into his belt and put the old Webley in the sack that he carried in his left hand. He prised at the boards again, higher this time, and two came loose, although the nails made a small screech that made him pause and listen. More prising and he made a hole that he could enlarge until the space was big enough for him to step through. He took the lamp back to its original location, so that its glow might be seen from outside, then exited into the night from the back of the barn.

The land in front of the manor house was still lit by arc lamps. The captives sat on the ground. Three of Muldane's army were preparing a bonfire around the stone cross at the crossroads. They had put a two-wheel cart against it to provide a platform, and were packing the area beneath the cart with combustibles. Lights were on in the manor house. Armed men patrolled the spaces in between the village houses, moving from light into shadow. A motorcyclist rode from the parking area in front of the manor house up the hill towards the guard post near the front gate.

The village houses were unlit, although dim lights showed in the Farmer's Boy. Reaper took out the Bowie knife and moved back, away from the barn and into darkness, before making his way up the hill behind the open lorry that held one of the machine guns. He crossed the road that went over the hill, and moved into the cover offered by one of the unlit cottages. He studied the area in front of him for a long time before moving again, silently across the grass, until he was behind another cottage. The pub was two buildings down, towards the light. He stayed in the shadows, crouched low and moved slowly. He made the next cottage. He listened at the door and windows. He knew it was empty. His sixth sense told him so. The pub was the next building down.

He continued to stay low and move with caution. He eased himself down the sloping ground and saw the sentry outlined briefly as he caught the light from the village square. Reaper left the sack on the ground and went forward silently until the area he was in was obstructed from the arc lamps, even if he stood upright. He was sure the man was alone. The moon was hidden and the clouds were making the night claustrophobic, but they were on his side. Reaper got to his feet and strode forward, the knife held at his side.

'Got a light?' he said, waving his left hand in the air as if it held a cigarette.

'What?'

The guard was taken by surprise at Reaper's sudden arrival from nowhere, but his instinct was to reach into a pocket for a lighter rather than to raise a gun. It was all Reaper needed to get in close and bring the knife up through the stomach, between the curve of the ribs, and into the heart. The man gasped and drooped briefly against Reaper before he was pushed away to fall silently into the grass. He cleaned the blade on the man's clothes.

Reaper went back and recovered the sack, then checked the man for weapons. He had one of their Heckler and Koch carbines, and a Glock in a holster belt that was stuffed with spare magazines. He unfastened the belt and put it in the sack. He hoisted the carbine over his shoulder and went deeper into the shadows at the back of the pub, the knife still in his right hand. Light spilled from the rear window of the dining room that had doubled as a concert room. Shaggy had played in there. How was Shaggy now? How were Pete and Ashley and all the other members of the disparate group who had become his friends?

He peeked through the window. The light was dim and diffused, reflecting from the rough white walls. It was coming from what he guessed was a battery powered lamp, that was in the front room. He could hear Sinatra singing *Fly Me To The Moon*. Kate was standing in the middle of the room, her hands cuffed behind her back, while a fat man in black jeans and T-shirt swayed to the music in front of her. Kate's T-shirt and bra were raised and the man's hands were on her breasts.

Reaper controlled his breathing. He leant back against the brickwork of the wall, felt its solidity and pressed against it. He focused on the reality of brickwork and a warm night, the breeze and the sound of an insect, the prowl of a cat along the roof. He made the world real again while channelling his rage. He opened himself to the night, allowed his senses to range wide and went to the back door. It was unlocked, as usual, and led into the bottle bank and ground floor pub cellar. He stepped inside. A cat followed him in, brushing against his legs.

The interior door opened directly behind the small bar. He stood flat against it and listened. Male laughter, a woman's voice, a hard slap, hand on flesh. He opened the door and the cat slipped through. Frank Sinatra got louder. He bent low and eased himself behind the bar. He left the door half open behind him.

'What the fuck?'

'It's the cat.' Sandra's voice. 'He's always doing that.' The cat squawled obligingly as someone aimed a kick at it. 'Hadn't you better warn your mate upstairs? Wild animal on the loose.'

Good girl. She had guessed, or perhaps hoped, the entry had not been achieved solely by the cat and was telling him where they were. She got another slap for her cheek, but did not cry out. Reaper rose from behind the bar with a throwing knife between thumb and forefinger of his right hand. Sandra was sprawled along one of the bench seats. Her T-shirt had been raised and the tops of her trousers were open. The man responsible was so ordinary that

Reaper was almost disappointed. Medium height, medium build, clean shaven, regular features. He wore the regulation black shirt and a pair of black trousers which were open at the front. At the squeak of floorboards, he turned and saw Reaper. Reaper smiled and threw the knife. It took the man in the throat and he fell backwards against a table that Sandra stopped from toppling with her feet.

Reaper went round the bar, eased the man to the floor, and used a clean knife to cut the plastic cuffs behind Sandra's back. Her eyes looked past him, an indication, towards the dining room, and she mouthed, 'One in there. With Kate. One upstairs.'

He nodded and walked to the arched doorway that led into the dining room. Sinatra still played. Some other song, but Reaper wasn't listening. He took the knife from his ankle sheath and walked into the dining room without hesitation. The man was facing away from him. He was behind Kate, his groin pushing against her tied hands, his hands upon her breasts. He was humming along to the song. He was on his way to Monterey.

Reaper stepped behind him. He put one hand softly over the man's mouth and the blade of the already bloody knife against his throat.

'Remove your hands,' he said softly, and the man gasped and lifted his hands sideways.

'Who the—'

'Your worst nightmare.'

Kate stepped away and turned, love and relief in her gaze, and he indicated with a turn of the head that she should move. She walked past them. Reaper slit the man's throat and the blood gushed from the carotid artery. He held him until the flow eased and then lay him down quietly in his own gore. He wiped the blade roughly on the back of the man's shirt and returned it to its sheath.

Sandra had cut the plastic cuffs binding Kate's wrists. Kate had pulled her top back down and now came into his arms. They said nothing, simply held each other for a moment. When she let go, Sandra hugged him too.

'We thought . . .' Kate said.

'I knew you'd come,' Sandra said. 'I knew.'

'I hoped,' said Kate.

'How many upstairs?'

'One,' said Sandra, in a low voice. 'He took James and Jenny. They were told not to rape us, not yet at least. But they planned on having some fun. I don't know where upstairs they are exactly.'

'I've heard movement in both bedrooms,' Kate said.

Reaper took them back into the bar area and produced the sack of weapons. He put a finger to his lips and said, 'I won't be long.'

He opened the door that kept the upstairs private from the public area of the pub and listened at the foot of the stairs. If the man with Jenny was similarly involved as his two companions had been, he could be likewise distracted. He went upstairs silently in the dark, missing out the steps that creaked; the ones he had learned to avoid when he had so often returned late from a vigil in the motor home and didn't want to disturb Kate. Two bedrooms and a bathroom led off the landing. One bedroom door was locked but someone was kicking at it. He guessed James. The other bedroom door was open and the light from another battery-powered lamp spilled onto the landing. Jenny lay on her back on the bed where Reaper and Kate had slept and made love. Alongside her was a thin man who was intent on discovering her body.

The time for subtlety and silence was past. Reaper strode into the room, gripped the man by the throat with his left hand, forcing him onto his back on the bed, and thrust the knife into his stomach. The first blow didn't kill him, so he did it again. Twice, three times. The man gurgled and died . . . not a man - only a spotty, weak-chinned teenager.

Jenny had rolled off the bed and Sandra was already there, cutting her loose. Kate opened the door of the second bedroom, where James had been held captive, and cut him loose too. Reaper stood and saw himself in the full-length mirror, and was shocked at the sight. His face and upper body were covered in blood. His hands and arms looked as if he had been butchering an ox. The glare in his eyes was intense. He felt he was death and he feared no one.

The others stared at him in something approaching awe and perhaps a degree of fear. He opened the door of the pine wardrobe and lifted the flooring. Beneath it were handguns, belts and ammunition, another sheath knife and another set of throwing knives. Kate was the only other person to know about the cache.

He went into the bathroom and washed his hands, but left the blood on his arms and his face and body. Tonight, he wanted to look as if he had returned from hell. Back in the bedroom, his special forces were arming themselves. Sandra had brought upstairs the sack of guns and ammunition he had brought, as well as the arms belonging to the dead men from downstairs. He fastened on the double-holstered belt he had secreted away and replaced the throwing knife he had left embedded in the man downstairs.

Sandra said, 'They came in the middle of the afternoon, front and rear entrances at once. Some came over the wall and silenced the lookouts. Arif . . .'

'I know.'

'The four of us were out. It was all over by the time we got back. They simply arrived in the village heavily armed. A few put up a fight.' Her voice quavered. 'Ashley and Gavin and Nick and some of the others took a beating. Jamie and Milo . . . were shot. Once they went down, the fight ended. James and I got here about four. We drove straight into an ambush. Nothing we could do. Same with Kate and Jenny when they got back half an hour later. Apparently, they had been planning it with Houseman for the last two weeks. They waited until you left before they moved in.'

'How many?' Reaper said.

'Muldane, his sergeant, Houseman and, I'd guess, at least thirty men. They came armed with an assortment of weapons, but most have now upgraded from our arsenal.'

'How many prisoners?'

'They took most of the community who were here.' Reaper made a quick and rough calculation: some two dozen men, thirty-plus women, five children. 'They haven't touched the villages or farms yet,' Sandra added.

'They will, tomorrow,' said Reaper. 'Then Scarborough, Filey, Bridlington. Unless we stop them here.'

'Muldane's army is now down three,' Kate pointed out.

'Five,' Reaper corrected.

'Those aren't bad odds,' said Sandra. She bristled with attitude as ever. But Reaper could see and hear other things there too. Hurt. Grief. Venom. Hate.

The fleeting thought went through Reaper's mind that today he had already killed eleven men and felt no guilt. Tonight, with luck, he would kill more.

'They have two machineguns covering our people,' Reaper said, 'and plenty of guards around the village. Is Muldane still in the manor house?'

Sandra said, 'He went in there when you were taken to the barn. Mr Muscles was with him, two of his officers and two guards. Houseman was there too. They took some of the women.' Reaper tensed. 'To cook, not fuck,' she said without embarrassment. 'They're planning a midnight feast.' She nodded out of the window. 'They've built a bonfire.'

'I know,' Reaper said. 'I was going to be Guy Fawkes.'

Kate put a hand on Reaper's arm in alarm. He didn't mention that Muldane's plan was to burn them, as well.

'We haven't got long,' he said. 'Pretty soon they'll discover I'm not in the barn, or someone will come and check here. I'll go into the house the back way and take out Muldane and his party.'

'I'll go with you,' said Sandra.

'I wish you could. But you have to take out the two machine guns and rescue our people. Believe me, you've got the harder job. Look, by my estimation there are at least twenty-one of them out there. Say two on guard duty at front and back gates. That leaves seventeen. There are four visible on the machine guns, another three by the bonfire and two on the front steps of the house. That leaves eight out there somewhere in the darkness.' He looked at each in turn. 'You have to find them all and take them out. And one thing to remember before we start . . . take no prisoners. These are rapists and murderers. They all need to die or they'll come back to haunt us. Like Houseman. No hesitation. And try not to take too many risks. No one is wearing a vest anymore.'

His eyes moved from face to face and he was satisfied with the looks he got back. Even young James was determined and committed. He moved the lamp onto the landing and closed the bedroom door, so the room was in darkness, and they moved to the window. The manor house was across the square, the barn where he had been held was to the right. The captives were huddled on the left side of the manor house. Below and on the edge of the square to the right, was an open back truck with two men sitting next to a machine gun. On the far side of the square, behind and to the left of the captives, was another truck and another machine gun crew.

'James and Jenny. You take out the machine gun down below. Take them out from here and then make sure no one else climbs up there to use it. As soon as they are down, target the other guards in the square, the ones by the bonfire and on the steps of the house. It's likely you will come under attack yourself. Barricade the stairs when we leave and, if you have to get out, use the window in the back bedroom. It drops onto the roof of the bottle store.'

They nodded affirmation that they understood his instructions.

'Sandra, you and Kate are with me. We'll circle round behind the other machine gun. I'll try to get a knife to our people so they can have a chance of cutting themselves free. Then I'll leave you and go into the house to find Muldane and Houseman. You have the hardest job.' He would have preferred to leave Kate in the pub, shooting from cover but he could not allow his personal feelings to dictate roles. Kate was motivated and she was good. She was best for the job he planned for her and Sandra. 'You two have to take out the gun team at close quarters – carbine, handgun, your choice. Then you'll have to protect the position.'

'How about using the machine gun?' Sandra said.

'You don't know how,' he said. 'I don't know how.'

She nodded and licked her lips. He could tell she wanted to get started; her husband had been killed and she wanted revenge. He put a hand on her shoulder. 'There's plenty to do,' he said. 'But it has to be done right. You'll also be protecting the rest of our people.'

Sandra took his meaning and nodded again.

'Ready?' he said.

'Ready,' they all repeated.

To James and Jenny, he said, 'Unless someone raises the alarm or comes knocking on the door, wait for us to fire the first shot. Then don't hesitate. Take them out.'

They nodded and he led Sandra and Kate from the room. He switched off the landing light and went down to the ground floor. James looked down at them from above, already moving a chest of drawers towards the top of the stairs.

Reaper called up. 'This door locks from the inside. You might want to make it secure and take the key.'

James nodded and they left him to his defensive preparations. They exited the pub by the back door through which Reaper had entered. Sandra and Kate both had handguns, but only Sandra had a carbine. They climbed the hill to the next cottage and, staying low, moved sideways through the dark. Reaper would have liked to take out the guards one by one but time was against them. It was 11:30, and Muldane would soon be coming out to start his midnight celebrations.

They were at the side of the village now and, between the outlines of the last two cottages, they could see the square in all its arc-lit glory. Low and silent, they hugged the shadows until they were about fifty yards behind the lorry with the machine gun. To its left was the huddled mass of their people, sitting disconsolate, some in despair. A few quiet sobs, a low murmur of male voices. Reaper saw the outline of a guard, strolling behind the roped captives. He held a rifle casually at waist level. Reaper indicated that his two companions should remain lying on the ground. He moved forward silently, the Bowie knife in his right hand.

He was one with the night. He was a shade of death. He felt the souls of those he had already killed that day around him in the dark and he wore them like a cloak. The guard never heard him and never turned round. He clamped the guard's mouth with his left hand and cut his throat with the knife in his right. There was a cough, a spurt and the man gurgled and sagged, and Reaper lay him down. His own blood raced through his veins. He turned and saw Sandra laying down the body of a second guard he had not seen.

The girl got to her feet, her face ashen in the glow of the lamps, his spare Bowie knife in her right hand dripping blood, more of it staining her front. The body at her feet still twitched, but made no sound. He went to her and they sank to their knees on the grass to remain out of sight.

'I didn't see him,' he said.

She nodded, eyes wide, shocked at taking a life in such a bloody fashion, destroying it while it breathed in her arms. He nodded in return and kissed her forehead. He lifted two fingers, meaning her and Kate, and pointed at the lorry and she gave another nod. She took the carbine of the guard she had killed and his spare ammunition. He took the Glocks of the dead men and the spare carbine, and moved into the shadows at the side of the house, giving thanks to the god of death for granting him a guardian angel in the shape of an eighteen-year-old girl.

The captive men were closest to the house. The first one to see him sat up in surprise and, despite Reaper putting a finger to his lips, a murmur rippled as word was passed. The noise was not great, but it caused the men on the back of the lorry to take notice. They stood up and stared and one moved a lamp as if trying to find the cause of the disturbance. The men immediately lapsed back into silence, and the moment passed. Reaper crawled among them.

'About time you showed up,' Ashley said, in a low voice.

Reaper grinned up at him and cut the plastic cuffs with a throwing knife. Ashley was tied to the Reverend Nick at the ankles.

'God bless you, Reaper,' Nick said, making it a benediction.

Reaper gave Ashley the knife and passed two more to other men. One, he realised, was Pete.

'Sandra and Kate will take the lorry,' he whispered to them. 'Jenny and James will take the other. They're in the pub. Stay low. The shooting is about to start.'

He left the spare weapons with Ashley and backed out from the group into the deep shadows at the side of the house. He was about to go round the back when the alarm was raised.

'He's gone!' one of the guards shouted. 'Reaper's gone!'

As the two men in the back of the truck stood up

again and stared across the square, two shots from behind threw them forward and off the end of the truck. More shots rang out: rapid fire from the upstairs of the pub. It had started, and Reaper was not where he had planned to be. Bugger the back door – he would go through the front.

He drew both handguns and looked round the corner of the manor house. The two guards on the steps were crouched behind the Doric columns, shooting back at the pub. Two more at the bonfire were aiming at the back of the lorry near the captives. More shots came from out of the darkness. The lights of a truck came over the hill and headed down towards the village square at speed. Someone directed a lamp from the back of the captured lorry and it picked out the approaching vehicle. In the back were at least six more armed men dressed in black. Shit. It looked like they had underestimated. The whole situation was about to get even worse.

A shadow rose from the crowd of captives and leapt onto the back of the lorry. First his size gave him away, and then his dark skin glowed in the lights and Reaper had his identity confirmed. Ashley grabbed the machine gun and lifted it into his arms, cradling it as if it weighed nothing. Legs spread for balance with the ammunition belt trailing, he fired across the square at the oncoming lorry. Sandra and Kate knelt by his side, firing their carbines. Ashley's action might just have tipped the balance.

Reaper shouted at two of the nearest men: Smiffy and Gavin.

'Get me up!' he said.

They hoisted him swiftly to the nearest window. It was single-pane glass that he shattered with the butt of a Glock. He felt inside, released the catch and pushed it up. For a moment he almost lost his balance and bullets hit the brickwork around them. One of the men holding him grunted as he was hit, but they didn't relinquish their support. He cut his wrist on the broken glass but then he was tumbling inside into the darkened sitting room. The battle outside continued, but Reaper had his own war to fight.

This was one of the manor house apartments. The door was unlocked and he let himself out into a lit corridor. Another apartment was to his left, but the corridor to his right led to the front hall. He was at the turn in three strides, glanced round and saw a guard crouching in cover and firing through a broken window. There was no time for assessments or plans; he simply went round the corner with both guns levelled and shot the man dead. Beyond him, a second guard turned in surprise from another window. He shot him, too.

He paused before stepping into the hall and bullets hit the plasterwork near him. He heard the rattle of a door and shouted curses. 'The bastards have locked it,' someone shouted. Then Houseman's voice saying,

'This way!' and footsteps on the stairs going up, and more gunfire from the dining room that overlooked the square.

Reaper went round the corner in time to see Muldane's sergeant disappearing along an upstairs corridor. He guessed Houseman was taking them to the servants' stairs at the back of the house. He was about to follow when he caught a glimpse of movement through the open doorway of the dining room. A man's rifle shot scored his left arm. Reaper fired back, put him down and stepped to the doorway. The second man in occupation, who had been firing through a broken window, threw down his weapon and raised his arms.

'No!' he shouted.

Reaper shot him: chest and groin. He didn't deserve a head shot.

Now he was up the stairs and in pursuit. He heard screams and shots and more curses. He went down the rear stairs and into a stone flagged lobby. The rear exterior door to the left was still closed, the door to the kitchen was open. He stepped inside. Muldane's sergeant was holding his eyes and shouting in pain and, from the colour of his skin, Reaper guessed that he had received the boiling contents of the upturned empty pan that lay on the floor. Jean Megson was also lying there. The warm woman with the eye-catching décolletage, who had been one of his first recruits; the woman with the generous spirit who had mothered four-year-old Ollie Collins through his own personal tragedy. Jean lay on her back on the kitchen floor, a bullet hole in her forehead.

Two other women crouched in a corner. Muldane stood over them, beating them with his swagger stick and screaming at them. Reaper felt a sudden calm as if he was in a film that had slipped into slow motion. Muldane was demanding the key to the back door. The women simply cried out at each blow. The sergeant had shot Jean. In his pain, he had dropped the revolver he had used. Reaper wanted him to have more pain. He shot him in the lower back so that the bullet would exit via his genitals. The large man fell screaming. The shot got Muldane's attention. Only now did he drop the swagger stick and reach for the holstered gun at his waist. Reaper levelled a gun at him and shot him in the stomach. No quick death for him. He, too, deserved pain.

The two women were looking at him in shock. He guessed he looked a sight.

'Where's Houseman?' They shook their heads. 'It's safer upstairs,' he said, and they went past him, one pausing to touch Jean's lifeless body, then they were gone.

Muldane rolled about on the floor, holding his wound. Reaper picked up the revolver dropped by the sergeant and threw it in the sink. He pushed Muldane to one side so he could take the gun from his holster and threw that in the same place. Muldane stared up at him, the pain distorting his face and making a mockery of his dimples.

'Please,' he said.

Reaper shot him again. Twice. Once in each knee.

Now. Where was Houseman?

The women had locked the door between the kitchen and the rest of the house and hidden the key. It seemed they had done the same with the back door. So where had Houseman gone? There was a pantry, which was empty, and a room that, in times gone by, had been a sitting room for servants. It was in darkness, but he felt the breeze from the open window as soon as he went in.

The bastard had got away.

Reaper realised the shooting outside had become sporadic. But who had won?

He climbed out of the open window and slumped against the wall. The guns were still in his hands, but he had no idea how many shots he had fired, or how many bullets he had left. He slid down the wall and sat on the ground, letting his senses explore the dark. Where *was* the bastard? He heard the swish of a sheet of canvas, and he knew.

Reaper ran round the back of the house to the barn. The door was open, not just the small access gate, but the full-sized door. Inside was Pete Mack's Harley, his pride and joy, a machine that could take Houseman to safety at 120 miles an hour. Reaper stepped into the doorway as the engine roared into life and the headlight was switched on. Blinded by the light, Reaper pointed both guns and fired, but was knocked sideways as the bike surged forward. He rolled on the ground and continued to fire, but he knew his bullets were going wildly into the night. The bike's rear tyre skidded but Houseman got it straightened. Cross-country on this machine in the dark was not an option. He needed the road and speed, so he turned it towards the village square.

Reaper's body was aching but he got to his feet and sprinted in the bike's wake.

'Stop him!' he shouted. 'It's Houseman!'

Some of the arc lamps were still on, and the square remained bright. Reaper reached the corner of the barn to see Houseman almost lose control of the bike as the rear wheel once more skidded on the grass. He levelled the handguns and fired, but had no more bullets. Houseman grinned back over his shoulder, sensing his freedom just up the hill. He didn't see the Reverend Nick step out from the unlit bonfire at the stone cross, where he had been checking on the bodies that lay there. He was unarmed. Nick stretched his arms out wide and walked directly into the path of the bike.

Houseman saw him only at the last second, as the

bike was gathering speed, and they collided with a sickening thump. The Reverend Nick was thrown sideways, his body suddenly limp, and the bike fell over with a scream of its engine. Houseman rolled through the dirt until his back was against the unlit bonfire at the base of the stone cross.

The man was shaken and confused but, as Reaper strode towards him, he got to his feet and reached for the handgun strapped to his thigh. As he pulled it free of its holster, Reaper kicked it out of his hand. For a long moment the two men stared at each other, one in fear, the other in contempt, before Reaper dropped his handguns and took the Bowie knife from the sheath on his right leg. He thrust it hard into Houseman's stomach. He held it in place, close enough to feel the man's anguished breath on his face, twisted it and thrust again, deeper.

Reaper stepped away and Houseman slumped to the ground, his hands clasped around the hilt of the blade, the arc lamps throwing the shadow of the cross over his body.

People were already gathering round the Reverend Nick and Reaper joined them.

'He's alive,' someone said.

'Reaper!'

Sandra's yell cut across the square and the tone in her voice filled him with dread. Please God, not Kate.

He started to walk towards the lorry upon which

he could see Sandra standing. Someone was crouching next to her. He began to run. As he got closer, he could see Ashley cradling someone in his arms. Reaper reached them, breathless, and looked for hope in Sandra's eyes. He found only pain. He climbed onto the lorry. Ashley was crying, holding Kate close to him. Reaper knelt next to him and the former soldier gently passed her body into Reaper's care.

Her life force had gone. Only the shell remained. She was dead – snatched from him – and there was absolutely nothing he could do. Reaper looked out over the square, at his people back in control and having to count the cost of their first war. Crying over other lost souls. But Reaper was empty. He had no tears. He held his love in his arms and silently cursed God. If this was the price of living, he would sooner be dead.

Ashley touched his shoulder lightly in sympathy but did not intrude. Reaper looked across the square again and saw the wounded being tended: Gavin dripped blood from his shoulder as he was being supported by Smiffy; Pete Mack was taking charge, directing help; Cassandra Cairncross and Manjit administered aid to a man with a bleeding leg; Judith, her grey hair catching the light, bent over the Reverend Nick; Pete's partner Ruth, sat on the steps of the manor house, holding seven-year-old Emma tightly in her arms; fourteen-year-old James Marshall stood by the body of

Milo like an honour guard and Sandra, the carbine still hanging from one shoulder, walked alone towards the body of her husband.

The living go on, Reaper told Kate.

If Kate's death was to have any meaning, he would have to help this community they had founded, to survive and prosper.

Oh Kate, he said, crying within. *Why did you have to leave me?*

Chapter 19

ASHLEY'S DECISIVE MOVE HAD BEEN THE TURNING point of the action. The toll had been severe but manageable, in the greater scheme of things. Eight men and five women died and as many injured. Dr Greta Malone came from Scarborough to help. The real toll was not in the numbers but in the individual loss. All shared a common grave, but the memories were personal; the mourning was personal. Reaper held hands with Sandra during the service. A dull day in September. Clouds in layers, and no rainbow or God-sent shaft of sunshine to offer a hope of life eternal. Just death and dirt.

Reverend Nick, his leg in splints, said words that made many cry. The outlanders from the nearby villages and farms that the Haven had helped to proper, swelled their ranks, offering sympathy and more tears.

All Reaper wanted was revenge.

The dead of Muldane's army had been thrown into the back of a truck. Twenty-seven bodies. With them went five wounded. Early that morning, Reaper had driven the lorry ten miles south to an uninhabited part of the country and parked it in a field. Sandra had gone with him in the Honda. She hadn't argued when he told her to wait by the roadside.

Reaper had climbed into the back of the lorry and shot the wounded. No compunction. They hadn't believed he intended to kill them, until he fired the first shot. The remaining four called out in fear and protest, begging for mercy. He had none, but he made the executions swift. He doused the vehicle in petrol and set it alight. Sandra drove him back in silence.

They guessed that perhaps five or six of their attackers had escaped in the confusion and darkness. After the funeral, with everyone still gathered, Reaper declared his intention to go to Whitby and remove the remnants of Muldane's army from there too, and liberate their prisoners.

'I'm going with you,' Sandra said, and she went to stand with him. Without hesitation, Jenny and James joined them, both in clean blues, wearing Kevlar vests and fully armed.

The Reverend Nick said, 'I wish there was another

way, but I accept there is not. There is evil in Whitby and it needs cleansing.'

Pete, Ashley and Smiffy joined them and, without debate, other men, including Shaggy, and a few women, swelled the ranks of Reaper's regulators. They donned vests and armed themselves.

They set off immediately. Reaper drove a military Land Rover, with Ashley alongside manning one of the machine guns that had been mounted on the front. Sandra was riding shotgun on the RAF truck they had liberated, with Smiffy standing in the back, the second machine gun mounted on top of the cabin. He had six armed personnel for company in the truck. Other vehicles followed, each commanded by one of his trusted few – Pete, Jenny and James. Reaper was primed for war once more, because he had nothing else. The life he thought he might have had, had been snatched away. It filled him with righteous brutality.

Whitby offered little resistance. They advanced through the suburbs warily, but the closer they got to the town, the more they sensed the enemy remnants had abandoned their stronghold. Reaper stopped the column and called Sandra to join him and Ashley in the lead Land Rover. He instructed the rest of the vehicles to proceed with the same caution, while they went ahead at speed to reconnoitre.

'You're crazy, you know that?' said Ash.

'I know,' he said.

They went in fast, straight down the hill and swerving around the roundabout alongside the inner harbour. At the bridge, they stopped. Their arrival caused panic among half a dozen men dressed in black on the other side. They were all that was left of Muldane's Army. They were trying to push two reluctant girls into a Transit van. At the sight of the Land Rover, the men abandoned the girls, who ran back towards the cobbles of the old town. Three of the men paused to fire shots across the water, the others climbed into the van.

'Okay?' Reaper said.

'Okay!'

Ash and Sandra said it together, both charging their weapons. Reaper drove across the bridge, straight at the enemy. The men tried to run but the attackers' firepower cut them down. The van rumbled into life and began to move. Ash shot out its tyres and pulverised its engine with machine gun bullets until it lurched to a halt. Reaper stopped the Land Rover and shouted, 'Cover!'

Sandra turned to face the narrow street that led into the old town and Ash kept the now silent machine gun trained on the lorry. Reaper jumped out of the Land Rover, leaving his carbine behind and taking both handguns from their holsters. He skirted round the front of the van, saw movement in the cab, and fired through the window. He jumped up onto the running board and looked inside. It was a six seater:

two rows of three seats. The driver was dead but two passengers were alive. They were terrified. Reaper shot them. This was one virus that would be eliminated.

The back doors hadn't been properly closed and Reaper grabbed one and pulled it fully open, safe in the knowledge that Ash had the machine gun trained inside.

'Clear!' shouted Ash.

Reaper looked inside and saw mattresses, a box of food and cases of beer. The battle of Whitby was over.

The captives were both shocked and grateful at the speed of their delivery. Muldane had left eight men to guard the town. Three or four more had turned up with the dawn, and the news they brought had caused panic. The convoy from Haven parked on the harbour side and its members mingled with the newly freed population of the town. While they exchanged experiences, the Haven members told the recent captives about Haven and the other peaceful communities that were attempting to achieve a normal life.

Reaper sat alone on a bench and stared at the boats in the inner harbour that had been unused since the plague. Maybe they would never be used again. The brief action of the morning had not been the catharsis he needed. It had only postponed his mourning. Only now, in the aftermath, did he realise that, while he did not particularly care about his own life, he had put those of Sandra and Ashley at risk by driving into the town looking for a fight. Even so, the revenge he wanted to expiate his loss had not been achieved.

He wanted more violence and he did not care if revenge was not the answer. Any number of psychologists – if any still survived – might try to tell him revenge was wrong, but they could go to hell. There were bad people still alive and preying on the good and vulnerable, and he would remove them, *permanently*, wherever and whenever he could.

It was a fact that the community he was intent on saving contained men and women who did not have his capacity for killing. They were the normal citizens that were essential for the recovery of the human race: people of a softer and more humane disposition, like the Reverend Nick. They would fight only as a last resort, and avoid the killing if they could.

Only God, Nick would say, had the right to give and take life.

Nick might be right but Reaper didn't care. He would be God's right hand on earth, a right hand that held a Glock or a Bowie knife, a right hand that would dispense justice without qualm or conscience. The bad guys needed to die, and Reaper would kill them.

The faces of those they had lost rose in his mind: warm-hearted Jean; likeable Milo; the smart-mouthed young rogue Arif; Jamie, to whom he had entrusted his adopted daughter; Kate, who had revived the heart he thought he had lost. Tears prickled the back of his eyes.

Sandra joined him on the bench.

'They want to come back with us. The girls they used are in a bad way. They are going to need a lot of rest and understanding. They'll need time.'

He nodded.

She went on. 'Before the guards tried to escape they shot people. It seems indiscriminate. Fourteen men and six of the older women. Those they called the drones. There are twenty-four men, twenty women and eight children left.'

'We'll bury their dead and take the rest home,' he said.

Heavy clouds were making the late afternoon prematurely dark, and it suddenly started raining. Neither of them moved.

'Tomorrow,' he said, 'I'm going back down the coast. To where I was yesterday.' Yesterday? It seemed like a lifetime ago. Yesterday was when he had decided to ask Kate to marry him.

'You didn't tell us what you found,' she said.

'I found more bastards.' He looked at her. 'And I made a promise to two very frightened girls that I'd be back. I'm going tomorrow.'

'I'm going with you.'

He nodded his agreement. They were alone again, as they had been when they first met and started out on the odyssey that had led them to found a community; that had led them both to find love and then have it wrenched from them. He guessed Sandra wanted vengeance, too. They were a good team. Tomorrow they would dispense more justice.

Reaper looked up at the sky and was glad of the rain. It hid his tears.

Coming soon . . .

The second instalment of
the Reaper trilogy . . .

JON GRAHAME'S

ANGEL

MYRMIDON

COLD RAIN
by CRAIG SMITH

"I turned thirty-seven that summer, older than Dante when he toured Hell, but only by a couple of years…"

Life couldn't be better for David Albo, an associate professor of English at a small mid-western university. He lives in an idyllic, out-of-town, plantation-style mansion with a beautiful and intelligent wife and an adoring teenage stepdaughter. As he returns to the university after a long and relaxing sabbatical, there's a full professorship in the offing- and, what's more, he's managed to stay off the booze for two whole years.

But, once term begins, things deteriorate rapidly. The damning evidence that he has sexually harassed his students is just the beginning as Dave finds himself sucked into a vortex of conspiracy, betrayal, jealousy and murder. Unless he can discover quickly who is out to destroy him, all that he is and loves is about to be stripped away.

" A slow burn thriller about a man's life being ripped apart. Vivid, authentic, and masterfully written."

Tom Harper in *Mean Streets*

"…an absolute gem of a surprise. This is good, solid writing piled with suspense and tension!"

It's a Crime! (or a mystery…)

978-1-905802-34-0   £7.99 PAPERBACK EDITION
978-1-905802-59-3   E BOOK EDITION

**SHORTLISTED FOR THE CWA IAN FLEMING
STEEL DAGGER FOR *BEST THRILLER OF 2011***

THE STONE GALLOWS
by C. DAVID INGRAM

"I guess the end justifies the means. At least that's what I believe. Most of the time."

DC Cameron Stone spent three months in intensive care before he could recall what happened: the high speed pursuit of a vice baron through the night streets of Glasgow that took the life of a teenage mother and her child. Then the message from Audrey on the back of a 'get well soon' card announcing that she had left him and taken their young son, Mark, with her. Booze, anti-depressants and therapy have all failed to enable him to resume his old job.

So now Stone lives in a one-room flat in the worst part of town. He pays the rent by running errands for a private detective. His tasks include tracking down a teenage runaway and surveillance for a woman who thinks her husband is sleeping with her sister. He's also paid by his former colleagues, doing the work that's not quite clean enough for them to do themselves-like putting the fear of God into any local scumbag who thinks he can't be touched.

It's been a bad week. Audrey has moved into the plush home of a plastic surgeon: and is getting difficult about access to Mark. He finds his runaway in a brothel and just gets roughed-up for his trouble. There's the knife wielding kids on the stairs outside his flat and the daubing on his front door: *Burn in Hell Baby Killer*. The only brightness on his horizon is his growing friendship with Liz, the sunny Irish nurse who lives on the next floor.

But things are about to get worse for Cameron Stone... Somebody out there is out to destroy him and everything he loves- unless he can get to them first!

"There were some stunning debuts this year, but if I had to pick one it would be this world class Scottish thriller...
Shari Low, *The Daily Record*

"This great first book makes me want to read the next instalment – Ingram having promised some interesting times ahead for Cameron Stone.
Paul Blackburn, *Eurocrime*

978-1-905802-20-3   £7.99 PAPERBACK EDITION
978-1-905802-63-0   E BOOK EDITION

Scotland has a new crime detective: a big man with a big heart... and very few scruples. His name is Cameron Stone.

SPY WHO CAME FOR CHRISTMAS
by DAVID MORRELL

A gripping seasonal thriller from the author of *First Blood* and *The Brotherhood of the Rose*

On Christmas Eve in snow-covered Santa Fe, New Mexico, tens of thousands of pedestrians stroll through the festively decorated streets. Among them is Paul Kagan, a spy on the run trying desperately to protect a special package; a baby who just might be the key to a lasting peace in the Middle East. He is pursued closely by three extremely dangerous men, members of the Russian mafia whom he has just betrayed.

Attempting to elude his hunters, Kagan seeks refuge in a quiet house on the outskirts of the town. Once inside he discovers it is occupied by a woman and her 12-year-old son hiding from other evils and whom he has now put in mortal danger as his hunters manage to track him down. In the tense hours that follow, Kagan tries to calm the woman and the boy by telling them the spy's version of the traditional Nativity story as he prepares the house for the onslaught he knows to be coming...

" Master storyteller David Morrell gives us an amazing holiday classic that thrills us with heart-pounding suspense while tugging at our emotions."
Tess Gerritson, bestselling author of *The Bone Garden*

"...the father of the modern action novel delivers a unique, edge-of-your-seat thriller with amazing twists and riveting characters."
Vince Flynn, bestselling author of *Power Play*

978-1-905802-18-0   £7.99 PAPERBACK EDITION

SHARAF
by RAJ KUMAR

Searing and controversial romantic thriller set in Saudi Arabia

Major-General Farhan Al-Balawi is a loyal soldier in the Saudi Arabian army, engaged in a struggle to defend the kingdom from drug smugglers, conspirators and fanatical insurgents. Farhan dotes on his beloved daughter, Maryam and delights in her intelligence and independent spirit.

Despite the love she shares with her family, her respect for her father, the pride she takes in her Arabian heritage and her loyalty to Islam, Maryam yearns for travel and the opportunity to continue her education in a European university.

When Farhan announces that she is to marry – the fulfilment of a solemn promise made before she was born – Maryam endeavours to stifle her bitter disappointment. Out of love for her father, pride in her Arabian heritage and her devotion to Islam she is willing to sacrifice her yearning for travel and the opportunity to continue her education.

Then she meets Joe, an American dentist- and a Jew.

As they embark on a clandestine and passionate affair, Joe and Maryam dare to dream of freedom and of a life together. But Joe draws the attention of the *Muttawa*, the feared religious police, and when fate deals Maryam yet another cruel blow she knows that she faces the struggle of her life.

"... brings to life a searing and realistic portrait of an oil rich land caught between ancient codes, overwhelming wealth and the romantic desires of a beautiful Saudi woman... powerful and compelling."

Jean Sasson author of *Princess, Love in a Torn Land*
and *Growing Up Bin Laden.*

978-1-905802-33-3   £7.99 PAPERBACK EDITION
978-1-905802-60-9   E BOOK EDITION